Praise for Topaz and the Green Fairies

"*Topaz And The Green Fairies* brings us to Cottersdamp Island, where the rising floodwaters threaten the lives of the fairy folk living there. It is up to young Bozel to find a way to Knownotten and seek help before everyone is washed away, but first he must face his inner fears and much danger if he is to find King Topaz. With no way back to Cottersdamp, Bozel must trust the conjure cat and his faithful friends, Daisy, Otis, and Dooley to think of a plan that will rescue all the Green Fairies and bring them safely to Knownotten.

As a writer of children's books, I can say that I thoroughly enjoyed the thought-out characters in this series. From the wise yellow conjure cat to the dangerous Buckwetcher, the Black Fisher Bats and the Spotted Gray Matoose, magic, adventure, and mystery abound in this tale. A perfect bedtime read for pre-teens and younger."

—Sandra Jane Maidwell, writer of children's and teen fiction

"Another fantastic book by Pat Frayne! *Topaz and the Green Fairies* makes a great addition to the Topaz series. Topaz is back, this time to help the Green Fairies and cure his land. It is a beautifully written story that intertwines many different elements. I loved the different story lines and seeing how they all come together. With a great cast of familiar characters and terrific selection of new ones, Topaz and the Green Fairies is a wonderful story. It is a must read for any child!"

—Robin C. Berry, Library Graduate Student

"Author Pat Frayne's *Topaz and the Green Fairies* is a story that will evoke and enrich children's imaginations. Her characters are fascinating in the descriptions she gives them and the settings she describes will surely intrigue young readers as they envision what they are reading. Even adults will enjoy this book, which would be a great one for adults and children to read together. *Topaz and the Green Fairies* would also be a great stage play for young audiences."

—Karen Despain,
Retired journalist whose career in the newspaper business
spanned more than 30 years.

Topaz

and the

Green Fairies

Pat Frayne

ISBN-13: 978-1518621154

ISBN-10: 1518621155

Disclaimer:
This is a work of fiction. This book is a product of the authors imagination. Except for the names of my grandchildren, the names of characters, places or situations have no bearing on any actual persons, living or dead.

*For all my children and grandchildren
who love fantasy and mystical adventures*

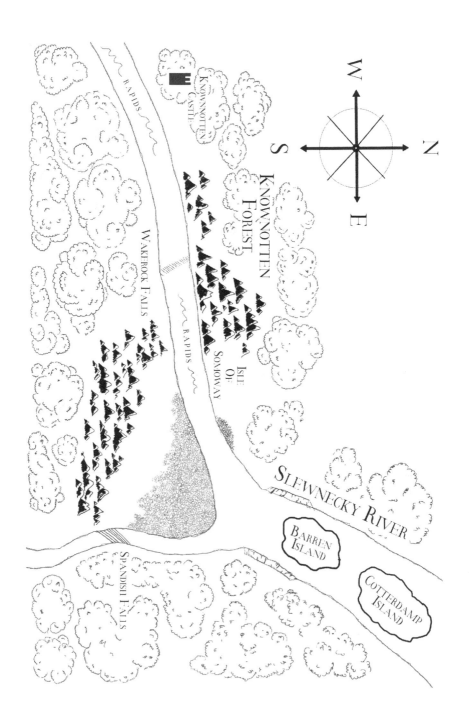

PART ONE

Barren Island

CHAPTER ONE

Otis had been on the wing since dusk the previous day. Weary, and half starved, the great owl looked for a place to rest and find a meal before completing his journey home. Far below and nearly hidden beneath its dense blanket of white fog, the wide Slewnecky River stretched out for miles.

Even though he was tired and hungry, the cool morning breeze and the endless gray sky seemed to be urging Otis to push on. Had the sun been shining, he would have given into his nocturnal nature and sought a shady place to sleep until evening. Now, he considered going on to Knownotten Kingdom instead.

With the wind in his favor, there was every chance he would arrive in plenty of time for Sunday afternoon tea at Knownotten Castle. The prospect of seeing his old friends sooner than he'd expected gave him a sense of renewed energy. Nevertheless, something to eat and a short nap were still in order.

This year's visit with his brothers in Wentloc lasted longer than he'd intended. Even so, it had been an enjoyable time. Otis looked forward to amusing his friends with his latest adventures, especially young Daisy. She was his best listener.

Barely visible through the fog, a narrow strip of dry land appeared almost directly beneath Otis. He circled round and dropped down for a better look. The island had been ravaged by fire, and though it hadn't been recent, he could see no evidence of new growth anywhere. This puzzled Otis. Nevertheless, the island would do for a place to nap after catching a fish for his morning meal. Otis circled round again. This time, he glided over the water, his attention focused solely on choosing his prey.

Just as he was about to sail down and grab his meal, two Giant White Osprey came out of nowhere, catching him off guard. In a flurry of gray and white feathers, the large raptors were all over him. Their thick curved beaks pecked hard against his skull, and their monstrous scaled claws grabbed his wings repeatedly as if they would tear them away from his body.

A paralyzing pain blazed through his left wing, leaving him breathless for a moment. When Otis recovered, he fought back with his beak, even as he struggled to wrench himself free. But he was no match for the osprey. They were larger and stronger, and he barely escaped their ruthless clutches.

The ospreys' screams were loud and terrifying as they chased after him. Otis flapped his powerful wings in stiff deep beats and swerved. This time he managed to stay out of their reach. He swerved again, and headed toward the mainland, only to discover that the larger of the two birds was ahead of him and about to cut off his path.

In an attempt to avoid the larger osprey, Otis made a wide turn. The smaller bird came up from behind with an unexpected swiftness and grabbed his left wing in both its huge spiked claws. Again, the searing pain gripped him.

Otis gave a loud screech. He pecked at the smaller bird's claws while he flapped his wings in an effort to get away. The spikes on the bottom of the osprey's clawed feet were used to hold onto a wriggling fish, but as Otis found out, these sharp spikes had other uses too.

The larger osprey circled round to close in. Aware of the larger bird's intentions, Otis thrashed about in desperation, trying to jerk himself away from the smaller bird's claws. When this failed, he nipped at his captor's face again and again.

Moments before the larger osprey was near enough to seize his other wing, Otis reached out and raked his captor across the breast with his sharp talons. Feathers flew, and blood dripped. The smaller osprey screamed and let go. Otis skimmed past the larger bird, barely managing to avoid a collision in his timely escape.

He'd been fortunate to dodge another brutal attack by the larger bird. Nevertheless, this battle was not yet over. The osprey were right behind him, nearly close enough to nip his tail feathers.

In spite of the pain in his left wing, Otis did his best to remain airborne. Even so, the wing was too weak to support him, and the osprey were closing in on both sides. How many times could he cheat death in a day? He hardly had time to wonder.

Otis screeched in anguish as he felt himself falling out of the sky.

CHAPTER TWO

When Otis finally came to his senses and opened his eyes, he found himself lying half on his face, his injured left wing crushed painfully beneath him. His neck ached and his head throbbed. A moment later, the jolting memory of the attack by the two Giant White Osprey came rushing back to him. *Why didn't they finish me off?*

He'd hit the ground hard, and he was grateful the fall hadn't broken his neck. As for his left wing, Otis remained doubtful; the pain was awful. He had to get his weight off it. He struggled to get himself upright. He dug his talons into the earth and flapped his right wing until he had both his feet under him. The effort it took to accomplish this feat was draining and extremely painful. Yet somehow, he managed it.

He swiveled his throbbing head for a better look at the injured wing, extending it as far as the pain and stiffness would allow. Besides the injury, two long feathers were missing. Otis groaned inwardly, worried about how the missing feathers would affect his flying. *How bad is this?* Right away, he began to work at stretching the wing, hoping to relieve some of the stiffness.

He was grateful to be alive. All things considered, he shouldn't be. The osprey could have come in for the kill when he'd fallen. Unconscious, he would have been easy game for them. *Food for their nestlings.*

After a few more stretches he became used to the discomfort of moving his wing, and the wing did move more easily. He spread both wings and flapped them to test their strength. Next, he attempted to lift himself in flight. The pain in the injured wing was severe enough to let him know he wouldn't be flying away from here today. Even so, he did manage to gain purchase on the lowest limb of a charred madrone tree.

The tree's malformed trunk jutted up from the earth at an odd crooked angle. It looked as if it had been blown over by strong winds when no more than a sapling. Its stout snake-like branches were only inches from the ground. Otis thought they resembled boneless arms reaching for the sky. Though the tree appeared as if it might fall over at any moment, it proved to be quite sturdy.

Otis was glad to be up off the barren earth. Instead of hopping, he used his strong beak and sharp talons to inch himself along the tree's charred bark until he reached the top. This was less jarring to his injured wing, and he thought he'd be less likely to lose his balance.

He blinked and rotated his head in slow motion to take-in the details of the ruined landscape. It was hard to imagine a fire so fierce as to destroy this island's entire forest. The black and twisted remnants of the madrone trees, and the charred spikes of the tall cedars were all that remained.

It sickened Otis to see such utter destruction, and yet, the island was not a total loss. Judging from the droppings he'd seen, a number of bats had settled here. They'd made their homes inside the burned out hollows of these huge ruined trees.

Apparently nothing had grown here since the fire, not even a blade of grass. Nothing lived here now except the bats, not even a bug. Otis could see no reason why any living being would come here ever again, except the bats who'd laid claim to this wretched island. Who, but they, would chose to live in such a dismal lifeless place? For them, this island was a refuge, and it seemed unlikely that anyone would care to disturb the solitude of these reclusive creatures.

Had it not been for the attack of the osprey and the injury to his left wing, Otis would be far away from here by now. As it turned out, the island had become a refuge for him as well. Unless the osprey were to come looking for him here amongst these scarred remains.

For the time being, at least, Otis felt safe. He believed he had nothing to fear. Had Otis been familiar with the local rumors about this island he would have known better.

CHAPTER THREE

Rain still poured and strong gusts of wind howled through the branches of the sycamore tree that grew outside Bozel's window. The tree's limbs scraped against the side of the house and across the roof. The noise gave Bozel a creepy feeling, especially since it was dark, and there was no light in his room.

When he was much younger, Bozel used to imagine the three-eyed giant was responsible for those eerie sounds. He pictured the giant scratching on the roof with his long fingernails, trying to get in. The giant, a villain from one of Bozel's bedtime stories, had been the source of more than a few of his scariest nightmares.

"Please, Bozel, may we come in?"

Bozel jumped and caught his breath, startled by the unexpected sound of Izzie's voice behind him. He turned away from the window.

His two younger sisters, Itza and Izzie, dressed in their nightgowns, stood hand in hand in the open doorway. Before he could answer, thunder rumbled overhead. Several streaks of thin white lightning zigzagged through the night sky casting brief waves of light that lit up the room.

Itza, the younger of his two sisters, let out a squeal. Both girls ran toward him, throwing their small arms around his waist and squeezing him tight. Thunder crashed again, and another bolt of instant white light flashed, much brighter than before. An explosive crack followed. Bozel felt the house shake, and his body tensed. Itza and Izzie fell to their knees and scrambled under his bed.

"It must have hit the ash tree on the hill," Bozel heard his father shout. From where he stood he could see his mother, Reza. She'd just left his sisters' room carrying a small gourd lantern with a candle inside. "Hirsol, I can't find the girls."

"They're in my room, Mum."

As soon as Itza and Izzie heard their mother's voice, they crawled out from under the bed and dashed down the hall to meet her. Reza set the lantern on the floor and put an arm around each of them, pulling them close. "We're safe, my little ones. Have no fear, it will be over soon."

Bozel knew that wasn't altogether true. No one was safe anymore. Cottersdamp Island was slowly disappearing into the Slewnecky River. That was a certainty, and every Green Fairy on Cottersdamp Island now knew it. Bozel could read it on their drawn green faces when they came out of their houses to inspect the damages after every storm.

Hirsol strode over to the window and looked out. "Can't see much out there in this light, but the old ash looks like it's still standing. I'll have a better look in the morning." Hirsol slammed the shutter closed and latched it. "Better take my lantern if you're going to be up for a while, Son."

Bozel nodded to his father as he took the lantern. He set it on the table beside his bed. "I won't be up long, Dada."

Hirsol clapped him on the shoulder. "Your mum and me, we'll sit with your sisters till they fall asleep. Call us if you need us for anything. Good night, Son."

"Good night, Dada. I'll be all right; don't worry about me." Although his father would never say so, Bozel thought his dada might be thinking thunder still frightened him.

After Dada left the room, Bozel opened the shutters. He didn't like being closed in, and he wanted to see the sky when he woke up in the morning. He sat down on the side of his bed and tried to finish the small sketch he'd started before supper. Thunder boomed again, but softer, somewhere in the distance. For the sake of his sisters, Bozel was glad to hear it moving on. Nevertheless, the rain was coming down just as hard, relentless as ever.

Bozel was reminded of the Flatlanders, the Green Fairies who'd once lived in the lowlands along the river. During the rains, their homes had been under water more often than not. Eventually they'd left the island to find another place to live. To leave the only land they'd ever known seemed a hard choice at the time, but a wise one as things had turned out.

As for the Green Fairies who'd chosen to stay behind, they were now stranded. The last big storm had taken all of their boats in its wake. Fortunately, one small boat hadn't been on the beach that day. The boat, not yet finished, had still been in the work shed. Until that day, Bozel's family and all the other Green Fairies who lived in the mountains of Cottersdamp Island had been foolish enough to believe they were safe.

Because they lived higher up, in the mountains, they didn't think they needed to worry as much about the rising water along the beach. Sooner or later, they expected the rain to stop and everything to return to the way it used to be. But that's not what had happened. Now, everyone worried, and the Green Fairies had come to realize they'd waited far too long to leave.

Bozel was awake even before the first gray light of day appeared. He dressed and made his bed. Afterward, he stretched out on top of the covers and listened to the rain beat against the roof and the back of the house, the side that faced the river. That side, the west wall of his room, always took the brunt of every storm. Inside, the house was quiet, only because Itza and Izzie were still asleep.

While he lay there, Bozel's thoughts turned to the journey that lay ahead of him. With only one small boat left, someone had to go and find help to rescue the remaining Green Fairies from Cottersdamp Island. Bozel, among several others, had offered to go. To his surprise, he'd been the one the old ones had finally chosen. Since then, time seemed to drag by while he and everyone else waited for a break in the weather.

After a while, he'd begun to think the old ones had made a mistake by choosing him. He began to wonder if he was really up to the task after all. Yet in spite of his doubts he wanted to get going before he lost his nerve altogether. Each day he delayed gave birth to new fears. *What if all my folk were to perish before I find someone to help me rescue them from the island. How will I live with myself if that happens?* These thoughts, too morbid to speak of, never left him.

Bozel sat up on the side of the bed and pulled on his house boots. In the beginning, he'd welcomed the chance to prove himself. Secretly, he'd been longing for an opportunity to impress his family and friends, especially Cazara. But as time passed, thoughts of leaving home and all that was familiar began to trouble him. *What do I know of the outside world? I've never even been on the mainland.*

He suspected this wish to have his family and friends believe him brave and able to face any challenge was the only reason he'd asked to go in the first place. Thinking about this now made him feel small minded and ashamed. He pushed the thought away as he tiptoed past his sisters' open doorway. Cocooned inside their thick quilts, the girls slept soundly, undisturbed by the noise of the pounding rain. Even though her head was covered, Bozel could hear Itza's snoring. He would tease her about it later.

Bozel found his mother in the main room of their wooden house. Seated by the table where the family ate their meals, Reza was busy cleaning the large gourd balanced in her lap.

Bozel leaned down and kissed her on the forehead. "Good morning, Mum."

He wondered what they'd be having for their morning meal, or if there was anything at all left to eat. But he didn't feel bold enough to ask. Anyway, it was too early.

Reza reached up and patted his shoulder. When she raised her head to look up at him, a smile crinkled the bridge of her nose. "You're up so early, Bozel."

"Guess the rain woke me, seems to be coming down harder than yesterday."

Still holding the wooden scraper, Reza pushed her hair back with the back of her hand. "You may be right about that."

Bozel noticed a small puddle on the stone floor near the leg of the table and placed a large gourd bowl under the drip.

"Your dada will have to make time to go up on the roof again today."

Bozel nodded, but made no comment. The room was cold, and the fire hadn't been laid. Bozel guessed they had no more wood, or what they did have was probably too wet to burn. He decided to ask anyway. "Shall I start a fire, Mum?"

"Not just yet, my dear. Your father will see to it."

Not quite knowing what to do with himself at this early hour, Bozel ambled over to the window. He looked out at the dark gloomy day, his mind still filled with misgivings about the impending journey. One of his biggest fears was one so terrible he didn't even want to admit it to himself. All the same, it haunted him.

He believed it was a fear that he and his father both shared, although neither of them could give voice to it. To speak of such a thing was forbidden. Green fairies never talked about the things they feared, especially their fear of death.

Even so, everyone on the island knew the risks he'd be taking. Some unpredictable misfortune could befall him on this journey. But to say it out loud was to give it power and make it real. Once said, it was as good as prophesy, and prophesy almost always came true. So Bozel kept this fearsome thing to himself.

Bozel looked over at his mother. "Do you think the rain will stop today, Mum?" He knew it wouldn't. All the same, it was something to say, and he needed to break the silence.

Reza brushed a long wisp of brown hair from in front of her face. She made an attempt to laugh. "Oh, Bozel, you ask me that every day."

Bozel shrugged. "I do?" Then crossing the room, he took a chair and sat down beside her. He watched his mother remove the stringy green substance from the gourd with her scraper, its slimy contents embedded with small clusters of flat white seeds. She scooped it into a bowl that sat at her elbow on the table.

The gourd's contents would be put aside for his sisters to rinse and hang on a rack of sticks for drying. Then it would be combed and straightened and woven into cloth. His father was a clothes maker by trade, and this was the fabric his father used. When dried, it was soft and stretchy and extremely durable.

"It has to stop raining sometime, Mum. Maybe it will tomorrow."

"I think it will be soon." His father came in from the covered back porch wearing the dry clothes Reza had left hanging on the peg just outside the door. He draped a damp towel over the back of a chair and rested a hand on Bozel's shoulder. "In the meantime, Son, we all have work to do. That roof is going to need another layer of twigs and moss. Let's hope the winds don't blow too hard for a while. The next big one could take this old roof right along with it."

Bozel was already halfway out of his chair. "I'll get right to it, Dada."

Hirsol pressed him back down. "You can gather the twigs and the moss, Bozel. It's better if I go up on the roof, though. I'm used to climbing up there and walking around. But we'll eat our morning meal first."

Bozel looked up at his father and smiled. He was glad to know there was still some food left.

As for mending the roof, he knew his father didn't want him to do anything that could result in him getting hurt. Should that happen and the rain stop, someone else would have to take his place on the journey downriver to find help. Although his father hadn't wanted him to go on this journey in the first place, he'd come to accept it, and he was proud of Bozel for stepping up.

Above all those who'd come forward and offered to make this journey, his father had said he believed Bozel was the only one who had the skills and the knowledge to succeed. Hearing that from his father, Bozel felt more encouraged than ever. His father had taught him to sail and to fish at an early age, and Bozel had learned his lessons well. Since his tenth birthday, his father had trusted him to take the family boat out whenever he wished.

Reza placed the gourd on the table. "Did you see much damage from last night's storm, Hirsol? How did our neighbors fare?"

Hirsol's forehead bunched. "I didn't want to tell you this, but there's been another slide."

Reza's face paled a little. "Whose house was it this time?"

"Stanzer's place, but thanks to the Good Spirit, they all got out in time."

Reza shook her head. "Who would have thought it could ever come to this, Hirsol. That's the third house in a fortnight."

"And two deaths," Bozel added, thinking about the furniture maker and his son. "What will the Stanzer's do now, Dada?"

"They don't have any relatives left living on Cottersdamp, I'm afraid. They're staying with Ozzen for now."

"It's good of Ozzen to take them in," Reza said.

Hirsol pulled a chair out from the table and sat. "They're talking about moving into Mezer's old place sometime tomorrow. It's badly rundown, but at least it will be a roof over their heads." Hirsol glanced toward the window. "Tomorrow, if the rain's not coming down too hard, me and Stanzer might go back to his place and see if there's anything to be salvaged from the rubble."

"I always get a little worried when you do that, Hirsol. Everything on this island is so unstable now."

"I'll be careful, Reza. You know I will." Hirsol looked at Bozel. "That big boom we heard last night? That was the ash tree that got hit. One of its big branches is down. Those two maples by Mezer's old place went down sometime during the night too. Both of them uprooted. It's fortunate neither one of them fell on the house."

Reza got up to clean her hands and start fixing the morning meal. "That was fortunate."

"A few of us plan on sawing the trees up for firewood within a fortnight."

"I can help with that, Dada."

"Let's hope you'll be gone from here sooner than that, Bozel." Hirsol gave Bozel a wink and a grin. "Now you'd better go and wake your sisters, or they'll sleep all day long."

Bozel left to do as his father asked, thinking this was probably an excuse to get him out of the room. More than likely, his parents wanted to discuss the growing food shortage. He wondered if it was as bad as he imagined.

The Green Fairies had always relied on fresh fish as an important part of their diet. Now, without boats or safe weather to sail in, fish was no longer a reliable source of food. Bozel figured their supply of dried fish was probably all gone by now. A lot of the food stuffs his mother had dried and stored for hard times had mildewed or rotted because of the island's muggy conditions.

The inhabitants of the islands to the north of Cottersdamp had fared no better. All had left the region several seasons back, not long after the Great Hurricane. Those living in the low lying areas close to the shore had been forced to leave much sooner, for they, like the Flatlanders on Cottersdamp, had suffered the worst of every storm.

Where they'd gone, no one ever found out; those who'd left had never returned to visit. Bozel wished he knew where they were, especially now that the responsibility for finding a new place for his folk to settle rested with him.

Itza and Izzie were already up. Bozel heard them singing as soon as he started down the hallway. He stopped a little ways from their doorway to listen, a lump filling his throat. The song was one they'd made up. He'd heard it once before.

"Rain and mud are here to stay. All our flowers washed away. We never see a sunny..."

CHAPTER FOUR

After their morning meal of bitter raw roots, Bozel went outside to collect the things his father would need to mend the roof. He took a flat wooden shovel and a large gourd bowl with rope handles along with him. Mindless of the pummeling rain, Bozel climbed the small hill beside their house and stopped at the ash tree that had been struck by lightning in last night's storm. The fallen branch looked as if it had been ripped from the tree by the hand of an angry monster. The jagged rawness of the exposed wood reminded Bozel of fresh open wounds. He bent down and broke off a few of the limb's smaller branches. After he stripped off the leaves and stacked the branches in a neat pile, he looked around for some moss.

The tapered edge of his wooden shovel slid neatly into a thick patch of moss. While he worked, he thought about what his father had said when he'd asked if he could help with the sawing. He hoped his father was right about him being gone by then. Yet there were times, like today, when he honestly thought the rain would go on forever. He leaned forward and pushed on the shovel, feeling it slice through the tight network of thin roots that grew beneath the ground.

Today, he seemed to be caught in one of the worst cycles of his gloomiest thoughts ever. He couldn't remember when his spirits had been so low, and the harder it rained the worse he felt. The old ones wouldn't give him permission to leave unless they were certain it was safe to sail. They were fearful of losing the only boat left on the island.

Bozel wondered if they weren't being a bit too cautious. What if the rain never did stop? What if it never even slowed down? He could be stuck on this island waiting, maybe forever, while the river continued to rise, and life for the residents on Cottersdamp became more unpredictable with every passing day.

After placing several small slabs of moss in the large gourd bowl and piling the twigs on top, Bozel carried the gourd down the hill. He left it on the back porch for his father. He then changed into the dry clothes he'd left hanging on one of the pegs by the door and went to the work room to begin his new venture.

He wished he could feel some enthusiasm for his work, but most gourds took quite a long time to finish. Although he expected to be on Cottersdamp Island for a while longer, it wouldn't be nearly long enough to finish a gourd. Knowing this took the heart out of the work. The dried gourd he'd chosen to work on was about half the size of the one he'd seen his mum cleaning earlier that morning.

He opened the drawer in his work table and pulled out a roll of paper that Itza and Izzie had made from wood pulp. On it was a sketch of his new design. This was the one he'd planned on carving into the gourd's outer surface when the finish was complete. Carving the design was the part of the work he enjoyed doing the most, but it was weeks away. The gourd had to be finished first, and the finish, both inside and out, must be as hard and as smooth as a pebble.

Bozel dipped a small piece of cloth into a thick paste that contained fine grains of sand. Then, beginning at the center of gourd's bottom, he rubbed the gourd's outer skin in a circular motion for several minutes. The results were encouraging. The spot he'd been buffing was already smoother and shinier. Even so, it was only one small spot, and it still needed work. This gourd would take a lot of rubbing before the job was done.

Finishing gourds was one of the main pastimes for youngsters on the island. It was more a labor of love than a chore. Every year, at the Festival of Gourds, contests were held to judge the best designs, and prizes were given. It was an honor to be chosen to compete, but to win was every Green Fairy's dream. It took the better part of a year to prepare for the festival, and everyone on Cottersdamp Island took part in it. Bozel dipped his cloth again and began rubbing the gourd's bottom in a wider circle.

Before the Great Hurricane, residents from neighboring islands used to come too. Sometimes they'd stay for the entire week of the festival. Those who didn't have relatives to put them up brought their own bedding and camped on the beach for as long as it pleased them. Seeing old friends again and making new ones were some of Bozel's best memories; it's how he'd met Cazara.

Although it was called the Festival of Gourds, it wasn't just about gourds. There were other special events too, like parades and games and dances. Youngsters helped their mums make special treats to eat. Some of these were foods they only got to enjoy once during the season. One of Bozel's favorite treats was tanga fruit. The last tanga tree on their island had fallen over in the same storm that had taken all their boats.

"Mind if I watch you work?" Itza came into the room and plopped herself on the stool by the door.

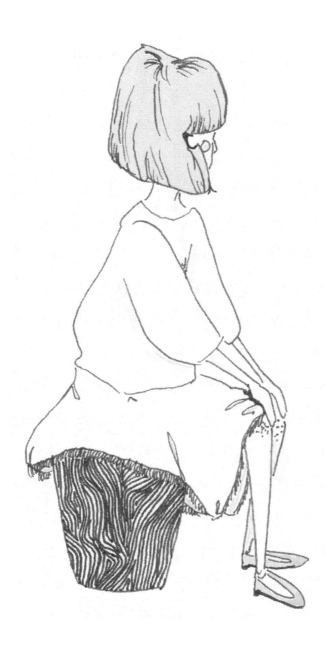

Bozel looked up from his polishing. "Nothing to do?"

"Not until Mum is finished cleaning the gourd. Are you making that for the festival?"

"It's something to pass the time. I'll be leaving before it's finished.

"Do you think we'll have a festival this year, Bozel?"

"Maybe not here, but we might have it someplace else." Bozel smiled and tried to sound cheerful, not wanting to disappoint her.

"It won't be the same though, will it? That's what Izzie said when I asked her about it."

"Izzie's right about that, but it will be just as much fun. You and Izzie can still help Mum make special treats to eat during the parade."

"Will we still have banners and beads to decorate the fronts of our houses? Izzie says we won't be able to take anything with us when we leave."

"Izzie's right about that too. But we can always make more."

"What about all of our beautiful lanterns? We won't be able to take those either."

Bozel thought about all the gourds he and his father had turned into lanterns over the years, piercing each one with its own unique design. His mum and his sisters made the scented candles they stuck inside to light them. This was an old family tradition, and he'd enjoyed the time he and his father had spent making the lanterns together.

They'd made a new lantern every year until there was one for every window. Even then, Bozel and his father continued to make the lanterns, because they took such great pleasure in the work. The extra lanterns were bartered at the festival. Bozel had given one of them to Cazara as a gift.

"We can make more lanterns too, Itza. It will be fun."

Itza scooted around on the stool to face Bozel. "Do you think we'll live near a beach? I love eating our supper around the big bonfires every night after the parade. It's one of my favorite things to do at festival time, that and the singing and dancing on the beach under the stars."

"Maybe we'll still be able to do some of those things even if we don't live as close to a river as we do here."

Itza's soft brown eyes became wistful. "I'll miss the singing and the dancing the most, I think. I can't imagine living anyplace else, can you?"

"Don't be sad, Itza, we'll still be able to do most of those things. We'll find lots of other things to do at festival time too, better things."

At last year's festival, Bozel and Cazara had met for the first time. Since then, Bozel had often thought about the nights they'd spent dancing together on the edge of the river in the smooth wet sand. Last year the rains had stopped just long enough to give everyone hope that life on Cottersdamp might return to normal.

Itza slid off the stool and went to the shelf where Bozel's favorite gourds were on display. He'd intended to barter them at the festival, but he hadn't been ready to give them up. Now it didn't seem to matter. The only thing that really did matter now was finding help to get his folk off this island.

"Is that the one you won a prize for?" Itza pointed to a blue gourd shaped like a pitcher, its design etched in darker shades of blue. "It's so beautiful. It would be a shame not to take this one with you."

Bozel looked up and nodded. "That's the first time I ever won anything."

"Itza?" Reza's voice rang out.

Itza looked at Bozel." Guess Mum wants me to help Izzie now."

"See you when it's time to eat. Guess it'll be raw roots again for the noon meal."

Itza rolled her eyes. "I don't know if I can stomach another raw root, Bozel. Maybe I'll give my share to you." Itza skipped out of the room, wearing a grin.

Bozel shook his head and chuckled. It was a bit of silliness they shared amongst themselves, he and his sisters, always threatening to give away their share of the raw roots. Though they kidded one another about this, they were glad to have food on the table. Such as it was, it filled their hungry bellies.

He went back to polishing the gourd. Last year, Bozel's gourd had won second place for color and smart design. As a special reward, his father had given him a fine set of carving tools for his birthday. The tips had been shaped from a special kind of quartz called flint, and the handles had been carved from a hard wood. With these new tools he'd hoped to take first place in this year's contest, but it was not to be.

Of all the islands in the Slewnecky River, Cottersdamp Island was considered to be rather special. A unique variety of gourds grew here. The old ones who'd traveled to other lands had often remarked that these particular kinds of gourds didn't grow any place else. Bozel found that strange. He couldn't imagine what they'd do without them. The gourds that grew on Cottersdamp Island were of all shapes and sizes because there were several different varieties.

Many useful things were made from gourds, depending on their size. They could be turned into storage jugs, pots for planting, or pots for washing up in. Smaller gourds were made into cups, plates and bowls. Some gourds were so tiny a bunch of them could be held in the palm of a youngster's small hand. Itza and Izzie collected them to make the strings of beads used for decorations at festival time.

Other gourds were large enough for a man, or even two or three of them, to sit in. These were the gourds used to make boats for travel and for fishing. Boats were vital to this island community, and a gourd that size had great value. Such gourds not only took a long time to grow, they took as much time or more to clean and cure. It was not uncommon for an entire family to spend a season or two drying and finishing a gourd for that purpose.

A boat was the most important thing a family could own on Cottersdamp, and it was more valuable than their house. The fibrous material that grew inside the larger gourds was cured and used to make other goods. Because of its strength and durability, it was commonly woven into nets for fishing. Without gourds how would they make nets, Bozel wondered, and without nets, how would they fish?

CHAPTER FIVE

Mum was in front of the fireplace when Bozel came in from the workroom. She looked over at him and smiled. Bozel smiled back. It seemed to him his mother was always in a pleasant mood. Lately, Bozel couldn't understand what she found to smile about. But at least there was a fire in the fireplace, and the room was warm for a change.

A sudden flicker of excitement ran through him when he noticed his mother was stirring something in the large kettle over the fire.

"It's good to have some hot food once in a while." She spoke as if she'd been reading his thoughts. "We have a little dry wood left."

Bozel grinned. "I'll set the table, Mum." He knew he ought to be grateful for what they did have instead of grumbling to himself all the time. Some families had lost everything they owned when their homes collapsed in the slides. Some had even lost their lives, crushed beneath the weight of their own houses. Still others had gone down the mountain with their house and been drowned in the river or been buried alive beneath an avalanche of eroding earth.

He took the gourd bowls down from their shelf, and set one at each place around the rectangular table. It wasn't hard to guess what was boiling in the pot. Since fish and other foods were in short supply all over the island, Green Fairies had come to rely more on roots to supplement their diet.

Roots of the gourd plant had become their main staple. As of late, roots were sometimes all there was to eat. Those of the large tuberous variety were the most tender. Peeled and boiled until soft, they were then mashed into a mush. Reza used herbs to season the mush if there were any. Otherwise, the dish was a little bitter and somewhat tasteless at best. Nevertheless, eating them cooked was far better than eating them raw. By now, Bozel could smell a faint herbal fragrance, and his stomach growled.

Itza smelled it too. She sniffed the air. "Something smells good, Mum. It's making me hungry."

"Me too," Izzie said from the back of the room where she and Itza were hanging the fibrous strands from the gourd over the rack to dry.

Reza's laugh was soft. "It will be ready by the time you and Itza are finished, and remember, Izzie, it's Itza's turn to collect the seeds.

"Yes, Mum."

Bozel didn't want to think of only the things that could go wrong in their lives, yet he couldn't help wondering how long it would be before they ran out of roots too.

Outside on the back porch, Hirsol stomped around, trying to knock the large clumps of mud from his boots. He was barefoot when he came into the room carrying a small muddy sack. Streaks of mud stained his clothing too, and bits of forest debris were stuck to the front of his shirt and his pants. A puddle of rainwater grew at his feet as he stood there. Soaked through to the skin, his baggy wet clothes clung to his tall frame.

Bozel could see how thin his father had become in the past few weeks. With his dark hair matted and plastered against his skull, he looked more like a specter from a nightmare than a Green Fairy.

"I'm going to need some dry clothes, Reza."

When Reza looked up and saw her husband, her hand flew to her mouth. "Hirsol, what happened to you; did you fall off the roof?"

Hirsol laughed. "Not today, Reza."

Izzie pointed to the small muddy sack. "What's in there, Dada?"

Hirsol grinned. "You won't believe what I found." He placed the sack in the gourd basin Reza used for washing things.

Reza ran over and looked in the sack, her smile broadened. "Where on Cottersdamp Island did you find these lovely mushrooms?"

"I tripped over them."

Reza raised her eyebrows. "Before all these mud slides, Hirsol, I might have believed you. There were mushrooms a plenty then, and lots of other plants too, but now..."

"Truly, I did. I tripped on a stone half buried in the muck and fell right into a whole patch of them. I didn't even know they were there at first. They were hidden under a heap of rotting leaves... I didn't steal 'em; they were on free land."

Reza smiled. "Of course you didn't, Hirsol, and I would never think such a thing of you."

Hirsol pressed his lips into a thin line. "I hope it never comes to that. It's hard to say what folks will do to keep their families from starving."

"Where were they, Dada? Can me and Izzie go look for more after we eat?" Itza asked.

"Found 'em down by the creek. They were growing under that big old tree you and Izzie used to climb. I suppose there's no harm in looking, but don't get your hopes up, Itza. I believe I took all there was."

Reza rinsed the mushrooms and placed them on a clean cloth to drain. There's so many. I'll try to dry some to store."

"Will you make soup, Mum?" Bozel asked.

Reza glanced at Hirsol.

Hirsol nodded. "Soup would be good, Reza. I think I know where I can lay my hands on a few more pieces of dry wood. Might as well use what's left of the supply we laid in."

"Then we shall have mushroom soup for our supper. And Bozel, you can take a few of these to the old fisherman. No telling when he's had a decent meal last."

"You're right, Reza. It wouldn't hurt for us to share with those who have less, or can't do as much for themselves. The old one is getting weaker these days, and I believe it might be because he ain't eating."

"Would that be Sezel, Dada?" Bozel recalled the good times he and his father used to have with Sezel when they'd fished on the river together. Bozel missed the old fisherman's stories.

Hirsol nodded. "He has a hard time getting around in this muck. I sometimes wonder if he still cares about living now that his poor wife has gone to the Good Spirit."

Izzie looked at her father. "He must be lonely, Dada."

"I know he is, Izzie, but I can't seem to find the time to get up there to see him these days.

"Shall I take some soup along too, Dada?" Bozel asked.

Hirsol was quiet for a moment. He seemed to be considering something. "Sezel would like that, Bozel.... And, I think I'll come along with you. Now, how about those dry clothes, Reza, unless you want me dripping all the way through the house and messing up your clean floors."

CHAPTER SIX

Dusk came early to Barren Island, as it was still known to some. The nights were long, and the bats preferred it that way. Two different species of bat lived on this island: the Black Fisher Bats and the Brown Bats. The Black Fisher Bats were the largest. They possessed strong claws and could fly exceptionally low over the river, low enough to grab fish swimming close to the surface. The Black Fisher Bats had extremely good eyesight and excellent hearing, but they actually did see much better at night. This was true of the other bats as well. This was why the bats waited until darkness was about to fall before they left the island to hunt.

Each night the Brown Bats went off to feed on the insects that lived on the mainland and on the other islands several miles to the north. Their funnel shaped ears allowed them to hear the bugs by listening for their echo. One Brown Bat could eat thousands of bugs a night, and in this region there were plenty of mosquitoes for them to feed on. Catching them couldn't have been more simple. The bats merely opened their mouths and scooped them in with their wings.

Just as the bats were leaving the island, Otis awakened to the sound of their wings beating the air. He watched in awe as a colony of small Brown Bats swept across the sky in the fading light. There must have been thousands of them. Then came the swift wings of the powerful Black Fisher Bats, also numbering in the thousands. Their huge black bodies and wings created immense silhouettes as they thrust forward at an even greater speed to take the lead.

Squeaking voices called out in mutual greeting as the Black Fisher Bats flew past. They were a magnificent sight against the fiery orange backdrop of the setting sun. Otis looked after the receding swarms until they were only a scattering of tiny dots in the distance. Then he eased into slumber once again.

Otis hadn't been asleep for long when the singing woke him. The light soprano voice rang out in the foggy darkness like soft chimes. His feathered ear tufts twitched and pivoted toward the sound. Though his eyes were still heavy for the want of more sleep, he strained to keep them open.

Otis watched as the singer's eerie image glided toward him, moving backward as though she floated on the rising mist that had begun to gather along the ground. *That's odd. Why's she backwards?* A chill ran through him and Otis shuddered, all at once wide awake. He stared at her, spellbound by his own curiosity.

Silver hair streamed down her back in long shiny ribbons. Her gown of white satin gleamed with a shimmering essence that might have been borrowed from the pale moon's glow. Yet the moon itself couldn't have been more than a sliver. The gown flowed gently over the contours of her slim form, then seemed to melt into the filmy vapor that collected all about her.

Otis thought her the most mystifying being he'd ever seen, peculiar yet fascinating. The melody of her wordless song was one Otis hadn't heard before. He felt a surging desire to join in the singing though he knew nothing would come of his trying. Owls simply couldn't sing. He sat there on his perch and stared down on her in silence while she swayed to her own rhythm, waving her long slender arms in graceful movements on the air.

"H'hoooo," Otis called to her the moment her song ended.

Abruptly, she turned as if hearing his voice had startled her. Nevertheless, Otis sensed she knew he'd been there all along, watching her.

When she spoke her small silver beak barely moved, and her voice was like an echo on the wind. "Who are you?"

Otis blinked, his posture straightened. He could barely keep from gawking. Her facial features were not at all what he'd expected.

She moved closer, weaving her way effortlessly through the ruined forest with uncommon grace, a luminous unearthly vision wrapped in a cloud. Otis wondered if she floated on the mist, or if she was instead a part of it. He couldn't see her feet. Who was this mysterious enchanted being? Could this be a dream?

"Who are you?" she asked again, gazing up at him with pale round eyes lashed in fine silver feathers.

He blinked again, trying not to stare at her so openly. "My name's Otis," he said finally. "Some call me the great owl."

"Tell me, Otis, what makes you great?" Her voice now sounded more like the faraway tinkling of many small bells.

Otis shook his head, thinking it might improve his hearing. On second thought, he wasn't sure this mesmerizing creature had spoken at all. This time he hadn't seen her beak move. Perhaps he'd heard her thoughts instead. If so, it would certainly be unusual.

He'd never been able to hear anyone's thoughts before. There'd been times when he'd known what his friend, Topaz, was thinking, or what he was about to say. But that had never seemed at all unnatural. They'd been close friends for many years. They understood each other's ways and each other's way of thinking.

"Oh, I'm not great," he admitted, finding his voice at last. "'Great' is just a nick-name, short for Great-Horned Owl."

"I see." She spoke in the peculiar tinkling voice again.

Otis' ear tufts twitched. "Now, you must tell me your name."

Her feathered lashes fluttered. "My name? I haven't any."

"Everyone has a name."

A moment of silence passed.

He waited, giving her more time to answer; while he did, he happened to notice something about her arms that hadn't been apparent to him until now. They were layered with tiny rows of pale silver feathers. The longer he stared at them, the more he realized the long slender appendages he'd assumed were arms were actually a pair of wings, but much too narrow for flight.

After several more moments passed, and still she had not answered, Otis changed the subject. "Then tell me who you are and why you're here on this dreadful island?"

"Who I am?" She seemed to be confused by this question. "I am no one, and that's why I'm here."

Otis flicked his ears, bewildered by her answer. "Everyone is someone. Why won't you tell me who you are?"

"Because, I am no longer who I was, nor will I ever be again. Therefore, you may call me whatever you please."

"I don't understand. Tell me what you mean?"

"I have, and there's nothing more to tell."

Otis blinked, wondering why she chose to speak in riddles, but this time he didn't bother to ask. He stretched both wings, and changed his grip on the perch while he tried to think of an appropriate name for his unusual acquaintance. "Then I shall call you Silvera."

"I shall answer to it," she said simply.

In spite of her puzzling behavior, Otis was enchanted with this lovely curious being. He longed to hear her sing again, but he didn't think it would be proper to ask. Instead, he decided to ask his first question again. He thought she might give him a reasonable answer if he worded it a bit different. "Do you live here on the island?"

"Yes, if you would call it that, but I would say, this is where I am bound."

"Where you're bound?" Otis repeated. He was baffled by her statement. When she said nothing to enlighten him, he went on, "How do you survive in such a place? What do you find to eat here?"

"Eat? I have no need of food."

Otis rocked on his perch and flicked his ears. He didn't know what to make of this so he let it pass. "Where is your real home then?"

Silvera spun round in a graceful pirouette, then glided to a stop at the base of the charred madrone tree where Otis was perched. The mist swirled about her as though disturbed by her sudden activity. When she looked up at him, the metallic feathers of her face and lashes sparkled like stars. "As I've told you, Otis, this is my home."

"Where is there to live?" Otis glanced around, taking in the ruined landscape Silvera called home. "How can you live in this barren place?"

"Where would you have me go?"

He ignored the question. "Aren't you lonely here? What about friends?"

Silvera threw her head back, and her small silver beak opened wide. Her laughter was a soft tinkling echo that seemed to go on and on.

Otis found it delightful, a warm glow washed over him and a surge of joy filled him.

When her laughter finally ended, Silvera spoke aloud, "You're my friend. Aren't you, Otis? Who else could be?"

CHAPTER SEVEN

Early that evening when Hirsol knocked on the door of Sezel's one room cottage, he called the old fisherman by name.

"Come on in, Hirsol," Sezel hollered back.

Bozel hadn't heard Sezel's voice for quite a long time. He thought it sounded weak and thin. He glanced at his father, but Hirsol seemed not to have taken notice.

As soon as they entered the small rundown structure, Bozel caught sight of several gourds sitting on the floor around the room. Most of them were already filled to overflowing. There were more drips than gourds to catch them, and the plank wood flooring was soaked. Without waiting for a look from his father, Bozel set the covered kettle of soup on the table and went about taking the gourds outside to be emptied.

"I was just about to get up and do that, Bozel." Sezel winced a little as he strained to sit up in bed. "But I'm sure glad you got to it when you did. That old roof springs leaks faster than I can get up there to fix 'em."

Hirsol ambled over to the bed, the small clean sack of mushrooms still in his hand. Sezel motioned to a chair and a stool sitting in front of the fireplace. Hirsol picked up the chair and set it beside the old one's bed. "Are you ill, Sezel?" He gave the old fisherman a questioning look as he sat down, placing the small sack on the floor beside him.

"The dampness gets to the bones these days." Sezel let out a long breath. "You look well, Hirsol. How's your family?"

"My family is well, and they've asked me to tell you they send their best good wishes."

Smiling, Sezel nodded, then leaned forward to look at the sack on the floor. "What's in there?"

"Reza thought you might like to have some mushrooms." Hirsol held the sack up so Sezel could get a better look. "She rinsed them off, but said they might need another wash before you eat any."

Sezel's long, withered face broke into a grin. "Are you sure you can spare them, friend?"

Hirsol's eyebrows went up. "Would you have me take them home again?"

Sezel laughed aloud. "Not if I can keep you from it."

When Bozel returned from emptying the last gourd, Sezel and his father were talking about Stanzer.

"Would you like some mushroom soup, Sezel? My mum sent a kettle full, and it's still hot."

"If you would be good enough to serve it, I would be happy to eat it, Bozel, and when you get back home, tell your mum I'm grateful for her kindness."

Hirsol handed the sack of mushrooms to Bozel to put away. He then got up to add a few sticks of wood to what was left of the glowing embers in the broad stone fireplace. Built from river rock, the fireplace divided the cooking and sleeping spaces, and it served to heat both of them quite well.

A short time later Sezel sat on the side of his bed slurping his warm mushroom soup from a bowl he held in both hands. "I hear it won't be long before you're gonna leave us to go and look for the new land, Bozel."

Bozel sat on the stool next to the fire place. He used his small flint knife to carve a long handled cooking spoon. The spoon was to be a surprise for his mother's birthday. He flicked the unwanted woodchips into the fire. "I hope to leave as soon as the rain slows down some." Bozel stopped carving to look up at Sezel. "Everyone says I should go south."

"That's good advice. There ain't much use looking to the lands that lay north of here. It's too cold up there for Green Fairies now. I'd say Cottersdamp is getting colder too." Sezel waved a hand in the air. "The islands up that way have already been ruined by floods anyway, or soon will be. But you probably know about all that."

Bozel bobbed his head. "Are there any islands south of here?"

"There's only one island south of here in this river, and it's one you want to keep well away from."

Tiny shivers crept up Bozel's back. *Barren Island.*

Sezel slurped a mouthful of soup and swallowed. "You'll have to go a lot farther than around here to find a place fit for Green Fairies to live in. We don't take to the cold, nor any of those rocky places."

"Why can't we just go farther south and live on the mainland?"

Sezel swallowed a large gulp of his soup. "Good soup." He wiped his shirt sleeve across his mouth. "That's where the Green Fairies used to live a long, long time ago. My great granddada used to tell stories about what it was like to live on the mainland when he was a youngster. Things were different there back in his time. We couldn't live there now though."

"Why not, Sezel?"

"Wild beasts, that's why. The mainland just ain't safe no more. That's the reason the Green Fairies came here to Cottersdamp Island in the first place. Wild beasts was roaming the woods and killing other beings, and sometimes they'd kill Green Fairies too."

Bozel's eyes widened. "Why did they kill them?"

"'Cause, that's what they ate. They didn't eat too much fish, 'cause they were afraid to go in the river, afraid they themselves might get eaten. Back in those times, there was great river beasts living in the Slewnecky River. They were just as big as the land beast and just as mean, too. Those river beasts were the only thing the land beasts were afraid of."

His carving forgotten, Bozel's hands lay idle in his lap while he fired more questions at Sezel. "Did the river beasts eat Green Fairies too?"

"I don't believe I ever heard any stories about the river beasts eating Green Fairies."

"Did your great granddada ever see the river beasts?"

"My great granddada never did see one, but there were a few Green Fairies who did. Not that the beasts weren't around, more like they wanted to keep to themselves. So they stayed hidden."

"Are the river beasts still around, even now?"

"If they are, I ain't seen 'em. Seen plenty land beasts when I was fishing though. They'd come to the edge of the river to drink. Mostly, they keep to the woods." Sezel coughed to clear his throat before he swallowed another long slurp of his soup.

"When Green Fairies lived on the mainland they took to building their houses in the tops of the trees. Back then, it was the only way they could keep out of danger's way. But, after a while, there got to be too many wild beasts, and the beasts took to climbing trees to find enough to eat."

"Green Fairies had no way to protect themselves against creatures that size, so there was nothing left for 'em to do but find another place to live. Cottersdamp Island was the closest. So that's how we come to be here instead of one of the other islands we might have gone to." His voice still a bit raspy, Sezel coughed again to clear it.

Bozel loved to listen to Sezel talk. He learned something new every time. The old fisherman had traveled to many different lands in his youth, some of them a fair distance from Cottersdamp Island. Sezel's stories always made him want to explore those places, if only to see how the other beings lived, how they dressed, what they ate.

Bozel went back to his carving. He needed to finish it before it was time for him to leave the island.

Sezel started talking again. "Now that the weather's changing in the lands around here, things won't never be the same. Even if the rain were to stop today, it's unlikely any of us will live long enough to see this island return to the way it once was. It don't make sense to stay here now. It's time to look for a warmer, dryer place to settle, someplace where there's trees, and plants, and streams with fish. But there's lots of things we're gonna have to learn to do different when we go to live in another land.

"Is every place so different?"

Sezel thought about it for a moment. "Well, let me put it this way, Bozel; there ain't no other place like Cottersdamp Island. So there ain't no need to look for a place you won't ever find."

Bozel nodded, not quite sure he understood how other places could be so different. "Will the beings in other lands treat us like we're trespassers? I mean, like the Flatlanders did when our folk first came here to this island?"

"It might be like that. As for the Flatlanders, they simply didn't care for us, but at least they left us in peace."

Bozel scooted his stool closer to Sezel's bed. "Do you think the Flatlanders would have liked us better if our folk had come here before theirs did?"

"Hard to say, Bozel. Could be they just wanted to keep the island to themselves. Part of it was, Flatlanders were afraid there wouldn't be enough of everything to go around if they had to share it with the Green Fairies from the mainland; there were so many of us compared to them back then."

Sezel finished chewing a plump, spongy mushroom and swallowed. "Maybe they thought we would take the island away from them and they'd have no place to live. Every place may not be the same as it was here when those folks were around. Some beings may not let us settle in their land, even if we do keep to ourselves."

Bozel raised his eyebrows, feeling a twinge of anxiety. *What if I end up in a place like that?* "Do you know of any place we can go where we'll be welcome?"

"Well, let's see, there's one place I remember. Fairies and Elves and different kinds of animals lived there too."

"What was it like? Did they grow gourds?"

"Some gourds grew there, but not like they grow here on our island. The gourds there were small and there weren't very many of them. What I remember most about that place was the forest. There were lots of trees, some of them very old. Trees there were much bigger than the ones that grow on our small island. Different kinds of things to eat grew there too."

"What about fish?"

"There was fish, but in the Land of Knownotten, there were no great rivers like the Slewnecky River. So fishing was done different, 'cause the fish lived in streams and small lakes."

"Where is Knownotten?" Hirsol asked.

"Not that far if you go by the west fork of the Slewnecky River. It's tricky going through that way though."

Bozel was intrigued. He wanted to know more about this place Sezel called Knownotten. He leaned forward. "Tricky? How, Sezel?"

"Well, the west fork leads to the rapids."

"What are the rapids?"

Sezel drank the last of his soup and set the bowl on the table beside his bed. "It's a place in the river where the current runs fast, so fast it can cause a boat to turn over or crash into the rocks. There's lots of big rocks in water like that." Putting his feet up, he pulled up his old frayed blanket and leaned back against the pillows.

"In the Slewnecky River, there's a long narrow gorge before the rapids start. It's risky going down that gorge, a being can end up going too far. It's in that gorge that the water starts to get a bit rough. The current running through there is strong enough to pull a boat right into those rapids before a being can help his self."

Bozel felt his throat tighten. "Will I have to go through the rapids?"

"Nobody in their right mind would go through those rapids."

Hirsol leaned toward Bozel. "What Sezel means is, the rapids are to be avoided altogether. The Slewnecky Rapids are some of the worst rapids you'll find anywhere, Bozel. The rocks will tear a boat to shreds and a Green Fairy along with it."

Bozel frowned, tilting his head to one side. "I don't understand. If I don't go through the rapids, how will I get to Knownotten?"

Sezel scratched at the few scraggly hairs that grew beneath his chin. "You got to beach the boat before you reach the gorge. Otherwise, you can get trapped in there. Before the gorge, there's a small patch of rocky beach. It's just a little ways into the west fork. It's easy to miss, so you got to be careful you don't row past it, especially if it's dark. That small rocky beach is where you leave the boat. You'll have to go on foot from there."

"What's the east branch of the river like?"

"The east branch goes over the falls; you don't want to go that way. There's a part of the east branch that looks a lot like the narrow gorge on the west branch, but the gorge on the east branch is not as deep or quite as narrow."

Sezel tugged on his blanket, pulling it up to cover his chest. "If something happens, and you end up in the east fork, get out of the boat as quick as you can. Then go south-west on foot. It will be a long journey, but you can still make it to Knownotten Kingdom from there. No matter what, don't get too close to the falls. If you go over the falls you'll drown for certain."

The more Bozel listened to Sezel talk the more his emotions wavered between dread and excitement. He rubbed his sweaty palms against the knees of his pants. "Traveling over the land, will it be dangerous? I mean, are there wild beasts or other beings I should be on the lookout for?"

"Hard to say, Bozel. Nobody's been down there for a long time, so you'll need to be careful. Might be best to stay out of the woods, though. Just like on the mainland, the woods is no place for a Green Fairy, especially when it starts to get dark. But things could be different in Knownotten. The woods is where most of the Fairies and Elves live."

Bozel nodded. "How far is Knownotten Kingdom from the rocky beach?"

Sezel sat up, pushing his knees up, he wrapped his long arms around his legs. "From there, I'd say it's about two days of hard walking, maybe more. That's if you get out of the boat where you're supposed to. Keep going west; you'll find it."

"Have you been to Knownotten Kingdom more than once, Sezel?"

Sezel paused to think. "I been there a few times. Some years have passed since I saw it last. I thought the name a bit strange when I first heard it. It's a good place though. The land is ruled by an Elf king, and he's kind to all beings. Fairies and Elves live there in peace together. Most of the animals do too. But, as I've already told you, things there are done different. Most places are like that. You have to get used to it."

"Are there any Green Fairies there?"

"When I was there, I didn't see any Green Fairies. All the same, I was welcomed. They treated me as if I was one of their own."

"Like you said, that was a long, time ago," Hirsol reminded the old fisherman.

Sezel looked at Hirsol and raised his eyebrows. "Not so long ago that I don't remember hospitality, Hirsol."

"I beg your pardon, Sezel. It's not your memory I question."

"Could folks be so different, now, Dada?"

"Rulers change, Son, and sometimes, when that happens, the customs of the beings that live there must change too. I'm only saying, you should be cautious when you go to any place that's strange to you. There might even be wild beasts there too."

"It's still the best place I know," Sezel insisted, speaking a bit loud. His voice was edged with conviction. "Knownotten has mountains, and woods, and meadows, and streams of clear running water with plenty of fish in 'em. The land is rich in everything a being could need, and it will be the same. There will be room enough for Green Fairies as well. You must trust me on this, Hirsol."

Sezel looked at Bozel. "All the same, there may be creatures in the forest you should be wary of. The few I happened to see weren't a danger to the other beings who lived there... But your dada is right too, Bozel. It's true that beings can sometimes change toward outsiders when there's a new ruler. It's good to be cautious."

Bozel turned to his father. "I want to go and see it, Dada; if it's not a welcoming place I'll look for another. But at least Knownotten Kingdom is a place to start. There must be someone there who'll be willing to help us."

Hirsol looked into his son's earnest young face, taking in every feature as if he were seeing Bozel for the first time, or perhaps the last. In Bozel's eyes he saw hope, anxiety, determination, and a need for a father's approval as well as a father's blessings. Hirsol believed Bozel would be more likely to succeed if he knew where he was going to end up, if he had a special place in mind. Maybe Sezel was right after all, how much could Knownotten Kingdom have changed?

Hirsol's voice was husky with emotion when he spoke again. "I guess we should be more concerned about getting folk off this island. We can worry about how others will treat us later."

He got up and went to the fireplace and picked up several charred twigs that had cooled. Bringing them back to the bedside, he offered them to Sezel along with a scrap of cloth he'd taken from the pocket of his shirt. "Please, Sezel, my son will need a map."

CHAPTER EIGHT

The following day when Otis awoke, he couldn't remember
having fallen asleep, nor could he call to mind when the
visit with Silvera had ended. He tried to recall his conversation
with the remarkable bird-like creature; nevertheless, he could only
remember the strange melody of her song.

He did recall hearing the chirps of the bats as they returned to
the island before dawn. He would have watched their homecoming
if he'd been able to keep himself awake that long. Even now, as he
tried to preen his feathers, he felt sluggish and tired. He wondered
how he could feel so worn-out when he'd slept nearly all day and
most of the night. He wondered too, why he wasn't hungry or
thirsty, and he knew he should have been.

Otis longed for home, and he regretted missing afternoon tea
with his friends at the castle on Sunday. Seeing the sky was still
overcast, he saw no reason why he shouldn't leave now. It would be
dusk in a few hours. He could be home before the sun rose again.

In an effort to test his strength, Otis extended both wings and
lifted himself several inches off the perch, then settled back down
again. The injured wing was still stiff and sore. Even so, he could

move it well enough. The discomfort was bearable, and in spite of the two missing feathers, he knew he could fly, although his lift and speed were likely to be affected.

Nevertheless, in spite of his desire to go home, Otis couldn't will himself to leave his perch. He couldn't leave it even for a drink of water at the edge of the river. Like a worrisome insect that buzzed 'round his ear, an unnamed foreboding nagged at him. He knew he ought to leave the island. He wanted to. And yet, Otis fell asleep instead.

CHAPTER NINE

Four days after Bozel and his father visited Sezel, the rain stopped. But as always, the sun remained hidden behind its dismal gray shade, and the day was as cold and dreary as ever it had been. This was especially true on the edge of the river where Bozel's boat waited. The cold gloominess of the morning was a familiar sign to the inhabitants of Cottersdamp Island, a sign that the rain would not stay stopped for long.

Everyone on the island had come down the mountain to see Bozel off, and all were dressed in their warmest clothes. Nevertheless, nothing they owned could keep out the dank chill that hovered over the beach this morning. Those who gathered closest to the water's edge felt the cold even more. They stood stiff legged, arms close to their bodies, and hands jammed into their pockets, while they shuffled their feet in the sand, trying to get warm.

The gourd boat was already stocked. It bobbed up and down as the small waves lapped against the shore. The wooden paddles Hirzol had carved and waxed rested secure in their holders, one on either side. Reza had prepared the food and water. One small gourd was stuffed with edible roots and a few leftover mushrooms that had been dried and wrapped in a waxed cloth to prevent them from spoiling. Another gourd contained a small portion of dried fish.

A fresh supply of rainwater filled the tall gourd with the long narrow neck. In addition to the food and water, Reza had packed a blanket, a gourd lantern with a candle, and a flint to light it. A coil of strong rope was looped through a hole below the railing for securing the boat whenever Bozel went ashore. The boat would hold nothing more.

"I'll be back before you know it." Bozel spoke to Cazara in his most reassuring voice. Then in a softer tone, barely more than a whisper, "Don't forget me, Cazara."

Cazara, a head shorter than her companion, looked up and smiled. Her kind hazel eyes searched his face. She seemed surprised by his remark. "Bozel, you're my best friend, how could I ever forget you?"

Bozel felt his cheeks grow a little warm. "Of course you wouldn't. It was a dumb thing to say." Then he reached inside his shirt pocket. "I, ah, made you something. I made it especially for you, that is." He held it out to her. It was a necklace made from the dried seeds of a gourd. The seeds had been dyed in several different colors and polished before they'd been strung together.

"Oh, Bozel, you're so clever. Did you really make this necklace especially for me?" She took it from him and fingered the seeds.

"Of course I did. I wasn't sure you'd like it though. I wasn't sure I would even give it to you until now."

Cazara pulled the necklace over her head. "It's perfect; every seed is exactly the same size. It must have taken a long time to make."

He grinned at her. "I was happy to do it, and it made the time go faster."

"It's the prettiest necklace I've ever had, and I'm going to wear it every day until you come back." Then she handed him a small cloth package tied with colored string. "It's only dried tanga fruit. Try not to eat it all at once."

"Only." Bozel laughed, his grin spreading across his face. "It's my favorite fruit, and it's been ages since I've had any. Could be, this is all that's left of it on this island."

Cazara giggled. "I'm so glad you still like it."

Although they were both laughing, tears glistened in their eyes, and for a long while they stood there looking at one another, not wanting to part, yet not knowing what else to say. Cazara spoke first. "I must let you say good-bye to your family. Good journey, Bozel."

Cazara seemed about to walk away, but turned back to him unexpectedly. She reached up and threw her arms around Bozel's neck and hugged him tight.

Bozel hugged Cazara back, not wanting the moment to end. He'd never felt so happy and so sad all at the same time. It was a strange and wonderful feeling, and one he hoped would last until he saw her again. When Cazara finally moved away, Bozel went over to where his family stood talking to neighbors. After chatting with everyone for a time, he gave each of his sisters a hug, then hugged his mum.

Reza wrapped her arms around Bozel and squeezed him to her in a long embrace. "Take care of yourself, Son."

"I will, Mum. But you shouldn't give me all of the dried fish." He'd spoken only loud enough for his mother to hear.

"You must not worry about us, Bozel. We have plenty, and you weren't supposed to open those gourds until it was time for your next meal."

"I know, Mum, sorry." He suspected his mother had begun to put the fish aside when she learned he'd been chosen to go on this journey. He was truly surprised there was any fish left. As for there being *"plenty"*, from what Bozel could see, there didn't seem to be plenty of anything on Cottersdamp Island except mud and water. Nevertheless, he didn't contradict his mother.

"I left you something, Mum. It's for your birthday. Itza will keep it for you until then."

Reza, gave Bozel a watery eyed smile in return. Bozel could see his mum was too choked with tears to speak.

Hirsol grasped Bozel's hand and held it in a strong clasp. His eyes instantly filled with tears. Bozel had never seen his father look so solemn.

"You are a son to be proud of. You're just a youngster now, but someday soon, when you come back to us, you will be older and wiser than many of the old ones who live here on Cottersdamp now."

Hirsol paused to clear his throat. He placed his other hand on Bozel's shoulder. "Whatever happens after you leave us, Bozel, remember this. Life can be uncertain, and you won't always be able to foresee the outcome of some things ahead of time. There will be times when you'll have to take each day as it comes. This journey will be like that. But I want you to know that however things turn out, I will know that you have done your best, just as you have always."

Bozel felt himself being crushed in his father's arms. He swallowed hard to hold back a sob that had just lodged in the back of his throat.

"Dada," he managed, finally. "I love you, Dada."

His father blinked rapidly, as if to clear away the tears. "I know you'll be careful. Safe journey, Son."

It was time to go. Bozel stepped into the boat and undid the rope from around the post that had kept the boat from drifting. Right away the boat began to coast away from the shore. A burst of happy shouts rose up from the crowds of Green Fairies gathered on the beach. Everyone waved. Bozel smiled and waved back, then sitting down in the boat, he took hold of the paddles.

All at once, he saw old Sezel hurrying down the beach toward him.

"I didn't think I'd make it here before you left." Sezel huffed and wheezed as he came up parallel to the boat, just on the edge of the water. He reached a long thin arm out to Bozel. "I almost forgot to give you this; here take it, quick."

Bozel was just fast enough to shove the paddle in its holder and grab the object from Sezel's outstretched fingers before the boat moved out of range. He turned it over in his hand to get a better look at it. It was a hollow cylinder carved from wood, and no bigger than his middle finger. There was a small hole on one side at the tapered end. "What is it?"

"It's a whistle," Sezel yelled.

Small waves lapped at the sides of the boat as the current pulled it farther away from the beach.

"A whistle?" Bozel had never heard of a whistle. "What do you want me to do with it?"

"Blow on it," Sezel shouted, putting his fingers to his lips.

Bozel yelled back. "Blow on it? But why would you want me to do that?"

"You must use it to call the Spotted Gray Matoose when you get to the Isle of Samoway. If he hears that whistle, he'll come and take you to the Land of Knownotten. Wish I'd remembered to tell you about it when we had our talk a few days ago."

Bozel couldn't hear Sezel's last words clearly. The boat had already drifted beyond his range of hearing. "What's a Spotted Gray Matoose?" he shouted as loud as he could.

Sezel hollered an explanation, and at the same time he waved his thin arms up and down by his side. But by now Bozel couldn't hear anything Sezel said. He slipped the whistle inside the tight pocket of his shirt and took hold of the other paddle. He then maneuvered the boat into the mainstream of the river as he tried to make sense of what he'd heard Sezel say. *The Isle of Samoway? Did I hear that right?* He was sure Sezel hadn't mentioned it before. Was it even on the map? He didn't remember seeing it.

CHAPTER TEN

Dusk followed the murky day with barely any warning, except that the air became noticeably cooler. Only then did Bozel think of looking for a place to put the boat ashore. With night approaching so quickly, he wished he'd considered the notion much sooner. His tense overworked muscles were in need of a rest from rowing.

After he'd secured the paddles in their holders, Bozel reached for the tall narrow-necked gourd. He pulled out the stopper and took two long swallows. He then felt around in the bottom of the boat for his blanket, finding it he wrapped himself in it, then leaned his back against the boat. He stared up at the darkening sky.

The moon, already visible, was no more than a quarter of the size it would be when full. Bozel released a deep breath, knowing he should have taken another look at Sezel's map before it had begun to get dark. It worried him that he had no notion of how far he might be from a place to make land.

The long day of sitting at the paddles had put a strain on his whole body. The rowing was harder than he'd imagined it would be. It had been far too long since he'd worked at it this hard, and it would definitely take some getting used to.

For now, it felt good to be still and let the boat ride the current while he allowed his kinked muscles to relax. The motion of the boat was soothing, and he soon came to realize how easy it would be for him to fall asleep. *That must never happen,* warned the little voice inside his head. The thought instantly sobered him.

He sat up straight and took several more swallows from the tall gourd before he replaced the stopper and put it away again. The cold water tasted good, but his eyes still felt just as heavy. To fall asleep with the boat adrift was too risky. No telling where he might end up. He slid an arm over the side and scooped up a hand full of water to rub over his face and neck. The water was colder than he'd expected.

Somewhat refreshed, he sat up again and grabbed the lantern. He wanted to find a place on the map where he could land the boat before it got any darker. At exactly the same moment he managed to light the candle inside the lantern, he heard a loud squeaking sound directly overhead. When he looked up, a large cluster of black bats swooped toward him. For a moment, they hovered over his boat like an enormous black cloud. The noise of their high pitched screeches sent a piercing chill straight down his backbone. His breath caught and he felt his chest tighten with fear.

In the next heartbeat, the bats were so close Bozel could see the details of their shiny bead-like eyes and their hideous pinched faces, their pointed ears and their glistening black noses. When they screeched, their mouths opened to reveal double rows of white teeth, sharply pointed and incredibly long. Bozel sucked in a quick breath and held it as he slid further down into the bottom of the boat.

The bats passed over him, and as they did, Bozel sucked in another short breath of air. Some of the bats flew so low Bozel could have reached up and pulled a few of them from the sky. That's if he'd wanted to.

Seconds later, the bats' thick claws broke the surface of the water a short distance away. Bozel peered over the side of the boat and watched them skim along the top of the water. Their wings never touched. When they lifted off again, he could see fish wriggling in their claws. Another cluster of bats followed, hitting the water with their claws just as the others left. Another cluster followed and another after that. Bozel stopped counting, astonished to see so many of them.

Bozel knew where the bats came from. Although more than one species of bat lived on Barren Island, the old ones talked only about the large Black Fisher Bats. They were the most memorable because they were the biggest and the scariest, their faces thought to be gruesome. Now that he'd seen them up close, Bozel could agree. The bats were appalling to look upon. Even more frightful than their hideous facial features was their size, which was several times larger than a Green Fairy's.

From time to time, Bozel had seen these huge bats fly across the late evening sky above Cottersdamp Island. To see the bats come that far north on the river was not unusual. They went wherever fish were plentiful.

The inhabitants of Cottersdamp were horrified by the sight of them. All their lives they'd been told tales about islanders carried off by black bats and fed to their young hungry offspring. No one knew where these stories came from, and no one presently living on Cottersdamp Island had ever witnessed such a thing.

Nevertheless, the Green Fairies warned their children to take shelter at the nearest house if ever they saw a bat of any kind. Bozel found it hard to believe so many bats could live together on one small island. He was even more surprised the river held enough fish to keep them all fed, but apparently it did.

The bats continued to show up, wave upon wave. Bozel watched them make their appearance into the night sky as if they'd come through their own secret portal. He envisioned an undisclosed gateway behind a dark curtain somewhere in the heavens, its existence known to the Black Fisher Bats alone.

Bozel clenched his teeth and grabbed one of the paddles, his only means of self defense. Although it wouldn't be much protection should the bats actually attack him, having a weapon made him feel safer. He looked on in fearful fascination as the bats fluttered over him, some of them diving again and again to catch a fish, others simply passing through, a catch already squirming in their black claws.

Of all the bats that flew over, the ones with their fresh catches worried Bozel the most. *What if a fish gets away and it falls inside my boat? Will the bat come to fetch it?* The thought that such a thing could happen made his flesh want to shrivel on his bones. Bozel gripped his paddle a little tighter.

For the first time in his life he understand the meaning of *cold sweat*. It was something he'd heard the old ones say whenever they wanted to explain how they felt in the midst of a terrifying experience. Bozel shuddered. All at once he started to shake. He shook from fright as much as from the cold. He drew his limbs in close to his body and curled himself up into a ball, his blanket pulled tight around him.

Long after the bats were gone, Bozel remained there in the bottom of his boat watching the candle's small flame flicker in the darkness.

In spite of his misgivings about drifting into danger, exhaustion overcame him, and he slipped into a long deep sleep.

CHAPTER ELEVEN

The approaching light of day woke him. Frantic to untangle himself from his blanket, Bozel ignored his stiff aching muscles and struggled to sit up. He looked all around. Nothing about this part of the river looked familiar, and he had no notion of where he was.

When he looked behind him, he saw the river had taken a wide bend during the night. He guessed he was now headed in a more easterly direction. The river itself had narrowed by half, and up ahead, steep rocky cliffs bordered both sides. The cliffs appeared to go on without end.

As the morning sky brightened, Bozel noticed a faded ribbon of pink and orange light drifting above the surface of the water. Soon, the rim of a golden orb began to rise behind it. Bozel stared in wonder as the slow growing orb gradually became a massive ball of brilliant orange.

For an instant, he was given to the illusion that this breathtaking vision might actually be climbing up out of the river itself. He knew better, of course; this was not a reasonable thought. Yet he half expected to see sheets of water cascade over its fiery orange face as it emerged.

When the specialness of the moment finally became real for him, he knew he was witness to something extraordinary. This was something he hadn't seen in many months, something he used to take for granted - the miracle of a sunrise. For Bozel, this was a magical experience, and his heart filled with a happiness that brought tears to his eyes. Not too long ago he'd given up the hope that he'd ever see the sun rise again.

He celebrated this miraculous event by breaking the night's fast with a piece of dried tanga fruit. While he savored its sweet tangy taste he tried to remember every moment he and Cazara had shared together on the beach barely a day ago. He was tempted to eat another piece of the dried fruit, but he thought he'd like to save the last two slices for the next special occasion. What that might turn out to be, he couldn't be sure, but it would be something out of the ordinary.

As the day wore on, the sun grew hotter. By midday, the sun was high in the bluest sky Bozel could ever remember having seen, and there wasn't a cloud anywhere. Eventually, the sun's heat and its unfamiliar brightness became a bit overwhelming for Bozel. His energy drained quickly, and he found himself taking more and more time away from rowing. Even so, time away from the oars gave him the chance to study Sezel's map a little closer.

There wasn't much detail to it. The map was hardly more than a crude sketch. He recalled Sezel's last words and thought he ought to look for the Isle of Samoway. Nevertheless, having gone over the map several times, he couldn't find it. This came as no surprise since Sezel had forgotten to mention the whistle or the Spotted Gray Matoose beforehand.

The Spotted Gray Matoose had to be a bird of some kind. Why else would Sezel have waved his arms up and down as he had if not to imitate a bird's wings flapping. Remembering the whistle now, Bozel felt the pocket of his shirt to be sure it was still there.

By mid-afternoon Bozel could feel his face, ears, and neck burning. He got some relief from sloshing water over his upper body. The effects weren't long lasting, and all he could think about was how he could get away from the heat. He considered jumping into the river for a quick swim. In the end, caution won out over his desire to cool off.

Here in the sunlight, he could see clear to the bottom of the river in places. The water looked extremely deep. If he were to judge from the ripples he saw on the surface of the river, the current moved much faster than he could swim. To leave the boat in these waters simply wouldn't be wise. Had there been a place to beach the boat, he would have welcomed the chance to take a swim close to the shore.

In the meantime, Bozel did what he could to make his life bearable. He soaked his blanket in the river and draped it over himself in a tent-like fashion. It worked well to protect his head and body from the sun, and it gave him the respite from the heat he needed. Soon enough, the sun would go down.

Hunched forward and cloaked in the still damp blanket, Bozel chewed on a mouthful of dried fish and mushrooms. His paddles secured and the boat adrift, he gave his bunched muscles some time to loosen up. With night about to descend, the faint outline of a crescent moon became visible once again. Bozel was relieved to see the moon waxing. *If only the stars would come out.* He couldn't remember when last he'd seen them. *Now that would be something to celebrate.*

A clammy, bone chilling cold found its way up through the bottom of the boat and Bozel's feet felt icy cold. He wished he had another blanket. Exhausted from the almost constant rowing of the past two hours, he yearned for sleep. Yet high cliffs still bordered both sides of the river, and once again, there was no place to put ashore for the night.

Sleep would have to wait. All the same, Bozel needed to ease the tension in his upper body. If he leaned his back against the boat, he knew he'd be fast asleep in moments. He dare not take the risk. He rested his chin on his knees instead. Yet it seemed to make no difference; moments later he found himself fighting the urge to close his eyes.

This will not do, he scolded himself and sat up straight. After a drink from the narrow-necked gourd, he poured a little of the water into the palm of one hand and rubbed it over his face. It seemed to help.

Since he'd already used up his only candle the night before, he thought he'd better take another look at Sezel's map now. There was barely enough light left to read it. With the map smoothed out over his knees, he traced his finger over Sezel's sketch of the river. His finger stopped at the spot where the river divided into two separate waterways. The west branch veered right. That was the one Sezel advised him to take when the time came. On the map, it was narrow in comparison to the east branch, and more narrow still inside the rocky gorge.

Bozel slid his finger back to the rocky beach, the place where he was supposed to abandon his boat before he was to set out on foot. Sezel had marked it well. The beach was located on the right bank of the west branch. He figured the Isle of Samoway must be somewhere down river from there, although Sezel had forgotten to include it on the map.

What if the Isle of Samoway came up before the rocky beach? No matter, Bozel was certain he'd find it. He may have to follow the river on foot after abandoning the boat on the rocky beach. Even though it would mean he'd go out of his way, it would be worth it to find the Spotted Gray Matoose, if the bird could lead him to the Land of Knownotten.

He looked again at the place where the river divided. It seemed a long way off as it appeared on Sezel's map. Chances were, he wouldn't reach it until sometime the next day. That's if he found a place to put ashore for the night. Tracing his finger over the course of the river once more, he looked for a place to lay in and get some sleep.

This can't be. His stomach tightened. According to Sezel's sketch, high cliffs lined both shores all the way to the place where the river divided. There was nowhere suitable to make landfall before that. Bozel felt a rush of anger. *Why didn't I notice this sooner?*

Why hadn't Sezel bothered to point this out? Bozel shook his head in disbelief. He couldn't imagine why his father hadn't mentioned it. Did they think he could row all day and all night without any sleep? How was he even supposed to know where he was going when there was barely enough moonlight to see by?

Sick with fear and the fear beginning to cloud his judgment, Bozel berated himself for allowing his only candle to burn down to nothing his first night on the river. *What if I miss seeing the rocky beach and my boat gets caught in the rapids?*

His mind churned for several long moments before a sudden truth struck him. *What if the map's wrong?* Neither Sezel nor his father had been to this part of the river in years. Now that he thought about it, Bozel figured Sezel had simply left out some of the finer details.

Whether the map was accurate or not, he'd just have to keep his eyes open and stay sharp. Unless he was able to find a place to get off the river sooner, Bozel guessed his boat would reach the rocky beach sometime during the night. He didn't dare sleep until he found it. Maybe the rocky beach wasn't as far away as it appeared on the map. So much the better.

Once the anger passed, Bozel tried to reason with the negative side of himself, wanting to make himself feel better about his circumstances. *Tonight's moon is a bit bigger; it's bound to lend enough light for me to pick out the rocky beach in time. I'll find it, why worry?*

Bozel had no notion of how long he'd sat there staring at the map and not chewing. He'd only been conscious of the emotions that boiled up inside of him as he tried to make sense of his situation and cope with his frustrations. Now he realized the dried fish and mushrooms had turned sour in his mouth while he fumed over the map.

He spit what was left of the mess into the river. As soon as he lifted the narrow necked gourd to his lips to drink, he caught sight of a fair sized land mass in the middle of the river a few yards ahead of him. In fact, if he kept to his present course, his boat would be on its beach shortly.

He instantly knew he was fast approaching the fire ravaged shores of Barren Island. The gourd slipped from Bozel's fingers as he grabbed for the paddles. It was a small island, and the twisted branches of its blackened trees stood out like specters silhouetted against the late evening sky.

Better to risk the rapids than land here. *It's dusk. Where are the bats? They should be leaving the island to look for food. Could they already be gone?* But then he heard them. Random chirps and squeaks echoed from the island as if the bats had awakened at his bidding. As soon as he heard the bats, Bozel paddled faster while he steered the boat toward the river's right bank, desperate to avoid washing up on the beach of Barren Island. *Good Spirit, help me. I must not land here.*

A distant memory from his youth stirred, and an old fisherman's tale bubbled to the surface of his mind. Bits of conversations he'd overheard long ago were instantly recalled along with stories about this island and the creature who haunted it. His skin prickled, and he gagged on the sour taste of dried fish and mushrooms that was still heavy on his tongue, but he was determined to keep it all down. There was no time to be sick.

While he rowed he prayed aloud for the current to carry him past the island as quick as possible. Yet, the opposite was actually happening. The current, instead, had begun to pull his boat toward Barren Island. If he intended to avoid the shallow waters close to its beach, he knew he'd have to row much harder than this.

Without wanting it to, the vivid image of Sezel's friend, Mezer, came to mind. The old fisherman's face was still alive in his memory in astonishing detail, a gray boney mask covered with blisters, blind eyes embedded deep within dark hollowed sockets.

Mezer had been missing for days. Sezel and several other fisherman had been out looking for him. It was Sezel who finally found him and pulled him from the Slewnecky River, and it hadn't been far from Barren Island. Poor old Mezer, he was near death by the time Sezel brought him home to Cottersdamp.

Stick thin and unable to walk, Mezer had only lasted another day. His wild ranting about being held captive on Barren Island started a rash of rumors that have never been put to rest since that dreadful day. Because of the long and unsettling uproar that followed, many Green Fairies thought everyone would have been better off if Mezer had not been found at all.

Rumors of Mezer's condition and what he'd had to say about his time on Barren Island set off a wave of mind numbing terror. Alarming rumors washed over Cottersdamp Island and all of the other islands to the north of it. Soon the old legend of the princess who had defied her father was resurrected. For a long time after that, the legend was all anybody on any of the islands talked about.

The fishermen had always told bizarre stories about Barren Island. One got used to hearing them. Many of the islanders believed the stories. Still, there were as many others who thought such talk nothing more than a fisherman's wild imaginings. These skeptics refused to give credence to such tales, saying that those who told the tales had spent too much time alone on the river, suggesting they had gone a bit daft. Green Fairies didn't like to dwell on such things as ghosts, curses, and evil spirits. It was against their beliefs.

Fishermen, on the other hand, were a superstitious lot, and so were the Flatlanders who lived on Cottersdamp Island at that time. After they'd seen Mezer in that unspeakable state, many nonbelievers changed their minds about Barren Island. All at once, the story about the princess and the curse was no longer some old legend passed down through the ages to entertain family and friends on stormy nights.

The Green Fairies who had cared for Mezer had heard Mezer's account of what had happened to him from his own parched and blistered lips. Although a good deal of what Mezer had said was jumbled and incoherent, his listeners believed every word of it.

Of course, these gentle folk were struck by the condition in which Mezer had been found; however, where he'd been found was the most telling of all.

CHAPTER TWELVE

The young princess who had been exiled to Slewnecky Island - its name before the fire - had been sent there by her father, King Renzel. Exile was the punishment imposed on her for poisoning the being her father had intended she should marry. But this was not her only vile deed. She had been the cause of a great deal of suffering in the past. Nevertheless, murder was more than King Renzel was willing to put up with.

Legend was, the king feared his daughter. The princess had inherited special powers from her queen mother that King Renzel was unable to control. For that reason, the king knew mere exile would not keep the princess on Slewnecky Island. Something more would have to be done.

The king struggled with this decision for many days and as many nights before he finally did what he believed his poor dead wife, the queen, would have advised under such circumstances. He summoned a powerful witch from the Land of Boarsbreek to place a curse on his daughter. The curse altered her physical body in such a way that she would never be able to leave the island.

Even so, the princess retained her power to cast spells, as anyone foolish enough to ignore the warnings against visiting Slewnecky Island soon witnessed. Had King Renzel been able to discover a way to control his daughter's powers, or her behavior, it never would have come to this.

Some years after the princess's exile, a fire broke out on Slewnecky Island. No one knew what had caused it. It might have been a lightning storm, or the sun so hot it had scorched the trees, causing them to ignite. Perhaps it had even been deliberate. Nevertheless, the king's daughter perished in it.

After the fire, the island was barren of all life. Nothing has grown there since, hence its new name, Barren Island. But that was not the end of the story, nor was it the end of the wicked princess. Tales about fishing boats being drawn to the island against the fishermen's will caused a panic that soon had fishermen traveling out of their way to avoid the waters anywhere near there.

Whenever a fisherman was late returning home from a long fishing trip down river, their wives and children couldn't help but believe the worst had happened. Until they learned otherwise, they feared the fisherman had been taken by the ghostly princess. So it was, that eventually, the island came to be called "Haunted Island" by the fishermen and the Flatlanders alike.

Hirsol had little regard for these tall tales, as he insisted on calling them, and he'd cautioned Bozel about listening to such tripe. Even after he saw Mezer, Hirsol continued to resist the notion, saying the old fisherman had been in the sun too long and had probably suffered a stroke.

At the moment, Bozel's heart would have been gladdened had his mind been able to dispel these stories about Haunted Island. It may have been easy enough to do in the full light of day. Yet, here alone in this boat with another dark night descending, and the knowledge that the sky above him would soon be thick with large black bats, Bozel was close to wetting his pants.

His lungs and his muscles burned from rowing, but he was too afraid to stop. Bozel was beginning to lose faith in Sezel's recollection of this part of the river altogether. The old one's map had shown Barren Island to be much farther down river, yet here it was. Sezel's sketch also showed trees growing along the tops of the cliffs on either side of the river where Barren Island was supposed to be. That would have made perfect sense, since the island itself had once been covered by forest. Nevertheless, there were no trees to be seen on the tops of these cliffs.

Sezel must have gotten it wrong, that would explain it. What other reason could there be, unless the island itself had moved. Bozel wondered about that too. He'd once heard a story about a floating island, and it was supposed to be true. He guessed that was possible. But it was more sensible to believe Sezel had made a mistake about the location of Barren Island. *Islands in the Slewnecky River can't move, can they? Cottersdamp never had.*

A jarring bump threw Bozel backwards when the bottom of the boat scraped against sand and came to a dead stop. Since he was still several yards from Barren Island's beach, Bozel was fairly certain he must have hit a small sandbar. This had happened two or three times before when he'd been out fishing with Sezel and his father. He knew what he had to do to get the boat unstuck.

He considered getting out of the boat to push it off the sandbar. Nevertheless, leaving the safety of his boat so close to Barren Island was too scary to think about. The strange current in these waters around the island was another worry. The current was untrustworthy. Once off the sandbar, the boat could be pulled away from him before he had a chance to climb back into it.

In the end, Bozel decided to use one of his paddles to push the boat off the sandbar. When he'd watched his father do this, it hadn't looked too difficult. Two or three pushes was the most it had ever taken to get the boat moving again. He stood up and shoved his paddle into the sandbar. Then he leaned on the paddle the way he'd seen his father do. He pushed his full weight against it. He pushed until he felt his face grow hot, and until he thought his heart would burst, but the boat refused to budge.

The smaller Brown Bats were already beginning to leave Barren Island, and Bozel didn't like being out in the open. He considered hiding under his blanket until they were all gone. But he feared that by then it would be too dark to see what he needed to do. "Please, Good Spirit," he whispered aloud, "don't let me get stranded in this haunted place."

His skin was damp with the sweat of fear and he shuddered when a light evening breeze blew over him. Still praying under his breath, he leaned on the paddle and tried again, pushing with all his strength. He pushed against the sandbar until his limbs shook from weakness. This time the boat did move, but not enough to make a difference.

What is wrong here? Why isn't this working? Bozel decided it would take a lot of more pushing to get this boat off the sandbar. *Better to get out now, and give the boat a good shove. Then I can be on my way,* he told himself, calling on his courage.

When he jumped out of the boat, the water was past his knees and cold enough to send icy shock waves through his body. He sucked in a breath and felt the goose bumps spread over him as he sloshed his way toward the rear of the boat.

He dug both of his feet into the sand for leverage and began to push against the back of the boat. He continued to push until he was breathless and his limbs felt limp and useless. Still the boat would not move. Bozel stood up and blew a forced breath through his lips, his insides shaking.

About to push again, he noticed the chirps of the bats getting louder. Their wings fluttered above him. Without even looking up, he knew these were the large Black Fisher Bats he'd seen the night before. Crouched as low in the water as he dared, he pressed his shivering body against the boat and covered his face with both hands. He prayed he wouldn't be seen as the bats flew over.

When fairly certain all the bats had left, he got up and gave the boat another hefty shove. The result was same. The boat didn't move. Tears began to roll down his cheeks as all the nightmarish thoughts about this journey and failing his folk came rushing back at him.

If he didn't figure out how to get his boat off this sandbar everyone on Cottersdamp Island would perish, and it would be his fault. He'd been chosen because everyone, including his father, believed he could do this. He wondered what Dada would advise under the circumstances. *What if my father was here right now; what would he do?*

Bozel took in a few slow breaths and tried to quiet his mind so he could think properly. *Something's in front of the boat.* With this thought in mind, he tromped through the icy water to the front of the boat to see if he was right.

When he got there, he discovered a huge mound of sand in front of the boat, blocking it. Bozel wanted to laugh. If he hadn't been in such a panic, he might have thought to look in front of the boat a lot sooner. He cupped his hands and bent over to throw water over his burning face.

Back inside the boat, Bozel pushed against the sandbar with his paddle. But this time he pushed from the front of the boat and in the opposite direction.

When he pushed in this direction, the main current was in his favor. This would make it easier; however, once he was off the sandbar, he'd once again be at the mercy of Barren Island's bizarre mesmeric pull, and his boat would be dragged toward its haunted shore. That's why the fishermen were afraid to sail too close to the waters around this island. That's what had happened to Mezer.

Bozel took in a deep breath and summoned his courage. He was ready for this. He expected he'd have to paddle even faster and harder than he had before. He was afraid, too. But fear no longer ruled over him to cloud his judgment as it had before.

From inside the boat, Bozel pushed against the sandbar until he felt the Slewnecky River's mainstream current lift his boat. The sudden thrust of the boat forced him to sit down hard. He grabbed the other paddle. With a good grip on the handles of both paddles,

Bozel pulled back and began to row, but in the opposite direction from the way he'd pushed to get off the sandbar.

This time he rowed with purpose, intent on breaking away from the magnetic pull that threatened to deliver his boat to Barren Island. His paddles sliced through the water with steady even strokes. Bozel was determined to make every one of them count. He rowed until he felt the cords of his neck stand out, and until he thought his back would break and his lungs would surely burst.

The muscles of his arms and shoulders burned from overuse. Yet his body endured the hardship. Even when he thought it was impossible to row another stroke, Bozel discovered he could row anyway. He rowed until he felt the Slewnecky River's mainstream current liberate his boat from Barren Island's wicked pull and carry it downriver once more.

As soon as the mainstream current took over, rowing instantly became easy. The boat would have moved along all on its own at this point. Even so, Bozel chose not to slow down. Only when the menacing image of Barren Island had faded completely from view did he feel safe enough to allow himself to stop rowing.

Much later that night, Bozel saw an ancient evergreen forest on top of the high shale cliffs above the river. Some of the trees grew on the edge of the cliffs. The roots of these trees were exposed and they cascaded down over the cliff's rocky shale face all the way to the river below. Bozel had never before seen the roots of trees growing in this manner. He imagined the roots must have caused the rock to split as they'd grown, pushing their way through the shale and its thin layers of soil. Unable to bear the strain, parts of the shale cliffs had fallen away.

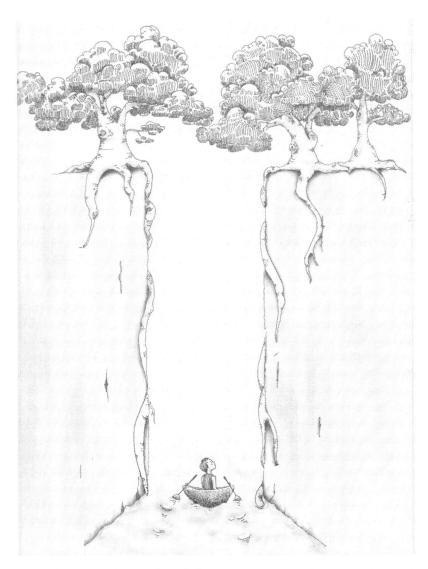

The trees that had ended up growing on the very edge had not only survived, but they were thriving as well. A coating of bark had grown over these once fragile roots to shield them against the harshest weather. Bozel was fascinated by their intricate patterns of growth and how the roots had woven their way through and around the shale in their efforts to hold on.

As he studied the roots in the moonlight, he noticed a few sturdy ones had grown below the water level. He stopped rowing and looped the rope around one of them. After tying the ends of the rope together, he curled up in his blanket to sleep.

The first thing Bozel noticed when he opened his eyes again were the cliffs above him. They looked quite different from the way they had the night before. All at once it struck him: the boat was moving. It was actually traveling rather fast through a narrow gorge. Glancing at the coil of rope now, his eyes widened. It was clear what had happened. Sometime during the night the knot in the rope had slipped.

Barely breathing, he sat up and gripped the sides of the boat as yet another unsettling realization came to him. The boat had already gone well past the place where the river divided. Even worse, Bozel wasn't sure which branch of the river the boat had taken. He yanked the map from his pocket and rolled it out on his knees. Yet not until he saw the sun coming up did he realize he was actually headed east, toward the falls.

Just how far out of the way he'd gone, there was no way of telling. That portion of the map was poorly drawn. Sezel hadn't bothered to sketch in unnecessary details. Only a little of the east fork of the Slewnecky River had been included. All he really knew for certain was that he was traveling through a narrow gorge in the wrong direction, and that his life would soon be in danger.

Bozel groaned inwardly, wondering if he'd be able to turn the boat around and find the west fork. It would be tough to row against this fast current, but what else could he do? He reached round for the paddles. They were gone.

CHAPTER THIRTEEN

A brand new fear swept over him. He was certain he'd secured the paddles properly before he'd tied the rope, but they were gone, nonetheless. His mind raced. To go back to the fork in the river without paddles was impossible. He studied the map again, and then he dragged his eyes along the rugged, rocky face of the cliffs that loomed above him on both sides of the narrow gorge. The cliffs were steep, but if he wanted to come out of this alive, he knew he'd have to make the climb and begin his trek over land.

If he was to judge by the increasing swiftness of the current, and the loud sounds of rushing water, the falls weren't that far away. Bozel knew he'd have to make his move soon, while there was still enough time for him to make the swim to the cliffs.

He stuffed the map into the pocket of his shirt, and wrapped the remainder of the dried fish and mushrooms together in the piece of waxed cloth. The packet of food he tucked inside his shirt next to his skin. Afterward, he climbed over the side of the boat and slid into the river, gasping aloud as the frigid water embraced his thin body. Bozel knew he'd have to keep moving before he became paralyzed by the cold if he expected to reach the rocky face of the cliffs in time.

Bozel kicked his legs out behind him, cutting a diagonal path through the water as he swam toward the cliffs. Any attempt to swim straight across would have been futile. The swift current would have pulled him farther down river anyway. Fortunately, there were only a few yards to swim before he'd be there.

Upon reaching the rocky face of the cliff, he grabbed on with both hands. As an afterthought, he looked for the boat. It was nowhere to be seen. He was sure it had gone over the falls by now. Even though he would have had to abandon the boat anyway sooner or later, Bozel felt a small ache for its loss and the way it had come about. Nevertheless, he was grateful to have gotten out when he did.

While clinging to the rocks with his toes and the fingers of one hand, Bozle reached inside his shirt to feel for the packet of food. Thank the Good Spirit it hadn't been lost during the swim. At the same time he remembered the dried tanga fruit. In his haste to leave the boat, he'd forgotten all about it. A wave of sadness and disappointment washed over him. *Cazara, forgive me.*

Cold water lapped at his back while his toes searched for the next foothold. Finding it, he reached up, grabbed onto the rock above and pulled himself up. He felt around for another placement, then dug his toes in and pulled himself up a bit higher. The rocks below the waterline were slick with algae. That alone would make the climb slow and tedious.

His body had become accustomed to the temperature of the water. Nevertheless, the unrelenting cold wind that blew through the gorge and against the wet clothes that clung to his back, his arms, and his shoulders chilled him through and through. This did not improve as more and more of his body became exposed to the cool, breezy air during the climb.

In spite of everything, Bozel was determined to keep climbing. He grabbed hold of the rock above him and then found the next foothold. One rock at a time, he pulled himself up. He was nearly half way to the top when his right foot slipped.

In the next moment, Bozel found himself sliding back down the jagged rock face. The palms of his hands scraped against the rough rocks as he grappled to get a hold on one that would stop his rapid descent. Before he could, his chin struck a protruding rock, and he plunged backward into the river.

The bone jarring blow shook his whole body. It knocked him senseless, and the pain brought flashing stars to his eyes. Bozel gulped water when his head went under. When his head came up again, he fought to catch his next breath. His chest heaved as he gasped for air while he thrashed about in the cold water.

He flailed the water with both arms while he tried to stay afloat. At the same time he struggled against the pull of the fast current. It could so easily drag him downriver and over the falls. If that happened...

Kicking and splashing his way back to the cliffs, he grasped hold of the slippery rocks. He clung there, waiting until his breathing was near normal and until enough time had passed to slow his pounding heart. His body felt stiff and awkward in the teeth chattering cold. His hands and face burned from the cuts and the scrapes he'd suffered on the rocks during the fall.

The experience was a brutal reminder of how easily things could go wrong. When he felt ready, his cold stiff hands and feet fumbled about in search of reliable placements amid the rocks. He couldn't afford to be careless again. He doubted he was strong enough to survive another fall.

Small hands and feet were to his advantage. Most times, they fit neatly into the tight spaces between the rocks. The soles of his boots were thin, but made of extremely strong fabric. This toughness protected his toes from the sharp-edged rocks closer to the top of the cliff. The same couldn't be said for his poor hands though. By now they were raw from the wounds they'd received on the rocks and rigid from the cold.

Along with the cuts and scrapes, his fingers were skinned and bruised and bleeding by the time he reached the rim. He held onto the rocky ledge with both hands, not daring to look down. Placing his toes in the next available space between the rocks, Bozel reached up and grabbed onto the first sturdy rock he could find. By repeating the process he managed to successfully grope his way over the rim. He crawled away from the edge of the cliff on hands and knees.

A safe distance away, he stood up. His first real glimpse of the treeless rocky landscape was a sinking disappointment. Nothing but rocks in every shade of gray stretched out before him for as far as he could see. He looked around with dread. There wasn't even a decent spot to sit down in comfort to catch his breath. *This is going to take a long time.* He grumbled inwardly as he started his trek across the rocky surface.

The journey over the rocks was just as slow and tedious as the climb up had been, and at times, quite painful on his feet. He found it tricky trying to keep his balance since his boots were still wet. He was prone to constant slipping. At first, it seemed as though he was more often on his knees than on his feet. By late morning his hands, feet, knees, and shins were a mass of throbbing bloody bruises.

It was difficult to think only of those things for which he should be grateful. Yet it was the best way Bozel knew of to keep his spirits up when things looked bleak. *At least it isn't raining,* he told himself. He was just as glad the sky was overcast, since he'd had to leave his water behind. The sun would have made the rocks hot and unbearable.

The map! Bozel pulled it out of his shirt pocket. He shook it out and looked at it. The charcoal markings had run. The whole thing was a mess, and it was altogether unreadable.

A tear slid down Bozel's face. Unconsciously, he wiped at it with the map. For an instant he wanted to be angry with Sezel. He wanted to blame him for everything that had gone wrong so far. Yet he found himself making excuses for the old fisherman instead. Sezel had done the best he could, and Bozel realized he didn't need the map anymore anyway. From here on in he was on his own.

Sometime that afternoon Bozel came to the bottom of the steep incline he'd been traveling since mid-morning. The terrain leveled off for a few feet before it began to slope upward again. He didn't welcome another uphill climb. His hands and feet were extremely tender, and he longed for a drink of water. Bozel figured the rocky landscape had been part of the river bed at one time, probably centuries ago, before the river had ever divided.

The enthusiasm he'd felt for this quest at the onset had slowly ebbed away. Lonely and discouraged beyond anything he'd ever known before, he loathed the thought of having to face another climb or another challenge. Yet there was even less energy to spare on the emotions of frustration and anger.

Driven only by self-determination, he pushed himself forward. In spite of his pains, his body had become something almost mechanical. And he was of a mind to keep it moving so long as all of its parts continued to work.

At some point, Bozel knew he'd need to take stock of his injuries. Like all Green Fairies, he possessed the power to heal himself. It was a magical power, and he'd need to take the time to focus all of his energy inward. Besides that, he had to be in contact with a large body of water in order for this inborn power to work.

Hours later, Bozel came to the crest of a rocky hill. All at once he was met by a remarkable discovery.

"Sand!" he whooped. He scrambled over the last few feet of rocks. *Glorious sand.* He fell upon its smooth, grainy, gray surface and wallowed in its cool softness. It felt good to lie down flat, to stretch out, to rest in comfort. Finally, he rolled onto his back and folded his arms under his head to gaze up at the dull colorless sky.

His thoughts turned inward. This mission had hardly begun, yet nothing had happened as he'd expected it to. So many things seemed beyond his control. Or had these mishaps been due to his own carelessness? No matter, it was done. He couldn't change any of it.

He'd always been taught to guard against those thoughts that threatened to keep his spirits down. No good would come of it. He must think of the lives that depended on him. Finding the Land of Knownotten was all that really mattered in the end.

In the short amount of time he'd been away from home he'd begun to think differently about many things. Maybe it was because he was alone and on his own. Perhaps being responsible for the future of so many others had changed him. This was the first time he'd had to think for himself in the midst of strife, the first time he'd had to make his own decisions.

As a result, he'd gotten to experience the consequences of the choices he'd made. There were no rules to abide by, and no one to consult with about what to do when things went wrong. Everything was decided on the basis of trial and error, and there wasn't even anyone to blame for all the unfortunate mishaps.

For once in his young life he had a sense of self-reliance and what a responsibility that truly was. Whatever happened to him on this journey had the power to make him stronger. Or he could let it destroy him. Only he could decide how this experience would be judged.

His father had said he'd have to live each day as it came. He'd said Bozel wouldn't always be able to see how things were going to turn out in the end. Blaming himself for everything that went wrong, or blaming someone else, wouldn't make him feel any better about the things that had happened. It wouldn't make him stronger either. It was more important to believe he was doing his best. It's how his father would see it.

What he did, and how he thought about the things that happened to him really did matter. His deeds and his outlook on life would determine the kind of being he was to become. There'd always be things he couldn't change or have power over, no matter how hard he tried. That much was plain already. He'd have to accept that and keep going. Should he fail, he vowed it wouldn't be because he'd allowed his own despair to bring him down.

Thoroughly exhausted from the difficult climb and the long journey over the rocks, Bozel welcomed the opportunity to sleep. He dreamed of a strange gray land where everything in it was made from rock, even the trees and the beings who lived there.

Half awake, Bozel became aware of something moving beneath him in the sand, a lump of some kind. He wanted to ignore it. He tried to, but the thing just wouldn't keep still. It seemed to get bigger rather quickly, bumping against him until he was fully awake.

Whatever it was, it had grown large enough to push against his shoulders and his back. A sudden rush of fear and anxiety catapulted him into a sitting position. He turned 'round to stare at the place where he'd been lying. Just as he did, the sand beneath his bottom began to swirl and churn.

Bozel jumped to his feet and moved out of the way just in time. Two broad scaly feet with long thick nails appeared on the surface of the sand. Next came two scaly legs, each limb several times longer than Bozel was tall.

Good Spirit, what is it? Feeling the hair rise on the back of his neck, Bozel started to run. This was not an easy thing to do in dry sand. He hadn't gone far when he heard a gravelly voice with a nasal twang speak out behind him.

"Where are you off to?"

Bozel stopped to look over his shoulder. A flat broad head now stuck up from the sand. Bozel stared at it. "Are you talking to me?"

As soon as Bozel turned around, the two wide nares above the creature's pointed snout blew open to spray fountains of sand through the air all around itself. Much of it cascaded over Bozel. Fortunately, he'd blinked in time to keep the sand from getting into his eyes.

The gravelly voice spoke again. "Who else is here." This wasn't a question.

Bozel answered anyway as he looked around with an edgy uncertainly. "I, ah, don't know. Only you, and me, I guess..."

The creature sneezed, making a loud shrill noise only to give Bozel another start. A light spray of sand followed. At the same time Bozel snatched a quick glimpse inside the creature's enormous mouth. Dozens of great saw-like teeth rimmed its long upper and lower jaws.

Bozel sucked in a short breath of air and held it.

"Green Fairies never come this far down river any more. What brings you here?"

Too frightened to move, Bozel watched the creature dig more of itself out of the sand. Its scaled exterior was of a pebbly texture in shades of gray, charcoal, and black. Bozel was sure he never would have spotted the creature had it been lying amongst the rocks he'd just traveled. He wondered if he might have passed any more of these creatures, unbeknownst to him, along the way.

Bozel spoke slowly, trying not to stammer. "I came to find the Isle of Samoway."

By now, two more of the creature's clawed feet had emerged. "Why would you ever want to go to that place?"

"I have to meet someone there." Bozel didn't feel comfortable telling this strange being too much about himself. Yet he couldn't have said why if he'd been asked.

The creature blew more sand out through its nares. "I see."

Bozel couldn't help letting out a loud gasp as yet another pair of clawed feet were unearthed, making a total of six in all. Only the rest of its thick spiny tail remained to be seen.

The creature lifted its long broad neck off the sand and gazed at him through unblinking orange eyes. Its dark vertical pupils contracted slightly as it spoke. "You seek the Spotted Gray Matoose." With that the creature flipped the rest of its spiny tail into view, flicking more sand over Bozel. The tail was twice the length of its long flat body.

Bozel stumbled backward as the creature's narrow grayish tongue licked out and snatched a large flying beetle from the air above his head.

"There is no need to fear me; I have never harmed a Green Fairy," the creature rumbled after swallowing the ill-fated beetle.

"I'm not afraid of you," Bozel lied, standing his ground.

The creature's feet plowed up the sand as it shuffled its way toward him, flinging sand in every direction.

Bozel found himself leaning away from the advancing creature as he struggled between standing his ground or fleeing for life and limb. "How-how do you know about Green Fairies?"

"For many a year now I've seen your kind on the river gathering their nets filled with fish."

At the thought of being watched by such a creature, Bozel felt a small chill overtake him. "Well, I've fished on this river for many a year too, and I've never seen one of your kind before."

The creature blinked. "Slanks like to keep out of the way. Our appearance is disturbing to others. But our ways are not so different from other beings."

"Your ways? What do you mean?"

"All beings must eat to live, and like you, we too eat the flesh of the fish, but only fish."

"Hah, I just saw you eat a beetle."

"That's different, everyone eats beetles, Green Fairy."

"I don't."

The slank's dark pupils contracted, but he did not comment.

"I suppose you could eat me in one bite too." As quick as these words were spoken, Bozel regretted having said them. "Not that you'd want to," he amended, feeling awkward and wondering why he kept making such dim-witted remarks. "We probably don't taste too good," he added, much to his horror.

"I can see why a little being like you would be wary of a slank, but it's not in our nature to eat Green Fairies. If times were hard it might be different, but there's always fish in the river, and fish flesh is more to my liking."

Although Bozel was somewhat relieved by what the slank had to say about his eating habits, he wasn't ready to trust the monster-sized being altogether. The slank's mouth was just too big, and then there were all those teeth to consider. He wondered why the slank had so many sharp teeth if he ate only fish. The bones of a fish were soft.

"Do you know how I can get to the Isle of Samoway from here?" Bozel asked the question to change the subject as much as to gain information.

The slank slapped his spiny tail against the sand. "It's down there on the other side of the river."

"The river's down there?" Bozel was surprised to find out that the west branch of the river was so close.

"Isn't that where your boat is?"

"I came over the rocks." Bozel moaned, recalling the grueling journey, and the fact that he'd had to abandon his boat, leaving his water and the tanga fruit behind. Afterward, he remembered his decision not to dwell on such things. "All the same, I'm here now."

The slank rolled his oval shaped orange eyes and blinked. "It's too bad you have no boat. The Isle of Samoway is much too far for a Green Fairy to swim, but I could take you."

Bozel brushed some of the sand from his face and forehead. "How? - How would you take me?"

"On my back, how else."

Bozel hesitated; he didn't think it wise to trust the slank nearly that much. Truth be told, he wanted to get away from him. "That's kind of you to offer, but..."

The slank wasn't fooled. Part of the reason he'd survived for so long in these parts was because of his size and his menacing appearance. That in itself was enough to discourage most other creatures with hostile intentions from bothering him, or attempting to move in on his fishing grounds. Even the Shaggy Red Buckwetcher stayed out of his way.

"I can't blame you for being afraid of me. Perhaps I'd feel much the same if I were you. So I'll leave you now, Green Fairy."

The slank turned away and began to claw its way through the sand as it headed for the river.

"Did you say the river was down that way?" Bozel shouted after the slank, nearly changing his mind. He had no notion of how he'd get to the Isle of Samoway unless he allowed the slank to take him across the river; nevertheless, there was this irksome uncertainty about the creature, and he couldn't ignore it.

"It's right over that sand dune. I'm going that way if you care to come along."

Bozel followed the slank at what he considered to be a safe distance. Although he knew it wasn't safe at all. If this powerful creature wanted to eat him, surely distance wouldn't stop him. At the top of the small sandy hill Bozel could see the west branch of the river and the tiny islet that was the Isle of Samoway. Although the west branch wasn't as wide as the east branch, and the Isle of Samoway didn't appear to be all that far, the swim to reach it would be impossible for Bozel. The slank was right about that.

The river was calm, leaving Bozel to believe that this part of the western branch was well above the rapids. How he wished he had his boat.

"It's not a big place." The slank looked out over the river. "I hope you'll be able to find the Spotted Gray Matoose."

This was another awkward moment for Bozel. He didn't know what to say to the slank, other than to thank him and let him be on his way. Even so, Bozel had no notion of how he'd ever reach the Isle of Samoway on his own. The slank began his trek down the sandy dune before Bozel could manage to get the words out of his throat.

"Thanks for your help," he shouted weakly, not even sure if he'd voiced it loud enough for the slank to hear.

Without a word, the slank slid neatly into the river and disappeared beneath its surface. When Bozel was sure the slank was far enough away, he followed its tracks down to the edge of the water. He knelt down and cupped his hands to take a drink. The water was cold and delicious.

It had been a long time since anything to eat or drink had passed his lips. Right away, he realized how hungry he was. He fumbled inside his shirt for the packet of dried fish and mushrooms. Finding it, he pulled it out to examine its soggy contents. Even though the food was ruined, he might have eaten it anyway, but the mess fell apart in his hands and dropped in the sand in front of him.

In spite of the promise he'd made to himself earlier that day, feelings of despair welled up inside of him. Sick to his stomach about missing his chance to get to the Isle of Samoway, he couldn't stop the loud sob that burst from his throat. Throwing himself onto the sand, he cried aloud until his emotions were spent.

The crying done, he reached for the old cloth map to wipe his eyes and blow his nose. When he yanked the map from his pocket this time the wooden cylinder Sezel had given him flew out along with it and landed in the sand by his feet.

With all that had happened, Bozel had forgotten about the whistle. He picked it up and dumped out the sand. Then he put the whistle to his lips and blew on it as hard as he could. The whistle sounded incredibly loud on the quiet beach. Bozel waited a few moments, then blew on the whistle again. He wasn't sure what he expected to happen next.

Barely conscious of his own actions, he pulled off his boots and stuck his bruised feet in the river. He tried to recall what he thought Sezel had been trying to tell him as his boat was drifting away from Cottersdamp Island on that dreary morning. He was certain Sezel had said the Spotted Gray Matoose would take him to the Land of Knownotten. Bozel hoped with all his heart that this was true. After everything that had gone wrong, he wasn't sure he'd be able to find it without getting himself lost a time or two.

He pushed the whistle back inside his pocket, then leaning forward, he cupped his hands for another drink. There was nothing he could do now but wait and watch the light fade from the late afternoon sky. He thought about Cazara and wondered if he'd ever see her or his family again.

Then, pushing all other thought aside, Bozel waded into the river until the water reached his waist. Once his body had adjusted to the extreme cold, he began to bathe his arms and then his chest. Finally, he ducked his head under. Now that he was completely wet, he could focus his attention on his healing energy.

It was long after dark by the time Bozel saw a large bird land on the wet sand at the edge of the river some distance away. He wondered if it might be the Spotted Gray Matoose. He'd been sitting there for so long, he was beginning to wonder if the Spotted Gray Matoose would ever come. He watched the bird dip its beak for a drink of water and waited until it had swallowed before he tried to get its attention.

"Are you the Spotted Gray Matoose?" Bozel called out to the bird, his timid voice laced with a trace of excitement.

The bird swiveled its long neck to look at him. "I am a Spotted Gray Matoose, but I am not the one you seek. My mate was killed in a battle with an osprey not two days ago. I have come in his place. My name's Menna."

Bozel stood up. I'm happy to meet you, Menna. I'm Bozel. I'm so sorry to hear about your mate, how terrible." Not knowing what to say to the poor bird he finished with, "What an awful thing to happen. I hope he didn't suffer much."

"Yes, it was awful, I saw it all. He died protecting me. Why have you come looking for him?"

The spotted Gray Matoose had the odd habit of ducking her head at the end of almost everything she said.

"This may sound a bit strange," Bozel admitted. "But the friend who gave me the whistle told me the Spotted Gray Matoose would take me to the Land of Knownotten."

The large bird gave Bozel an odd look, rotating her small head as if to look at him from a different angle. "I can take you to Knownotten Kingdom, but we must not delay. I will be too big to fly in a few days' time." She ducked her head again.

Bozel's eyes widened. "Too big to fly?"

"My eggs are growing fast. If I become much heavier, my wings won't be strong enough to lift me."

"Oh." Bozel hardly knew what to say to this, feeling even worse now than he had before about the bird losing her mate.

"I will need some time to find a suitable place to prepare another burrow for my chicks before my laying time, so if you're set on going, we can leave now."

"But this is your home, how can you leave it?"

The bird dipped her head a few times before she answered. "I have no desire to remain on the Isle of Samoway now that my mate has been killed. Here in this place, danger stalks me at every turn."

"Then it's better to leave. But how will I keep up with you if you are to fly?"

The Spotted Gray Matoose cocked her head to fix one small black eye on him. "You must sit on my back and fly along with me, Green Fairy. Have you never flown upon the back of a bird before?"

Bozel was stunned by the notion. "I've never heard of such a thing."

"If you were to walk, that would take many days."

"How long will it take to fly?"

"That would depend on how often I would need to stop and rest, I suppose. If you had come a day or so later, I would not be able to make this journey at all."

Bozel knew he had no choice but to fly with this bird, even though he was more than a little uneasy about it. But for some reason he trusted the Spotted Gray Matoose. After all, Sezel had told him about the bird, and there was nothing menacing in her behavior. He didn't feel the least bit frightened around her. Maybe fate had thrown the two of them together for a reason, both of them having to leave their homes and start their lives over in another land.

"I'm ready to go if you think this is a good time." Bozel sat in the sand to pull on his boots. "I don't know what I would have done if you hadn't been able to hear my whistle on the Isle of Samoway. I was afraid I was too far away for anyone to hear it."

The bird gave Bozel a peculiar stare. "Whistle? I heard no whistle."

"If you didn't hear the whistle, then how did you know I was here?"

The gray matoose cocked her head to one side and blinked at him. "The Six-Footed Sand Slank, 'twas he who came and told me you were waiting here."

PART TWO

Knownotten Kingdom

CHAPTER ONE

Topaz's sensitive pink nostrils quivered and flared as he breathed in the damp leafy fragrance mingled with the coming rain. This was the oldest part of the Knownotten Forest and he was standing on its deepest floor. The trees here were many thousands of years old and they'd stood strong in this forest long before his ancestors had arrived.

Distracted by a falling elm leaf, Topaz watched it drift toward him on its way to the ground. He thought of his old friend, Otis, and wondered what it would be like to fly above the tree tops and look down on his beloved forest from the sky.

Topaz didn't usually take his morning walks in the older part of the forest, but this wasn't an ordinary day. Today marked the one year anniversary of the death of his closest friend, King Kittle, the Elf king, who had ruled this land before him. Topaz wanted to pay his respects to the memory of his beloved friend in his own way.

King Kittle had been the longest living of all the Elf kings to rule in the Land of Knownotten. He'd outlived any royal heirs that might have succeeded him except for the one who'd called himself

Dominance. But that was another story, one Topaz didn't care to recall often.

This cool dark part of the forest was as familiar to Topaz as his favorite room in the castle. He thought of it as his secret place, his sanctuary. In another age it had been his home and the home of his ancestors, the Yellow Conjure Cats, a large, lean, muscular breed that had migrated here from another land centuries before.

Legend said they were from a faraway place across many great rivers. Topaz had his reasons for believing it must be true. Since they'd come, Yellow Conjure Cats had been loyal to the noble succession of Elf kings that had once reigned over this kingdom. In their time, these large cats had roamed this mountainous forest to protect it from intruders.

A breed unlike any other, these magnificent yellow cats could be identified by their pale orange stripes and their strange luminous eyes. Gifted with an extraordinary strength of mind, Yellow Conjure Cats possessed a unique natural power, a power to ward off evil and protect others. Nevertheless, the use of this power had to be taught, and like any other ability, it must be practiced to be perfected.

Remembering how his great grandfather, Amber Tiger, had nearly met his end, Topaz had learned firsthand that this was not a power to be taken lightly. Its overuse could be fatal. At the very least, its misuse could shorten a conjure cat's life.

Fortunately, Yellow Conjure Cats were endowed with long life spans. Some had lived for several hundred years. They might have survived in this world forever had their race not bred so few of them. Too many brave cats had died in battle at a young age protecting king and kingdom against the cruelty of evil wizardry and the greedy would-be conquerors so common to that day. Others had died from the outbreak of a terrible "fever" less than a century ago. As it happened, Yellow Conjure Cats had vanished from the forest. All except for Topaz, the last surviving cat of his breed.

Topaz padded along the ancient trail, stopping now and then to gaze upon the stillness of the natural splendor all around him.

For the past three hundred years, he'd been a witness to the slow growth and the minute changes that had taken place here. He'd watched these trees mature and spread, the ever increasing size of their trunks bringing them closer and closer together.

The Knownotten Forest was a shady haven for many woodland plants as well, like toad stools, mushrooms, fungus and lichen. Above them all, Topaz favored the moss for its vibrant green color and the way it grew. He marveled at how its dense layers traveled over the forest floor, spreading up the barks of trees and out onto their limbs to clothe them in tight velvet sleeves. He loved the way it spilled over the rocks and the fallen half-rotted branches of dead trees.

His elders believed that the spirit of every Yellow Conjure Cat was connected to the ancient untainted life force that flourished within this forest. Topaz had no reason to doubt it. He felt as much a part of this forest as the magnificent giants that were rooted in it. After all, it was his ancestral home too, as well as a living memorial to the history of his breed. This is where he'd been born, the place he'd spent his growing up years.

Whenever he passed the small ceremonial pit, he was reminded of that other age. This is where he and his young cousins had come to listen to the heroic stories told by the Elders. Topaz paused for a moment to take it all in, half expecting to hear his great grandfather's voice speaking aloud.

He guessed that was the reason he came here whenever he was troubled or when he felt the need to be alone. Yet he never felt lonely inside this maze of living green columns. Here in this ancient forest his courage and his power were renewed.

Thoughts of family and friends kept Topaz preoccupied while he traveled through the forest. The cushy dampness of the moss-covered path squished beneath his paws as he trotted along, even though his step was soft and light. Eventually the path widened and became one of bare, rich-scented earth. This part of the forest was younger, newer. The trees here were spaced farther apart, their trunks still slender.

Finally, the taller mountains receded into the background as the path he'd been traveling began its gradual climb up out of the darkness and mystery of the ancient forest's floor. The air here was not quite as cool, nor was it as still. High above him, he could hear woodpeckers drumming and squirrels chattering.

Through the thinner, more scattered tree tops, Topaz watched the dark storm clouds come together and ripen. Just then he felt a few large raindrops splatter the top of his head. Keeping to the dirt path he always took in the newer part of the forest, he moved a bit faster.

An intense itch behind one of his ears caused him to stop. While he was having a good scratch, he glimpsed something green dash across the path in front of him. It moved with such speed it seemed hardly more than a blur. A slight rustling noise followed, and the thick fronds of the giant fern beside him shuddered. The itch now forgotten, Topaz stared at the vibrating fern, his hind foot poised behind his ear. As still as stone, he waited. Yet nothing more happened.

The only living things he knew of that were green and capable of moving quite that fast were hoppers, lizards, and frogs. This creature was much too large to be any one of those. It was at least a foot tall, maybe more. Topaz inched closer to the fern, sniffing the earth around it. Then, sticking his head inside the plant, he examined each of the fronds. Finding nothing unusual between its ruffled leaves, he moved on.

Here alone in the forest, Topaz allowed his imagination a bit of freedom. He wondered about the sort of life he might have chosen if he hadn't been compelled to promise King Kittle he'd take the throne upon on his death...

A sudden heavy downpour jolted Topaz from his daydream. He ducked beneath the thick branches of a broad-leafed tree. While he sat there on his haunches watching the rain with a blank stare, his thoughts slipped back into the past. He recalled old conversations he'd shared with the former king. Some of them made him smile. Yet a lump of deep sadness still filled a part of his heart, and he guessed it always would in some measure. King Kittle had been his oldest and dearest friend.

When the shower ended, Topaz stretched and shook the beads of rain water from his outer coat before moving on. When he came to the place where the trail divided, he took the old familiar uphill path, the one he used to travel with the king by his side. Topaz, had actually been heavier than the king, his shoulders higher than King Kittle's waist.

Wet foliage dripped onto the muddy path, and water trickled toward him as the path curled up the steep hillside leading to the small sandstone castle. An abundant growth of broad leafy bushes and tall evergreens covered the grounds in front of him to conceal the first bend in the trail from view.

Anxious to get back to the castle, Topaz picked up his pace. The small green being made its second appearance almost as soon as Topaz rounded the bend. It darted across the muddy path and into the bushes so fast he nearly missed it. Topaz stopped short, and stared long at the place where the green being had disappeared.

This time, there wasn't the slightest disturbance in the foliage, and nature's protective camouflage didn't offer him a single clue. Yet he was certain that from somewhere inside the shrubbery, a small green being watched him. *Is nature hiding him, or can this small green being simply disappear at will?*

When Topaz reached the crest of the hill, he turned down the weedy path that led to the vegetable gardens and to the door of the castle kitchen. Half way there, the aroma of something baking drifted up to him, and he remembered that today was Sunday. This was the day the Elf cook had promised to bake his favorite pie for tea.

Weather permitting, today's tea would be served in the rose garden. Topaz had shared this old Sunday tradition with King Kittle for as many years as he'd lived in the castle, and he'd never consider changing it. The king would sometimes invite a guest or two. Most often it turned out to be Otis. Sometimes they indulged in lavish parties.

From their earliest years together as companions, Topaz and the king had shared many past times here in the rose garden. The king loved to hear Topaz tell stories about his adventures with Otis, or listen to his accounts of the missions he'd carried out on behalf of the kingdom. In turn, the king would read aloud to Topaz and teach him how to play table games.

The sun had begun to dry up the rain, and Topaz was happy to see the cook's helpers carrying trays of dishes and stacks of cushions out the back door on their way to the rose garden.

"King Topaz!" Heak Moot's voice boomed across the rows of ripening tomato plants.

When Topaz turned to face his friend, he was instantly stunned by the old Gnome's frail and shabby appearance. Sagging jowls had replaced Heak's broad stout cheeks, and dark shadows hung beneath his deep-set blue eyes. The purple knit cap he always wore was still too small for his oversized balding head; however, the baggy gray shirt Heak was so fond of wearing looked a great deal baggier than Topaz remembered.

"Welcome." Topaz tried to sound cheerful. He did his best to hide the shock he felt at seeing the sharp change in Heak since they'd last met a few months ago. He worked his way through the tall stalks of tomatoes, careful not to disturb the ripening fruit.

Seeing Heak as he was, Topaz was reminded of how King Kittle had looked not long before the Good Spirit had come for him. *Has he been ill? Why is he traveling all alone in such a feeble condition? Where's his cousin, Tad?*

Topaz put on his best cattish grin. "What brings you all this way from Gista-La?"

"I'm afraid it's bad news, my friend. I'm sorry to have to bring it to you."

A small chill seized Topaz's heart as he took in the elder Gnome's pale, somber face. He stepped onto the path in front of the Gnome. "Tell me, what's happened?"

Heak was about to answer when his attention was diverted. He stopped walking to look down the long path that lead to the rose garden. He jerked his chin toward the young fawn bounding up the path behind Topaz.

"It seems we are about to have company. If I am to answer your question, King Topaz, it would be better if I explain to you in private a little later."

Topaz sighed inwardly, disappointed not to hear the news straight away. He turned to see where Heak was looking and together they watched the approaching fawn.

"You remember Daisy." Topaz nodded to her as she came to an abrupt stop beside him.

"Indeed I do." Heak looked at the youngster and smiled. "You have grown some since I last saw you, Daisy."

"A bit." Daisy smiled back at Heak. She then turned to Topaz. "Cook sent me to tell you tea is almost ready."

"Thank you, Daisy, we'll be along soon."

Daisy dashed ahead while Topaz and Heak made their way to the rose garden at a much slower pace.

Heak changed the subject. "What of our friend, Dooley, did he finally come to settle here in Knownotten after all?"

"He has, and you'll be glad to know he's just as feisty as ever." Topaz knew the old Gnome enjoyed conversing with the spirited and curious raccoon. "He should be here soon. Dooley never misses tea on Sunday."

Heak grinned, and his blue eyes twinkled. "I look forward to seeing him."

"Could that be Heak Moot?" Dooley's disembodied voice spoke from a cluster of pink rose bushes on one side of the rose garden.

Daisy stared at the spot Dooley's voice had come from. "It is, and why are you hiding in there, Dooley, eavesdropping again?"

Dooley's gray head poked out from beneath the bushes, his black eyes accented by the white rings around them. "Of course not. Why would you say such a thing? That's just the way I came. Took a short cut, that's all. Nothing wrong with that."

"Sure, Dooley." Daisy used the mocking sing-song voice she resorted to whenever she spoke to the raccoon. "Hope you get a thorn, Dooley."

Most of the time, Topaz tried to ignore Daisy and Dooley's bickering. It was always the same with those two.

Dooley rolled his dark eyes at Daisy, then scurried out of the bushes to greet Heak.

CHAPTER TWO

Platters heaped high with tea sandwiches sat on either end of the table. An enormous deep dish pie with a lightly browned crust made an eye-catching centerpiece, and every chair had a cushion. Quite naturally, the pie was what caught Topaz's attention. Automatically, his pink tongue licked out and glided over his upper lip.

Heak grinned broadly. "This all looks so wonderful, such lovely plates. Who paints these fine flowers?"

"Fairies that lived long ago painted these ones." Daisy's eyes were aglow with Heak's praise for the dishes. They're my favorite ones, because the plates are yellow."

Heak traced a finger over the delicate blue and pink floral design. "I would like to have a set of these for Tad. He likes yellow also, but I suppose the Fairies do not paint them like this anymore."

"Some of the Fairies still do. Orange Blossom does, and she said she's going to teach me how to paint them too." Daisy's lashes fluttered as she spoke.

"Is that so, Daisy? How wonderful."

Daisy nodded. "But, first, I have to learn how to hold the paint brush in my mouth."

"Then you must teach me how to paint the flowers also."

Daisy giggled. "Yes, I will teach you, and Tad, too."

Dooley stood up on his hind legs and looked Daisy in the eye, a wicked little snicker on his gray face. "Good. Maybe, with a brush stuck in your big mouth, you won't be able to talk so much."

Daisy tossed her head back and looked away. "That will never, ever happen, Dooley." Again, she spoke in the taunting voice she always used for him. "I think you're jealous because Orange Blossom likes me."

Dooley didn't bother to comment. He merely dropped to the ground and swished his bushy striped tail.

Topaz glanced at Daisy. *She becomes more like him every day, or is it just her young age?*

"Let's eat." Topaz took his usual place at the head of the table, sitting in the oversized chair that had been crafted especially for him. The seat was low, and when he sat on his cushion, he was the proper height to eat from the table in comfort. Daisy preferred to stand. Her place was at the opposite end.

Mallory, the Elf cook, poured everyone's tea and passed the platters of sandwiches around before he left the rose garden.

Heak swallowed a sip of hot tea. "My cousin would have loved this. It is too bad he could not make the trip."

Topaz was worried. He looked at Heak, a small crinkle in his forehead. "Why couldn't Tad come; is he sick?"

Heak released a sigh. "Well, he has a bad knee."

"I'm sorry to hear that. I would like to have seen him again."

"He so wanted to come, but it would not have been a good thing for him to walk so far. His poor knee is swollen beyond belief."

"That's too bad, I hope he'll be better soon."

"Thank you, King Topaz, I will remember your kind words to him." Heak smiled. "I wanted him to stay with someone while I was away, but he complained that no one in the settlement has a bed long enough."

Topaz and Dooley laughed. Topaz thought back to the surprise he and Dooley both felt at their first sight of the unusually tall Gnome.

Daisy mistook the meaning for their laughter, and glancing up from her plate, she gave both of them one of her most scornful looks. "How can you laugh? Poor Tad." Then turning to Heak, she asked, "How will he take care of himself if he can barely walk, and he's all alone?"

"Oh, I would not leave him alone completely, Daisy. I would worry too much about him. Our neighbors will come by to look in on him a few times a day and bring in his meals. Also, someone will stay with him if need be. But, he truly is better off at home."

"That's good, he's not so alone then." Satisfied with Heak's explanation, Daisy went back to nibbling her rose petal sandwich.

Dooley had already finished a roll slathered in butter and stuffed with cucumber. He reached for another oozing with goat's cheese and honey. "Why is the knee swelling?"

"I wish I could say." Heak shook his large head and sighed. "Tad does not recall an injury."

"What do you do for the swelling?" Topaz asked.

"This is the sad thing, nothing seems to work for long. But you know, it is not only the swelling I am concerned about, the knee is also red, and it is very sore."

Daisy looked up from her plate. Her nose was slightly scrunched. "That's awful. Poor Tad."

"Yes, Daisy, I agree. I was hoping to find some juke root, growing here in the Knownotten Forest. It is the best herb I know of to treat such a condition."

"Don't you have any in Gista-La?" Dooley asked, his mouth stuffed with food. "I'm sure I saw some growing in the woods when we were last there."

"Not anymore, I'm afraid. There is not one leaf of it to be found in the whole Hamlet of Gista-La."

Dooley's eyes widened. No juke root? What could have happened to it?"

"I wish I could say." Heak looked down at his lettuce and tomato sandwich. He still hadn't taken a bite.

"You might ask the goats," Dooley managed between licks as he cleaned the honey from his long black fingers. "They must have eaten it. Goats are known to eat most anything."

"I heard it was raccoons that ate most anything," Daisy said under her breath.

Heak rested an elbow on the table."I only wish that were true - about the goats eating the juke root. Then at least I would know what had become of it. But, I must tell you, that is one plant the goats do not like."

There were a few things Topaz wanted to know, but decided it would be best to wait until he and Heak were alone before asking too many questions. He had a feeling the Gnome was deliberately keeping something to himself.

"There's plenty of juke root growing around my place. Take as much as you need," Dooley offered.

"Thank you kindly, Dooley." Heak looked toward the mountains as if he had just remembered something. "Knownotten Kingdom is surrounded by such a wonderful forest. I would like to gather a few other herbs and plants before I return home if you do not mind, King Topaz."

"Please do. I'll come with you. If you're up to it, we can go out early tomorrow morning."

"Yes, in that case, I shall be up at first light."

Topaz looked at Heak and nodded. "Now we must stop asking so many questions and give you a chance to eat your sandwich."

For a while they ate without talking at all. Nevertheless, at the end of the meal Heak's sandwich was barely more than half finished. A short time later Mallory returned to the table to serve up the dessert. Topaz sat up straight in his chair and watched Mallory's broad blade pierce the delicate crust and slice its way to the bottom of the deep pan. The first serving was, of course, placed in front of Topaz.

Eager to sample his long awaited slice of blackberry pie, Topaz leaned forward and stuck out his pink tongue. He intended to lap up the pie's juices as they were beginning to ooze onto his plate. All at once, he bolted upright to stare at Mallory instead.

Instantly, Mallory and everyone else craned forward to examine the curious bits of matter they saw floating in the thick greenish-brown liquid that still seeped from beneath the pie's crust.

"Grasshoppers!" Dooley shouted, as the pie filling overflowed the rim of the plate and began to drip onto the spotless white table cloth. "I hate grasshopper pie."

"What happened to the blackberries, Mallory?" Topaz's voice came out in a deep guttural meow that was hardly above a whisper.

Mallory's neck began to redden. "Well sir, there weren't any."

"Mallory, I saw blackberries by the bushel growing on the edge of the forest, not three days ago."

"Yes, Sire. I know, but as you say, it was three days ago."

Dooley's tail swished, his eyes fixed on the pie. "Well, what do you think could have happened to them? That's a lot of blackberries for the birds to eat in such a short time."

Mallory shuffled his feet. "I wish I could say where they went. Yesterday morning, I thought the same as you do now. When I sent the little ones out to pick the blackberries they came back straight away complaining there was hardly a berry to be found. I didn't believe it was possible. I wondered if they may have been looking in the wrong place for the blackberries. So I went to see for myself. But it was true. The blackberries were all gone."

Topaz wanted to scratch his chin with a hind foot, but thought better of it since he was seated at the tea table. Three days ago there had been blackberries everywhere. Daisy had seen them too. She had even remarked about how sweet they were and what an abundance of them there were this year. He looked across the table at the youngster. She was slurping her cup of warm tea.

In the same instant, Daisy looked up, and their eyes met. Her instincts must have told her what Topaz was thinking the moment she discovered his gaze fastened on her.

"Oh, no, it wasn't me this time," she blurted. Her hazel eyes flashed."I didn't eat all of those blackberries. You know I wouldn't..."

"I suppose not," Topaz said, his gaze shifting. "You couldn't have eaten that many blackberries, not without getting sick."

In spite of his complaint about hating grasshoppers and grasshopper pie, it was Dooley who ate most of it and most of everything else too. After the meal, Mallory filled the teacups again and conversation continued. Heak asked about Otis, wanting to know if he still lived at the top of the forest.

Topaz looked up from his teacup and swallowed. "He's visiting his brothers in Wentloc. He should return soon."

Daisy stared at Topaz. Her large hazel eyes held an intensity Topaz had rarely seen. "Otis never misses tea on Sunday. Why has he been gone so long? Do you think something bad could have happened?" Daisy and Otis were close. Had it not been for Otis, she would have drowned along with her parents during a heavy storm in the Scarford Mountains.

"I'm sure he's all right, Daisy. He may have decided to stay longer." Topaz made himself sound matter-of-fact. He knew Daisy worried about the great owl when he was away. He too was beginning to wonder why Otis had been gone so long.

After tea, Daisy and Dooley went their separate ways, leaving Topaz and Heak alone to talk quietly of everyday things. When the cook's helpers came to clear the tea dishes from the table, Topaz lead Heak inside. They retired to the great-room. The room's deep-set windows faced the rose garden, and the subtle fragrance of roses filled the room.

Four overstuffed chairs had been arranged in front of the gray sandstone fireplace. Three of the chairs were average sized. Topaz offered one of these to Heak, then took the oversized chaise lounge for himself. Curling himself up in the chair, Topaz stretched his great paws out in front of him. "Tell me, Heak, what is this bad news? I may be able to help."

CHAPTER THREE

Daisy was on her way outside when she passed by the open door of the great-room. The quiet murmur of voices made her stop and look in. When she saw Heak and Topaz, her first impulse was to go in and join them. She decided against it when she noticed how serious they both looked. If they were talking about something important, she didn't want to intrude.

As she was about to leave, she noticed a change in Heak's manner. She thought he looked upset, maybe even angry. Daisy hesitated, wondering if Topaz had said something to offend Heak. Then Heak began to talk extremely fast. At the same time, his broad chubby hands moved in small frantic gestures. Daisy had seen Heak do this whenever he wanted to give more meaning to what he was saying, as if the words by themselves were not nearly enough to express his true feelings.

At the moment, Topaz simply listened. His luminous eyes glowed brighter than usual, and his long white whiskers twitched every now and then. The more Heak talked, the more Daisy thought Topaz looked the way he usually did before he began to gag on a hairball that had gotten stuck in the back of his throat.

Daisy stepped away from the doorway. *What if Heak or Topaz happen to turn around and catch me watching them?*

Not wanting to feel as if she was spying, Daisy moved on. She stopped on the stone steps just outside the door to brood over the scene she'd witnessed. Still feeling a bit stunned and not quite sure what to make of it, Daisy merely stood there. She watched a lady-bug crawl over the stonework around the door.

When she heard Heak cough, she realized the windows of the great-room were open. On a whim she crept closer to one of the open windows and strained her ears to hear what was being said.

"So," said a familiar voice behind her. "You accuse me of eavesdropping. What do you think it is you're doing, Daisy Dearest?"

Daisy jumped, so startled she let out a gasp before turning her head to face Dooley. She spoke to him in a heated whisper. "I thought you went home, nosy raccoon."

"I came back. Somebody has to keep an eye on you."

"Go away, Dooley. This is none of your business."

"Well, I don't happen to agree with —"

"Dooley, be quiet," Daisy cut in. "They'll hear you."

"It's too late to worry about that," Topaz said, looking out over the window sill. "You two might as well come in and hear the rest of this."

CHAPTER FOUR

"I don't want to believe what I'm hearing," Dooley's small hands were spread open before him in a gesture of surprise. "Why didn't you tell us about this at tea?"

Heak sighed and wiped the perspiration from his forehead with a crumpled cloth he'd taken from the pocket of his baggy shirt. "It did not seem a good idea to talk about such a thing at tea." Heak glanced at Daisy. "In truth, I was not sure if you and Daisy should be told at all. But now, it seems this was not meant to be kept a secret."

Daisy's voice was an octave higher than usual. "But I barely heard anything."

Now back in his overstuffed lounge chair, Topaz had to lift his chin to look at Daisy. "I believe you may have heard just enough to make you worry. It's better to know the whole truth instead of being upset by what you think you know, because you believe something much worse has happened."

Dooley swished his bushy tail. "What could be worse than a blight on the plants in Gista-La Forest?"

Daisy tilted her head a little. "What is a blight, anyway? What does it do?"

Heak stuffed the kerchief back into his pocket. "It is a malady of sorts, Daisy, a sickness plants get."

"What could cause such a thing; do you know?" Dooley asked.

"I do. But what I do not know is what to do about it. The cure is yet to be found, you see, so I am afraid I do not know how I am to treat it. Everything I have tried has not made the condition one bit better. There may not even be a cure.

Dooley scratched his ear with a thin black finger. "If you know the cause, how can you not know the cure?"

"It is not so easy as you may think, Dooley. There is not always a known cure for everything under the sun and over the moon."

"You haven't told us the cause, yet, Heak. There might be something growing right here in the Knownottten Forest that could be used to cure your plants in the hamlet, something you haven't heard tell of before."

"Of course, that is true, Dooley. I am certain there are many plants I have never seen, and many remedies I do not yet know of. Even though I have studied these things all my life, it is possible that you may know something about plants and herbs I do not."

Dooley paced the stone floor in front of Heak's chair. "Then please tell us what has caused this terrible thing."

"You might as well tell them," Topaz urged. "It will worry them more if they are left to wonder."

Heak released a long breath. "I am not certain this is the best way to tell you, but I will tell you all the same. Remember what I said about the condition of my cousin's knee? Well, I did not tell you everything at the time. I did not want to scare young Daisy. I did not tell Tad all that I knew about his condition either."

Heak pressed his lips into a thin line. "Now, I am not so sure that was the best thing, but it was what I thought would be best for Tad at the time. I did not want him to worry. Tad is bad about that, so I must be careful not to say too much, lest I say something that might upset him."

"You see, the thing Tad suffers from is the same thing that is causing our plants in the forest to die. Thankfully, it does not seem to affect the trees. But that does not help Tad very much. It has gotten so bad, I am afraid to let anyone else go into the forest until I find out what can be done to stop this dreadful destructive plague." Heak paused to scratch his nose. "Perhaps this is why the goats are afraid to go into the woods. I had not thought of that until now."

Heak still hadn't mentioned what he believed to be the cause for the blight. Dooley, not known for his patience, began to swish his tail back and forth in a steady rhythm. This he did whenever he felt overly anxious or agitated.

"What kind of a plague is it that you speak of, Heak? Will you tell us, or will you have us all die of old age while we wait for your ramblings to come to an end?"

"Worms," Heak blurted.

"Worms?" Dooley repeated. "What kind of worms?"

"Tiny little worms. Worms so small they are almost impossible to see, impossible for my old eyes, it would seem."

An alarming thought came to Topaz. He stared at his uncommonly thin friend. Before he could even think the thought through it rolled off his tongue. "Heak, did you eat any of those plants or anything you may have harvested from those plants before you knew they were infected?"

Heak gave a hoarse little laugh. "Oh, no, I understand what you must think to see me like this. But I am not ill. I am worried about my cousin, and I am worried about the blight and what will happen if I cannot set things right again. I think of nothing else. That is why I do not sleep at night, and why I have lost the taste for food."

Topaz's whiskers twitched "That's a relief. I'm glad to know you aren't ill, at least. All the same, being sick at heart because of too much worry can make a being ill if it goes on for too long."

Dooley's eyes softened. "Forgive me, Heak, for pressing you so. We're all concerned about what's happening in Gista-La, and we want to get to the bottom of it. There has to be a remedy for it. I'd like to help out in some way if I can."

"There is nothing to forgive, Dooley. It is your nature to be as you are, just as it is mine to take so long to come to the end of what

I am trying to explain. I do ramble on. Tad loses his patience with me also, but still, I cannot stop myself."

Daisy laid her muzzle against Heak's arm. "I hope you'll find something to help your plants and something to help Tad's poor knee get better when you go to the forest tomorrow."

Heak stroked Daisy's head. "There has been some small improvement in Tad's condition already, Daisy, and I too am hopeful that I will find the proper treatment here in your forest. I believe the juke root will be the cure for Tad's knee. It is the only thing I can think of that I have not yet been able to try."

Heak paused to wipe his eyes. "Tad must get better. I do not know how I would get on without him, Daisy. He is my best friend and my only cousin."

CHAPTER FIVE

Puffy white clouds drifted overhead, and the sky was a magnificent shade of blue. Dooley stood outside his temporary home, a large hole in the base of an old and decaying crabapple tree in the Knownottten Forest. He stared at the ground around his feet and shook his head. "I can't believe it. There was juke root growing everywhere only a few days ago. Now, there's not even one sprig of it left."

Heak poked the pointed toe of his boot into a small hole beside the crabapple tree. "I have seen many such holes as these in the forest in Gista-La.

"Looks like something's been digging here, too. And here." Dooley pointed to another hole beside a large rock. "They're all over the place, everywhere you look."

Topaz sniffed the ground next to one of the holes and scratched at the earth with his paw. "Who eats juke root?"

"I cannot imagine who would eat such a thing," Heak paused to scratch his nose. "I have only used it to make a poultice for swelling."

"We can look in another part of the forest." Topaz arched his tail, ready to move on. "This can't be the only place it grows."

Heak grabbed the handle of his basket and followed after Topaz. "That is a good suggestion, King Topaz. I may even come across another remedy for Tad's sore knee while we are looking for the juke root."

They'd been walking for a while before Heak came to a standstill on the trail. "That looks like raccoonberry growing over there."

Heak tromped through the woody shrubs. "I must have a closer look."

Dooley followed right behind Heak, practically on his heels. "Raccoonberry? Why do you call it that?"

"This plant is known by many names, Dooley. Yellowberry is what the Gnomes call it because its fruit is yellow. Some other folk call it raccoonberry because raccoons are so fond of the fruit. You have never eaten any?"

"Can't say I ever have."

Heak kept going until he came to a place where the sun's beams streamed down through the tops of a small stand of oak trees. Topaz followed a little slower. By the time he'd caught up, Heak was standing waist high in a broad patch of the tall leafy plants.

"I have not seen this plant in many years. It likes to grow in the mountains and in places where the soil is always moist, like it is here in your wonderful forest."

By now Topaz was close enough to smell the fragrant white flower that blossomed beneath the two tall stalks of the plant's umbrella like leaves.

"I know this plant, but not by either of the names you mentioned." Topaz sniffed the air, breathing in the sweet flowery scent. "I remember this scent well, but I can't seem to recall what Great Grandmother called it."

Heak bent down to pick up a thin branch that lay on the ground by his feet. Snapping off the leafy end, he broke it down until the branch was about the height of a walking stick. "I have heard it called the devil's apple by some. Would that be the name you heard?"

Topaz shook his head.

"The fruit has a wonderful flavor. Alas, it is not safe to eat unless you know how to harvest it. Some of its parts are poisonous. But, the poisonous parts have good uses too."

"Poison," Dooley shrieked, rising up on hind legs. "How can poison be good?"

"That would depend on how you use the poison. The plant is poisonous as well. The leaves and the root can be harvested in different ways to treat bothersome things."

Dooley's eyes narrowed. "What kinds of bothersome things would that be, Heak?"

"Well, I myself have used parts of this plant to make a salve to cure warts and to treat rashes. But if I were to eat those same parts, I would become very sick. And if I were to eat too much of it, I could even become sick enough to die."

Dooley's eyes seemed to grow. "Have you ever eaten any of it?"

"I have eaten some parts of it. But, I would never eat the root, or the leaves of this plant, or even the stem."

Heak used his stick to lift one of the large umbrella shaped leaves to expose a small yellow bulb growing between the plants two leafy stalks. It resembled a lemon, only lighter in color.

"But, this, my friends, is the fruit, and it is quite edible." He bent down and plucked the yellow bulb. Smaller than a hen's egg, its skin looked smooth and waxy. "My mum used to make a jelly from the fruit. Tad is always making jellies and jams from the fruits we grow in Gista-La. I must take a few of these home to him."

Dooley's dark eyes grew wider still as he stood on his hind legs, gawking at Heak. "You aren't really going to eat that, are you? How can you eat something that has parts that are poison and parts that are not?"

For the first time since he'd arrived in Knownotten Kingdom, Heak laughed aloud. He was not at all surprised by Dooley's reaction. He quite enjoyed it. He took pleasure in the raccoon's blunt personality. Dooley was curious about everything, and Heak had come to understand that his sharp remarks were simply a part of his impulsive nature. He didn't believe Dooley intended to be rude on purpose, unless he wanted to annoy young Daisy, that is.

"The fruit by itself is safe to eat, Dooley, but I would not say the same for the rind and the seeds. But, as I have already told you, raccoons do love it. You might want to try it yourself sometime It may be that the poison would not affect you as it would other beings."

"Well, after what you've told me about this plant, do not expect this raccoon to eat any."

Heak laughed again. His laugh was gentle. "I can not say as I blame you, Dooley. It is good to be wary of such a fruit if you have never eaten it before. The next time you come to Gista-La for a visit, you may want to change your mind. You might decide to have a taste of Tad's jelly after all, once you see we have not died from eating it ourselves."

Still holding the fruit between his forefinger and his thumb, Heak held the fruit up to the sunlight to examine it more closely.

"When the rind becomes thin like this, the fruit is ripe and it will be sweet. I believe this fruit will make a fine jelly. But, I must show Tad a safe way to separate the fruit from the rind and from the seeds. He has never made jelly from this particular fruit before. I would not want anyone to become sick. When the seeds from this fruit have dried, I shall start some new plants in Gista-La. Then I will always be able to make enough salve to treat different sorts of rashes." Heak placed the fruit in his basket.

CHAPTER SIX

"The witches' umbrella," Topaz said all at once. "That's what Great Grandmother called it. When I was young, she used to tell us an old tale about this plant."

Heak scratched at the small red bump on his nose. "Yes, I have heard it called by that name also. I do not doubt that this is the same plant your great grandmother spoke of. I would very much like to hear the old tale if you would not mind telling it."

"The tale is long, and it's a sad tale, the way I remember it. I'll try to tell it as well as Great Grandmother."

Heak clapped his hands together. "Wonderful. I see a place where we can all sit in comfort." He used his stick to point out a level patch of ground covered with dry leaves several yards away from where they now stood.

Topaz padded over to it and stretched out on his belly, pushing his forepaws out in front of him. Although he was a large cat, there was still plenty of room for Heak and Dooley. When they were all settled, Topaz began to tell the tale.

"There once was an old Elven woman who lived in a small log house deep in the forest," Topaz began. "Her house was so small it had but one room with one window and one door. Right outside her door, the old woman kept a garden. In her garden she grew vegetables for her table, and because she liked flowers, she grew flowers too.

"Every day, after her morning meal, the old woman washed her dish, made her bed, swept her floor, and then went outside to work in her garden. There was always plenty to do, and the old woman liked to be busy. Nevertheless, all this work couldn't make up for the loneliness she felt inside."

"Why was she so lonely?" Dooley cut in.

"The old woman's husband had passed away some years before, and because there were no children, the old woman truly was alone in the world. Once she'd kept an orphaned baby rabbit, but the rabbit left her as soon as it was grown.

"For some years, the old woman had been longing to make friends with the other Fairy and Elf women who lived in the forest. But their houses were some distance from her own, and she was timid about going out of her way to meet strangers. Then one morning while she was tending to her garden, she thought of a way she could get to know her neighbors.

"So, that afternoon when her chores in the garden were done, she took a walk in the forest to gather some twigs to weave into baskets. The weaving turned out to be quite a chore for the old woman. Her knobby fingers were not as nimble as they once were, and it took many days to finish all of the baskets. By the end of it, her poor fingers were cracked and sore. Nevertheless, she was so pleased with the fine work she'd done she didn't mind it all that much."

Dooley sat up. "What were the baskets for, Topaz?"

"I'm getting to that, Dooley - patience. Now that the baskets were ready, her next task was to fill them with something useful. First she lined the bottom of one of her newly made baskets with soft dry grasses. Next she packed it with the vegetables and flowers she'd picked from her garden. Afterward, she took up the basket and walked to the house of a neighbor. When the neighbor opened the door to see why she'd come, the old woman gave her the basket as a gift. Touched by the old woman's kindness, the neighbor invited her in for biscuits and tea."

Heak smiled and nodded with approval.

"The old woman enjoyed the visit so much, she went out again the following week with another basket for another neighbor. Once again, she was welcomed into the neighbor's home. This time she was served a tasty hot stew for supper.

"Everywhere the old woman went with one of her baskets she was greeted with warmth and affection. It wasn't long before nearly all of her neighbors returned the visit, bringing their own homemade breads, and jellies, and cheeses. When they came, they stayed for tea, and they always complimented the old woman on her beautiful garden. Now, every day when the old woman woke up, she felt happy, because she had something special to look forward to."

Dooley's whiskers twitched. "I would think so."

"Early one morning when the old woman was pulling weeds in her garden she saw an odd little snake winding its way through the cucumber patch. The snake was quite pretty with its green and blue stripes and bright yellow speckles. Although she had never seen such a snake before, she did not fear it. She merely wanted it out of her way. So she lifted it with her garden spade, intent on putting it someplace else."

Dooley's tail swished, but he said nothing. Topaz went on with the story.

"The snake may have thought she meant to hurt it, or maybe she had done so without meaning to. Before she even knew what had happened, the snake turned and bit her on the hand. The bite was horribly painful, and her hand began to swell right away. By the end of the day her whole arm was swollen. The old woman treated the bite with herbs and salves; nevertheless, it did not get any better.

"On the following day, a foul green drainage began to seep from the wound. Long painful streaks of red ran up her arm all the way to her shoulder. Feeling ever so poorly, the old woman took to her bed, too ill with fever to help herself to food or water. During this time, which seemed like a long time to the old woman, not one of her friends came to see her. After a while, she felt as if no one cared about her, and she began to feel sorry for herself. When she thought about it too much, it even made her angry."

"How sad for her," Heak wagged his head.

Dooley's tail swished. "Poor old woman. Did she get better?"

"She did indeed." Topaz nodded. "Then one day when she was feeling better and her wound had begun to heal, a friend did come by to visit. But the old woman was still thinking her angry thoughts, and she treated her friend rudely. Not knowing the old woman had been sick, the friend didn't understand why the old woman was in such a terrible mood. Needless to say, the friend left soon after her arrival.

"Other friends who dropped by for a visit were treated in much the same way. Some of them scolded the old woman for her bad manners. This only served to make the old woman spiteful, giving her cause to play nasty tricks on them and do horrible hateful things. As time passed, the old woman became so busy with thoughts of how to punish her neighbors she lost interest in her house and her yard. Eventually, her garden became a mass of tangled, bug-infested plants and weeds.

"Yet, there was one plant among them the bugs did not trouble. It was a plant that usually grew in the wild. This was a tall plant with two long stalks, and a single flower of the purest white blossomed beneath its spreading umbrella-like leaves."

Topaz saw Dooley eyeing the raccoonberry that lay in the basket Heak had placed between them. He expected the raccoon to comment, but when he didn't, Topaz went on with the tale. "As the story goes, so long unkempt was the old woman's house that it became quite ugly indeed. Great Grandmother described what a frightful sight the house was to look upon. Its roof began to sag and lean, and its floor to crack and creak. The bugs that had once lived only in the garden moved inside the house. Because their eggs were no longer disturbed by the old woman's broom, they hatched everywhere inside her house, and their numbers grew and grew.

"During the day the bugs hid in the soil beneath the rotting floor, but at night they came out to search for food. Sometimes they crawled over the old woman while she tried to sleep in her bed. Those that had made a home in her mattress would even bite her and suck her blood in the night."

Heak shuttered, and Dooley began to scratch everywhere all at once.

"The walls inside the house that had not yet been taken over by the moldy black slime were inhabited by mites and ticks. Spiders hung their wide sticky webs in every corner. Mice and rats snuck in and out to steal her food. When there was not enough for them to eat they chewed on other things, including her mattress and even her clothes.

"Years earlier, a thick gray fungus had begun to take hold on the roof of the house. Unhampered, its scaly ridges grew over the old woman's only window and the top of her door as well. It grew until it hid the sunlight and until the old woman could no longer see out of her window, and her house became dark and gloomy.

"In time, the old woman even began to have trouble passing through her doorway, unless she bent way over. Eventually, her poor back became painfully bowed from practicing the tiresome habit. At long last, she decided to chop the fungus out of her way. But by now, it had become so thick that when she struck it with her hatchet, the handle snapped in two.

"As time passed, the old woman's bitterness toward her neighbors only grew. Her mind had become so filled with hate that she had nothing left to think about, except her grizzly, mean thoughts. Still believing her neighbors were to blame for all her troubles, she spent most of her time imagining evil ways to make them pay for their misdeeds. Finally, she came up with a plan that would make them all suffer."

Topaz paused, recalling the first time Great Grandmother had told this story to him and his young cousins. Crushed together in a tight little bunch, they'd been almost too frightened to breathe. Yet, whenever Great Grandmother had come for a visit after that, they would all beg and pester until she agreed to tell them the story again.

Dooley heaved a long heavy sigh, breaking into Topaz's day-dream. "Well... What did the old woman do?"

Topaz took up where he'd left off. "What she did was something so wicked that from that day on, no one ever spoke her given name again."

Dooley gave Topaz a critical look. "Not ever?"

"Great Grandmother said it was never again spoken while the old woman lived, or even after her death."

"Why's that?"

"Well, as we know, Dooley, names do have power. And because of the terrible deeds she'd committed, no one wanted to say her name, or remember it. Even after she died, everyone feared the mere sound of it would be enough to invoke her vile spirit to return from the wicked place to which it had gone upon her death."

Heak looked over at Topaz. "So, they believed the old woman was a truly evil being. Perhaps she was a witch."

Topaz nodded. "Even now, the Fairies and Elves do not dare to speak her name. I wonder if anyone can even recall what it was."

Dooley's tail swished. "What do they think will happen if the old woman does come back?"

Topaz spoke in a hushed voice as if he thought someone who shouldn't, might be listening. "The Fairies believe the old woman's spirit is more evil now than before. They fear she will take vengeance on the descendants of those she blamed for her troubles when she was alive."

Dooley sat up a little straighter, his eyes wide. "Do you think she really was an evil witch?"

"It's not an easy question to answer, Dooley. I guess that's because I never knew her, but the Fairies don't believe she was a witch. They believe she was something far more evil."

Dooley spread his small hands. "If not a witch, what else could she be?"

"Back then the Fairies called her the demon's wife, and I believe they still do."

Heak shook his large head from side to side. "She must have been evil indeed."

"Great Grandmother wasn't as sure about that as the Fairies seemed to be. She believed the old woman had a sickness of the mind that became a sickness of the soul. She believed it was this sickness that made the old woman do these evil things, and she was convinced that the snake's venomous bite had caused it. Still, there are many others who believe she was simply an evil witch. Nevertheless, you may judge for yourselves when you've heard the rest of the tale."

Heak and Dooley exchanged quick glances as Topaz resumed the story. "Not much time passed before she was ready to set out on her false-hearted mission. First, she cooked up a stew from what vegetables she could scrounge up from the woods and whatever was left in her ruined garden. Then she added her new, secret ingredient."

Dooley rolled his black eyes. "Guess I know what that is."

Topaz nodded. "When everything was ready, the old woman combed her hair and put on her best apron. She knew she had to make a good impression if she was going to entice her neighbors to sample her new recipe."

Dooley spread his small black hands. "But why would anyone trust her after all the terrible things she'd already done to them?"

"Well, Dooley, that's just it; at that time, no one knew the old woman was capable of such evil. All those terrible things she'd already done had been made to look like accidents. Or, someone else had been blamed for them."

Dooley scratched behind his ear. "It's hard to believe she got away with it."

"That's only because her neighbors were innocent good hearted beings, Dooley. No one suspected she was up to no good. She was clever, and with a bit of cunning, she managed to convince her neighbors that she'd been out of sorts for a while, and that's why she'd been behaving so badly. After all, it wasn't far from the truth, and after they'd seen her scars from the snake's bite, they had no trouble believing her.

"Once her neighbors began to show some sympathy and a bit of understanding, the old woman offered her stew as a token of her renewed friendship. She told them the stew was her way of making amends for her mean remarks and bad manners. Her neighbors were happy to forgive her, and they accepted her generosity without question."

Once again, Heak scratched at the bump on his nose with a forefinger. "What a crafty old crone."

"Did any of her neighbors die?" Dooley asked.

Topaz nodded. "Some got sick, and suffered terribly. Some even did die. Problem was, she ran out of stew before she'd had the chance to visit them all. Nevertheless, the old woman was so pleased with herself for tricking her neighbors into believing she'd changed, she decided to make up another batch of her wicked stew to finish the task she'd started. But this time, something she didn't expect happened.

"It may have been that the fire under the pot had been too hot. Or maybe she didn't notice when the stew began to bubble and boil. Whatever the reason, she must have been stirring her deadly brew when some of it splashed into her eyes."

Dooley glanced at Heak. "Guess she had that coming, nasty old witch."

"Nearly everyone heard the old woman's horrible screams as she scurried and stumbled her way through the forest. She crashed headfirst into trees and fell over logs in her rush to reach the creek and wash the poison from her burning eyes. Great Grandmother said the creek water helped to sooth some of the burning, but the old woman suffered in the worst kind of misery for days on end."

For a moment, Topaz stared at the ominous plants without speaking. The fragile white blossoms with their bright yellow centers and sweet apple fragrance gave the lethal plants a deceptive air of purity and innocence. The plants did have their uses, and if some of their parts could be harvested to make medicines to cure ills, they were plants to be valued. Even so, Topaz didn't like it that these plants were growing here in the Knownotten Forest.

"Did she die?" Dooley asked, jolting Topaz back into the moment.

"Not right away. She lived for some years after that, though she was blind, and she had gone completely mad from the pain. But as soon as she was able, she went about the forest destroying every plant she could lay her hands on. And that's the way Great Grandmother's tale finally ended."

CHAPTER SEVEN

Dooley stood up on his hind legs. "It sounds to me like the old woman was mad before the poison got into her eyes."

"Yes, it would seem so, mad and also evil. One must wonder about a being who would do such wicked things to others." Heak clucked his tongue. "This tale is a good reminder that one cannot be too careful with plants and herbs that are poisonous. There is always the risk that one may do more harm than good.

I am thinking that perhaps I should prepare the raccoonberries myself, before I give them to Tad for the cooking." Heak paused a moment. "Yes, that is what I will do, best not to take such chances. I will go and gather a few more of them now." He rose to walk back to the patch of raccoonberries.

Dooley was about to object to the name, raccoonberries, when he was reminded of something he'd wanted to remember. It was something Topaz had said when he was telling the story. For a long time Dooley stood there with his brow scrunched while he tapped on a front tooth with one of his long fingers. It's what he did when thinking especially hard.

"What is it, Dooley? Is something the matter?" Heak asked him.

"The fruit... I do believe you're going to need an awful lot of it."

Heak was about to ask why, but then he realized what Dooley was getting at. "Yes, yes, of course. This is the cure I have been looking for. Is it not? The extract from the rind and the seeds of the fruit may be just the thing to stop the blight. I will also collect some of the roots and leaves from the plants as well. I will make a solution to treat the plants that have been infected by those tiny worms. It is wonderful that you have thought of this, Dooley. Why did I not think of it myself?"

"I first got the notion when Topaz said this plant was the only one in the old woman's garden that wasn't bothered by the bugs."

Heak's blue eyes were alight with excitement. "Now that you make mention of it, that should have been a clue for me as well. Alas, I was enjoying the tale so much I did not consider it. I will gather what I can for now. I can always come back later if I think more will be needed."

Heak picked up his basket. "Not only will I make a special solution to treat the plants, I will make up a batch of salve too. I will try some of it on Tad's sore knee to see how well it works. The extract from this plant will be useful in treating more than one ailment. Of this I am certain."

Heak turned and began to walk back to the where the raccoonberries grew. Dooley and Topaz trailed along behind him.

"Will you have to cook it?" Dooley asked.

"I will indeed have to cook it to make the solution for the plants, Dooley. Why do you ask?"

"Ain't you scared that poison will get into your eyes?"

Heak's jowls wagged as he shook his head. "Not to worry, Dooley. I have just the thing to wear over my face to protect me from such a misfortune. This I do whenever I prepare a potion that has such properties. When it comes to noxious plants, one cannot be too careful. And of course, I will have this story to remind me that I must take the most particular care."

Heak leaned forward and reached out to pick a piece of the ripe fruit. As soon as he did, a streak of green zipped out from beneath the plant's tall leafy foliage and dashed through the undergrowth.

Like a shooting star, Topaz took off right behind it. His luminous eyes glowed brighter in the dimness of the shaded forest as he traced the creature's movements through the woody shrubs and bushes.

Dooley stood upright to get a better view of the chase. Heak's gaze followed Topaz as well, his basket dangling from the crook at his elbow, a gaping look on his face. After a moment, he turned to Dooley seeking an explanation, but the raccoon could only return Heak's puzzled look with a shrug and a wide-eyed stare of his own. They'd barely had a glimpse of what Topaz chased.

As soon as the shrubs and bushes stopped moving, Topaz stopped running. He assumed a low crouch, his shoulders hunched close together behind his neck, and his tall ears poised and listening for the faintest sound. As would any cat, he waited with the certainty of knowing that his prey would soon be on the move again.

A leaf trembled, and something flickered within Topaz's intense luminous eyes. His long white whiskers bristled and twitched. A faint noise, like the rattle of dry leaves somewhere in the distance, was enough to get him moving. The taut muscles of his hindquarters bulged as he crept forward with deliberate slow motion. His lean muscular body was slung so low his belly nearly touched the earth.

He made no sound as he advanced through the underbrush, placing each paw with care. The tip of his long tail twitched when a branch on the rhododendron bush in front of him shook, causing several of its pink petals to fall. Something else moved too, something green, but it wasn't a plant. The end of Topaz's tail twitched again, just before his back legs sprang and he made the lunge.

Topaz was quick, but the small green being moved even faster. It dodged away at the last moment and streaked ahead in the direction of the dirt path. Now, at least, the being was out in the open, and he could see it more clearly. Within two strides he was close enough to reach out with a front paw and push the creature down. As soon as it hit the ground, Topaz stepped forward and picked the creature up in his mouth. Immediately, the small green being began to kick and fling his limbs about in an effort to get away. But Topaz held its small body firmly between his teeth, using only enough pressure to keep the being from wrenching free.

CHAPTER EIGHT

As soon as he reached the path, Topaz dropped the being in the dirt at his feet. He intended to get a proper look at the creature, but the instant the squirming green bundle was on the ground it rolled itself up into a tight little ball and tucked its face between its knees. Topaz sniffed at the being. With his claws sheathed so as not to harm the creature, he pushed it gently, turning it around in the dirt as he tried to make out what sort of creature it was.

By this time, Heak and Dooley had caught up to him. Heak leaned over for a better look. "For such a small being, he moves with great speed."

Topaz looked at Heak. He was about to make a comment; however, before he could utter a word, the creature was up on its feet and running. Again with his claws sheathed, Topaz took a quick step forward and slapped a paw over the green being, smashing it to the earth.

Dooley stared down at the small creature who lay motionless in the dirt. "What do you think he is?" The being appeared to be about a foot and a half in length.

"He's larger than I thought." Topaz pushed the small being gently with his nose. "I don't know what he is though. I hope I haven't done anything to injure him."

Dooley crouched down beside the creature and watched him for a while. "It's breathing."

Heak removed his cap to scratch the top of his head. "What an unusual little being this is. I would say he is probably a Sprite, but the Sprites I have seen have all had wings. I have never before laid eyes on a green being such as this. He is not quite small enough to be a Green Goblin."

Dooley reached out with one of his long fingers to give the creature a poke on the shoulder.

"Careful, Dooley, he is very frightened, he may try to bite you. See how he breathes so fast? Yet, I do not think he is much hurt. More like he plays opossum; he waits for the chance to run away again."

Topaz looked at Heak and nodded. "Let's take him up to the castle. Someone there must have seen him or his kind around here before."

"Do you think he will talk?" Dooley asked.

Heak adjusted his basket "When he is ready, I am sure he will have quite a story to tell." He then turned to Topaz. "Would you like me to carry him? I can throw him over my shoulder. He may even be small enough to fit in my basket."

Topaz was silent for a moment as he studied the creature, "I think I'd better hold onto him, Heak. As you say, he will run if he has the chance."

Dooley finished scratching the inside of his ear. "What will you do with him, Topaz?"

"Find out where he came from and why he's here in Knownotten Kingdom."

CHAPTER NINE

The Spotted Gray Matoose watched everything from her hiding place in the brush. Her heart pounded beneath her feathered breast. She was too far away to hear their conversation, and she couldn't imagine why the huge four legged beast had chased her little friend out of the brush as he had. She wondered what would become of her friend now.

She didn't think the beast would eat him. All the same, her throat tightened at the sight of her friend's small body being pushed and mashed and prodded as he lay helpless in the dirt. The worst of it was when the beast picked her friend up in its large toothy mouth and trotted away, his companions with him. All at once she felt sick to her stomach. She craned her neck to see where the beast was headed. At the same time, she was seized with a powerful urge to attack the beast and free her friend. But her good sense prevailed.

This was not the time to interfere. There were too many of them, and her only means of defense was her beak. Even if she was a raptor it would be difficult to defend herself against a beast of that size. She'd already witnessed how quick and agile he was. One swipe from one of those huge clawed paws would kill her in an instant. She had to think of the eggs that waited inside her.

Her laying time was close at hand. Just as her eggs had grown, her body had grown too, until she had become stout and cumbersome and slow. Flying was now impossible. That had only happened since their arrival here a few days ago. Her short wings were no longer capable of lifting her awkward body off the ground. It had taken every bit of her physical strength as well as her strength of mind to reach the Knownotten Forest. The weight of her friend had been an additional burden, but only slightly.

Had it not been for him, she wouldn't have come here to Knownotten Kingdom, and now she regretted it. This place was not what either of them had expected. The Land of Knownotten, her friend had been told, was inhabited by Fairies and Elves. Yet they had not seen a single one of them.

She felt about as weak and feeble as she had when she'd watched her mate being torn apart by the osprey, the gray matoose knew there was but one thing she could do to help her friend now. She must find out where these beings had decided to take him. Later, she believed, she would discover a way to free him. It did seem to her that the beast made an effort to carry her friend without attempting to harm him.

How the beast would treat him later, she had no way of knowing. Nor did she know why the beast had taken her friend in the first place. Nevertheless, she intended to tag along until she had some answers. She hoped these creatures wouldn't travel too far from her burrow.

She had to keep up and yet remain hidden. To do this, she ran as fast as she could, making her own path parallel to the trail the captors had taken. Despite her oval bulk, she was quite adept at moving soundlessly through the brush.

Her feathers were arranged in a swirling, spotted pattern. The dull grays and browns allowed her to blend in with the woody thickets and shrubs. Even so, she kept her head down, careful to remain out of sight. She followed them as closely as she dared.

When the path began to wind uphill toward the huge stone structure, she had no choice but to slow down. The climb for her was not an easy one, and by the time she reached the hilltop she was nearly worn out. Even so, she waddled after them as quick as her short legs could carry her. Dodging in and out from under the thick bushes and thorny brambles, she struggled to keep up, ever fearful of being left behind.

The beast seemed to be headed for the stone structure. *What is this place?* Before she realized what was about to happen, the beast, along with his strange companions, entered the structure through a large stone opening, taking her little friend with them. She would have followed them, but she had lagged too far behind. By the time she reached the opening an enormous thick wooden slab had been slammed into it, sealing it tight.

In a moment of frustration and blind anger, she threw herself against the wooden slab, but it did not budge. With a heavy heart she slumped to the ground in front of the closure. Her body now felt as if it was filled with rocks instead of eggs, so great was her disappointment.

There was nothing more to be done here, she realized. Her eggs would come soon and she had to return to the forest to complete her burrow. Yet she hated the thought of leaving her friend behind. She knew he must be scared, and she wanted him to know that she knew where he was. So she made a long low-pitched call. It was a signal she'd used to let him know her whereabouts when they were out foraging for food in the forest. She only hoped he could hear it now and know that she would not abandon him.

CHAPTER TEN

From the moment she saw him, Daisy could hardly drag her eyes away from the small green being. His limp body, less than half the size of a Knownotten Fairy, lay sprawled over a soft blue cushion on the dining room table. Dressed all in green, his clothes appeared to have been woven from a fine thread; they clung to his thin form like a second skin.

Delicate pointed ears stuck out from beneath his shaggy greenish-brown hair. Daisy noticed that his skin looked a shade paler now than when he'd first arrived, and she wondered what that meant.

Mallory stood next to Daisy. He'd removed his apron before leaving the kitchen; nevertheless, he smelled of cinnamon, fresh butter and honey. A dusting of brown flour covered the backs of his hands and the tops of his dark red shoes. He'd been in the middle of baking an apple cake for the noon meal when Topaz had summoned him to the dining room.

"I wish I could say what he is, Sire. His color is a bit strange though. Do you think he might be sick?"

Daisy's nose scrunched. "He is a bit lighter than when I first saw him. I hope he's all right. He's so little and cute though, I wonder what I shall call him."

Topaz glanced across the table at Daisy; his whiskers stiffened. "He's not a pet, Daisy. He will have to go back where he came from when the time comes."

Daisy hadn't considered that. "Why can't we keep him?"

"Because, he probably has a family. He must belong somewhere."

Dooley, standing on Daisy's opposite side, leaned in for a closer look."Funny looking ears, those."

Daisy gave the raccoon a sharp look. "They are not, Dooley, I think they're nice. They're much better looking than yours are."

"Daisy," Topaz stared at her briefly. "Dooley meant no harm. Please, try to be polite to him once in a while."

Daisy's eyes filled with tears. She was sensitive to any sort of criticism from Topaz. On any other occasion she might have stomped out of the room and gone outside to cry, but today she couldn't bear to tear herself away from her new treasure.

A single tear slid down her cheek and dripped onto the small green being's face before she could do anything to stop it. She was sure she saw him flinch the moment the tear made contact, but she decided not to mention it. The green being must have his reasons for not wanting anyone to know he was conscious. For reasons she didn't quite understand herself, Daisy felt protective toward him.

It was then that Corra, the young Elven kitchen maid came in with a fresh table cloth over her arm. She'd come to set the table for the mid-day meal.

Corra stopped short when she saw the gathering around the table. "Oh," she gasped, catching sight of the little being on the cushion. "What's this? A poor Green Fairy; what's happened to him?"

Topaz's ears straightened. "Green Fairy?"

"Yes, Sire. But what's he doing here?"

Mallory seemed surprised. "You've seen Green Fairies before?"

"Why sure, on Cottersdamp Island. That's where they live, you know. We got ourselves stranded there once when our boat sprung a leak. The Green Fairies were good enough to help us mend it."

"You've been to Cottersdamp Island?" Topaz asked.

"Just the once, Sire. Can't imagine how this little being got so far from home. Is he by himself, Sire?"

"He's the only one we saw, but there must be others. He couldn't have made the journey from Cottersdamp Island alone."

Daisy looked at Corra. "Do you think he's sick?" The maid laid the back of her hand, ever so gently, on the Green Fairy's forehead. "I think he might need some water, I'll go and fetch some." Corra was about to turn away.

"No. Please, wait," Bozel cried out. He grabbed Corra's hand and sprang into a sitting position. "Please, I need to know about my family. Maybe you saw them."

Corra's blue eyes widened. "Your family? On Cottersdamp?"

"You said you were there, and Green Fairies helped you. So that means they're all right then. They've survived."

Corra stared at him, her eyes clouded with confusion. "Survived what?"

"The rain storms, the mud slides. Our island...it was but a lump of mud when I last saw it, and the river was still rising."

"Oh my," Corra breathed, beginning to understand. "I wish I could give you some good news, but the truth is, I haven't been to Cottersdamp Island in many a year."

Bozel's fingers slid from Corra's hand. His head dropped between his knees and his small body began to shake with loud sobs.

"Oh, I'm so sorry to tell you I don't know how your folks are. I truly wish I did." Corra spoke softly as she stroked his back while he cried. "How on earth did you ever manage to find your way here?"

The large bird's burrow was under a massive rotted out log. She'd begun the task of digging it out earlier that morning while her friend was still asleep. It was a good place to dig. The earth beneath the ancient log was already soft because of the plants and the fallen leaves that had been trapped so long beneath it. Best of all, she'd found many different kinds of bugs living inside and all around the rotted wood. There would be more than enough to feed on while she nested.

She had already eaten her fill of the juicy larvae hidden there and she'd feasted on a variety of other bugs as well. The large colony of termites could be saved until later. She thought her chicks might enjoy them. Some of these, like the millipedes, were new to her. These squirmy reddish-brown things were a lot too leggy for her tastes. The one she had eaten had stung her tongue, and she knew she'd have to be more choosy about what she fed to her chicks.

There were other strange looking crawly things inside the log and under it. Some of them she didn't care for the looks of, and she was sure they wouldn't be to her liking. One of them had a long spiny tail that curved up over its back, and there was a wicked looking stinger at the end of it.

Roots were another good source of food. Roots were one of her favorite foods, because they were easy to come by, and she foraged for all kinds. She'd become quite skillful at digging up the loose soil around plants by using her three forward toes. Then she could pull the root straight out of the earth with her slender curved bill. Her friend, Bozel, said he'd grown tired of eating roots long before he'd left his home on the island, so Menna ate most of the roots herself.

Blackberries were something they both enjoyed. She and Bozel had eaten nearly all of them in their first few days here. Aside from the blackberries and a small portion of roots, she had only seen Bozel eat a few other things. He seemed to like mushrooms, nuts and dandelion greens better than roots. She had finally given up on trying to persuade him to try bugs.

Whenever she could find them, she ate seeds and fruits of all kinds, and she wasn't shy about sampling something new and different. Some of the fruits she'd seen here in the Knownotten Forest were unfamiliar, like the yellow egg-shaped fruit that grew just a short distance from her burrow. Bozel had gone to pick more of them that morning, but the beast had snatched him before he'd had the chance. The ones he'd already gathered had been stored near her burrow to be eaten at a later time.

This denser part of the younger forest was dark and secretive, and it suited her needs well for the time being. Eventually she'd know whether or not she should stay here. It would depend on what happened to her little friend. Besides her burrow, she'd discovered many other places she and her chicks could hide from predators. It was always wise to have knowledge of a few safe hiding places before there was a need. That was one of the first things she did whenever she visited an unfamiliar place. She wished she'd made mention of this to Bozel. If he'd known where to hide, he might have saved himself from being caught.

When she felt the broad band of muscles across her belly tighten, she knew it was time to stop digging and test her burrow for size. Shifting from side to side, she waddled into the burrow backwards and settled herself into the space she'd made. It was a snug fit for her bulky shape. Once the chicks were hatched she would see about making it a little bigger. But, for now, the snugness was comforting, and the eggs would stay warmer if she had to leave the nest for a short while.

CHAPTER ELEVEN

When Bozel's long tale finally ended, he slumped back against the pile of cushions that had been stacked on the chair next to where Daisy stood. Topaz leaned forward from his own chair at the other end of the dining room table. "And where's the Spotted Gray Matoose now?" His stiff white whiskers twitched ever so slightly while he waited for Bozel to answer.

"When last I saw her, she was digging out her burrow, but I think she might have followed us here. I'm sure I heard her call out to me soon after you brought me inside."

Dooley looked at Topaz. "Now that Bozel mentions it, I too recall hearing some sort of a bird call around that time, a rather unusual one."

"I heard it as well," Heak said.

"Should I take a look outside?" Corra started for the glass paned doors that opened onto the courtyard. "Menna could still be there."

Bozel climbed down to the floor with Mallory's help. "Better let me come with you, Corra. She might not show herself to a stranger."

Outside in the courtyard, Bozel blew on the wooden whistle several times, aiming it in a different direction each time. He waited for a reasonable amount of time to pass. "If Menna was anywhere around here I'm certain she would have answered by now. She must have gone back to the forest."

"We could try again later. She might come back."

"Maybe. I hope she's all right. Her eggs could come any time now."

Corra put an arm around Bozel's shoulder. "You mustn't worry, Bozel. I'm sure your friend can take care of herself, and probably much better than you or I could, living all alone in the forest."

"I'll take you back to the forest as soon as we've eaten," Topaz called from the open doorway. "Your friend must be worried about you too."

When Bozel turned to make a reply, it surprised him to see that all the others were standing in the doorway as well. Heak, Mallory, and Daisy had managed to squeeze themselves in beside Topaz. Dooley, standing on his hind legs, was peering through the other half of the double door, his nose and long fingers pressed firmly against the glass. It seemed that all of his new friends were anxious to get their first glimpse of the Spotted Gray Matoose Bozel called Menna.

"I always say everyone thinks better on a full stomach," Mallory said as the group returned to their places at the table. "Shall I serve the noon meal now, King Topaz?"

"Please do, Mallory, I'm sure we're all hungry. After our meal, we must go to Menna."

Within minutes, the food was on the table, and nearly everyone had been served.

Topaz licked at a smear of goat's cheese on his muzzle before he spoke. "I didn't mean to scare you, Bozel. That's not how we usually welcome new visitors who come to our land. I only wanted to know why you were here in Knownotten."

Bozel nodded. "I guess the Green Fairies would be just as curious about any stranger that happened to turn up on the shores of Cottersdamp."

Heak swallowed a large gulp of his hot onion soup. "From what you have told us about your journey, Bozel, it seems you have had some frightful times. It is not an easy thing to know who to trust when you are among strangers. I too am cautious about other beings I meet in my travels, even more so when I am alone."

"I guess I didn't expect to meet so many different kinds of beings on this journey.

Topaz looked up from his plate. "Now that we know why you're here, Bozel, we must come up with a way to rescue your folk from Cottersdamp Island as soon as we can."

Bozel sat up straight on his cushion. Although he wore a grin, his eyes were wide and misty with tears. "You really will help us then?"

Topaz gave Bozel a small smile and nodded. "We will, and you and your folk are welcome to settle here in the Land of Knownotten if it suits you."

"Thank you, King Topaz. My folk will be grateful, and we'll work hard to be good neighbors."

"You're welcome, Bozel. Now please eat something. This has been a good season for berries, and the strawberries are especially juicy and sweet right now. Mallory will spoon some into a bowl for you."

Bozel watched Mallory dish up the plump red strawberries and pour on the fresh cream. All at once, he was hungry.

Daisy chewed on a strawberry while she talked. "Lots of Fairies and Elves live in the forest, Bozel. I'll show you where. They'll be glad to meet you and give you a proper welcome."

Bozel smiled at Daisy. "I'd like that a lot, Daisy."

"You know, Bozel," Dooley dipped his buttered roll into the warm honey, "I came here not so long ago myself. Knownotten Kingdom is a good place to begin a new life."

Bozel nodded to each one in turn as he acknowledged their comments, but his mouth was too full of fresh strawberries and cream to speak.

CHAPTER TWELVE

"I suppose you'll want to go in alone." Topaz spoke to Bozel over his shoulder, as they neared Menna's burrow. The Green Fairy was sitting on his back.

"I'll call out to her when we're closer. I'm certain she won't be afraid if she sees us together."

Topaz turned his head to look at Bozel. "She may even think you've captured me." He spoke in a low purr, a cattish smirk spread across his yellow and orange striped face.

Bozel laughed aloud. "I'm afraid Menna knows me too well to believe such a thing."

Just then, they heard Menna's distinctive call.

Bozel looked up. "She must have heard us talking."

The moment Topaz crouched down, Bozel slid to the ground running, forgetting to wait for Topaz.

Menna scooted out of her burrow and waddled toward the sound of Bozel's voice. "You're safe!" she tweeted as soon as he came into view. "I was so worried about you."

When Menna saw Topaz coming up behind Bozel, she stopped in her tracks, and began to inch backward, all the while dipping her head in a wild erratic fashion.

Bozel hurried over to her and stroked her broad feathered back in an effort to calm her. "We have nothing to fear, Menna. This is King Topaz. He's our new friend."

Bozel then turned to Topaz, who by now stood only a few paces away. "King Topaz, this is my good friend, Menna, from the Isle of Samoway."

Topaz barely had time to nod before Bozel began talking again. "I've told King Topaz everything." He then went on to tell Menna of his new friend's promise to help him find a way to rescue his folk from Cottersdamp Island and allow them to settle in Knownotten Kingdom.

Somewhat more at ease after Bozel's explanation, Menna settled herself on the ground next to Bozel, tucking her feet beneath her. She greeted Topaz with a tweet and a dip of her head. "I'm happy to know you as my friend, King Topaz. I would not want to know you as an enemy."

Topaz returned Menna's greeting while giving her a deep throaty purr. "Call me Topaz, please." Topaz then looked at Bozel. "Mallory and Heak Moot are the only ones who insist on using my title."

"You may still be wondering why I grabbed Bozel in the forest this morning," Topaz continued, his attention now on Menna. "I'm truly sorry to have frightened you. I merely wanted to know why he was here in Knownottten."

"Any wise ruler would be wary of strangers intruding into their lands. It all makes sense to me now that I know who you are." Menna ducked her head once at the end of her comment, as was her habit.

Topaz made a slight nod. "I was sorry to hear you'd lost your mate and how he'd been killed."

Menna dipped her head again, but said nothing.

Bozel stroked her back gently.

The Spotted Gray Matoose was indeed a large bird. Topaz guessed Menna must have a healthy appetite for a bird her size about to lay. The missing blackberries for his Sunday pie were no longer a mystery. "Bozel tells us your laying time draws near. My friends and I would like to do whatever we can to help out. You must tell us what your needs are."

"It's kind of you to offer, Topaz. I can manage well enough for now, but it will be harder once the chicks are out of their shells. I'll still need to keep them warm and watch out for their safety. They'll need to eat often, too. That means I'll have to leave the burrow to forage for the proper things to feed them."

Topaz sat down on his haunches. "I have a friend who lives nearby, and I'm sure Dooley won't mind doing whatever you ask of him when the time comes. He wanted me to tell you that he'd like to stop by tomorrow so the two of you can meet?"

"I'll watch for him then. Will you come too, Bozel?"

Bozel glanced at Topaz. "I will if I haven't already left for Cottersdamp Island by then."

"I think we're going to need at least a day or two to come up with a good plan to rescue your folk, Bozel. So you'll have time to visit with Menna whenever you like."

"Well, then." Bozel looked at Menna. "Maybe Dooley and I can come together."

"I'd like that, and I look forward to meeting Dooley. Will you be coming in the morning?"

A new thought came to Bozel, and he quickly turned to Topaz. "What if Menna comes to stay with us at the castle?"

Menna spoke up before Topaz had the chance to answer. "I would come, if only to visit. But my laying time has begun, and I must remain close to my burrow from now on." Menna shuffled backwards into her burrow as she spoke. Only her head remained where Bozel and Topaz could see it. "But you should go with Topaz, Bozel. You must think of a way to rescue your folk from the island as soon as you can."

"I'll come again tomorrow, Menna, and I'll bring Daisy with me too." That reminded Bozel of Daisy's offer to take him to meet the other Fairy and Elf folk who lived in the forest. He told Menna all about it. As an afterthought, Bozel asked Menna about food. "What will you eat? Don't you have to sit on the eggs all the time to keep them warm until the chicks are ready to hatch?"

"I do, but there are all sorts of things right here that I can eat in the meantime." Menna told Bozel and Topaz about the grubs and bugs she'd found beneath the rotting leaves under the log, and she told Topaz about the yellow fruit.

At Menna's mention of the yellow fruit Topaz stiffened. "You must not eat the yellow fruit." He'd spoken with such an unexpected force it caused Menna to start.

In a quieter, less intense voice he said, "The rind and the seeds contain a poison that could kill you, Menna. We'll bring you some fruits and vegetables from the castle gardens. I'll ask the Gnome to come along with Bozel and the others tomorrow. He can take the yellow fruit away; he has a special use for it."

Menna cocked her head. "You may have saved my life, Topaz. The fruit is already ripe, and I would have eaten it in a day or so. What will the Gnome do with poison fruit?"

"He knows how to harvest the parts that are safe to eat. The other parts will be used to make medicines to cure ills."

"The Gnome must be very clever." Menna dipped her head.

Topaz nodded as he stood up to go.

Bozel hesitated. "I don't want to leave you here alone. Maybe I should stay with you tonight."

"Menna will be safe here, Bozel. There's no need to worry. My raccoon friend won't mind watching out for Menna tonight." Then to Menna he said, "I'll ask Dooley to come by and see you this evening instead of waiting until tomorrow."

Menna gave Topaz a wild eyed stare while she ducked her head up and down.

"What's wrong, Menna?" Bozel asked.

Menna's eyes were still on Topaz. "Your friend, Dooley is a raccoon?"

Topaz nodded. "Dooley was with me in the forest this morning."

"The creature with the long bushy tail?"

Topaz nodded. "That would be Dooley."

"So that's what a raccoon looks like. I've never seen one before this morning, but I have heard stories about their treachery. They steal bird's eggs, you know, and then they eat them."

Topaz's tail began to flicker. "Dooley only wants to be your friend, Menna. He understands what it's like to lose those he cares about. He would never harm you or your chicks. He lost members of his own family when he lived in the Mountains of Scarford. So he'd be the first to understand how you feel."

Menna cocked her head. "How terrible; how did it happen?"

"All of them were killed by Trolls who simply wanted their skins to make fur coats."

Menna dipped her head several times. "That's dreadful, I'm so sorry to hear it... But if not eggs, what does the raccoon eat?"

"Dooley eats mostly fruits and roots when he's in the forest, and fish when he's near a stream." Topaz didn't think it wise to mention that Dooley had tried eggs once long ago and had given them up because they didn't agree with him.

Menna was quiet for a moment. Topaz had the notion there was something else on her mind, and he wanted to give her time to say it.

"I eat roots as well," Menna finally tweeted with a dip of her head. "I may have eaten most of the juke roots around here since we came. I hope he won't be angry with me for that."

"I ate a share of those roots too, Menna."

Topaz looked at Bozel and chuckled inside. The small portion of juke root Bozel might be able to eat would hardly attract notice. Topaz was sure Bozel had only said this because he didn't want Menna to take the blame alone.

"We were wondering what happened to the juke root." Topaz purred and his mouth curled into a smile. "But you mustn't be concerned about the roots, Menna. Juke root has too bitter a taste for Dooley, and anyway, there's plenty more of it to be found in this forest."

"I'm glad of that," Menna shifted her weight and settled herself a bit closer into the soft earth. "It's an easy enough root to find in most places, and I've always been fond of it. Though I've begun to tire of it myself lately." She glanced at Bozel, and he gave her a knowing smile. "I guess we both ate our fill of it on our way here."

"I see." Topaz was thoughtful. He couldn't help but wonder if they'd come by way of Gista-La.

CHAPTER THIRTEEN

Silvera came again that night as she had every night since Otis had been on Barren Island. As always, she sang her sweet bewitching song to him, lulling him into a deep and stuporous sleep. To sleep through the night was against his nocturnal nature, but Otis found himself powerless to resist the effects of Silvera's enchanting song.

Alone and confused, Otis had become another unfortunate victim of Barren Island and the infamous creature who ruled over it. He'd all but forgotten his former life and his home in the Knownotten Forest, except for those brief moments when hazy images of familiar faces coursed through his befuddled mind. Something was terribly wrong, and he knew it. Yet the answers he sought kept slipping away.

In those rare moments when his mind was reasonably clear, he knew he had to leave the island. It was in those particular moments that he sensed his life may even depend on it. He would have left already had he been able to act of his own free will. Although he did not know it, Otis was no more than a prisoner here, trapped by the bird-creature's enchanting spell.

This sense of danger Otis sometimes felt might have come from his intuition. Or perhaps it was his basic instinct for self-preservation giving him another gentle nudge. Sadly, Otis seemed to have little awareness about these things now. He was completely mesmerized by the lovely bird-like enchantress, and the influence she had over him was lethal.

His nights were dominated by her presence. When she wasn't there, he dreamed of her and her song. But not this night. Tonight his sleep was haunted by eerie shapes engulfed in smoke and flame. He could feel the scorching heat of the fiery blaze getting closer, hot enough to melt the feathers on his face. Even so, his poor numb mind was no longer capable of common sense or simple reason, and Otis was at a loss for a way to save himself.

The abrupt loud screams of an osprey broke through Otis' dreams. Believing these predators had finally come back for him, his eyes flew open and his body stiffened with fear. But when Otis found himself staring into the face of a raging firestorm, he completely forgot about the osprey. His attention was instantly consumed by the oppressive heat and the effects of its blinding brightness. The burning heat, he realized, wasn't a dream after all.

In reality, Otis was sitting face to face with the mid-afternoon sun. At first it appeared to him as an enormous sphere of red and orange flame. Spellbound by the bird-like enchantress, Otis had been isolated in this curious dim world for too long. Living in this dream-like existence, the sun couldn't have been more foreign to him. Its unexpected appearance had only added to his present state of confusion. He hardly knew what to make of it.

Owls didn't much care for bright sunlight. Usually, Otis did his best to avoid it. All at once, the great owl rocked on his perch, nearly falling as he grappled for a stronger grip on the branch. In his weak and dehydrated state, direct exposure to the sun's rays was an even greater danger than it otherwise would have been.

The osprey screamed again, and Otis shriveled inside. It worried him not to know where they were, and he wasn't sure what to do about it. Otis searched the skies, looking for the huge gray and white raptors that had nearly taken his life once already.

The sun's intense glare made it impossible for him to tell where exactly the osprey might be. When he didn't hear them again, Otis assumed they'd only been passing over. He hoped they hadn't spotted him.

He turned his attention to his surroundings and took a quick look around, thinking the osprey might have landed somewhere on the island. His feathered head rotated to its full capability in one direction and then the other. This was the first time he could recall seeing the island in the light of day since his misshapen arrival. Nothing about the charred landscape had changed. Barren Island was as disheartening to look upon now as it ever was.

His overview of the island included the surrounding beaches and the river. Now as he looked out over the water, Otis was reminded of his thirst and his crucial need to drink. Facing the sun as he was, this longing was impossible to ignore. Yet, as strange as this may seem, Otis felt compelled to remain on his perch. He might as well have been chained to it, for he was bound to it nevertheless. So powerful was Silvera's influence over him, he believed this charred tree was the only place he was truly safe.

At the same time, the sun was becoming more unbearable. Its intense heat poured over him. *I'm being roasted alive. But what can I do? There's no place else for me to go.* Finally, Otis decided to turn his back on the sun rather than leave the safety of his perch. This awkward attempt to turn himself around caused him to lose his footing when one of his talons caught on a raised piece of charred bark. When he tried to undo himself, he reeled forward and fell, only to land on the injured left wing.

The severe pain brought with it a shocking burst of clarity, sharp enough to rip away the false illusions that had kept Otis tethered to this tree. All at once the truth about his situation became clear, and he realized his life was in grave danger. Another hour in this heat without food or water would surely kill him.

Now that he understood this and understood too, why he'd stayed for so long on this wretched island, he was forced to take action to save himself. These may have been the great owl's first lucid thoughts since he'd heard the bird-creature's captivating song.

His new knowledge of what lay behind the bird-creature's innocent pretense made Otis quiver inside. Her song, like that of a spider's venom had kept his body and his mind paralyzed. All this time, he'd been under her control and unable to act on his own behalf. Now, for the first time, he had the chance to free himself.

His heart raced, and in spite of the sun's broiling heat, Otis felt a cold chill go through him. Propelled by this new understanding and his fear of what would become of him if he didn't act now, he ignored the pain in his wing and got to his feet. Next, he hopped down to the edge of the river and took a beak full of water.

One small swallow was as potent as a magic elixir. Not only was it powerful enough to revive his failing body, it gave him the spark he needed to get his dimwitted mind functioning close to normal again. Reason and logic seemed to follow. The shock of this new knowledge was beginning to wear off, but not his awareness of the peril he'd been courting.

Otis drank again while he allowed the cold water to flow over his feet and cool his body. He stretched his wings and flapped them. Satisfied that he was capable of flying in spite of the renewed injury to his left wing, he pushed off with his feet and flapped his powerful wings in hard waves to lift himself skyward.

If the osprey were anywhere around, Otis certainly didn't see them, nor did he hear their cries again. He flew west toward the mainland and avoided the river all together in case the osprey happened to be someplace nearby watching over their fishing grounds.

Glimpses of a narrow stream meandering through a shady forest of oak and maple were a welcome sight to Otis after he'd been airborne for a number of hours. The murky confusion of the past several days had cleared away, and Otis was beginning to think and feel more like himself. Now that he was off the island, he realized how fortunate he'd been to escape, thanks to the sun and his lucky accident.

His throat was sore and dry. Yet he was hungry, starving in fact. He had no memory of exactly how many days and nights had passed since he'd last eaten, but he knew it had been many. Feeling hungry was a good sign, he decided. It signified his body was returning to normal.

Otis dropped down and glided in through the tops of the trees to settle himself on a fallen branch that rested over the stream. It was lovely and cool beneath the large leafy trees. He filled his beak with water and allowed the cool liquid to spill gently down the back of his parched throat. It burned a lot, but not as much as the first drink he'd taken before leaving the island. Otis wondered if he would ever be able to drink enough water to quell the painful rawness he felt in the back of his throat at this moment.

Once his thirst had been thoroughly quenched, Otis fed on a school of minnows. After the small meal, his physical strength began to return again. It surprised him that so little nourishment could be satisfying. Ordinarily, these few tiny fish would have been no more than a mere nibble.

The shaded woodland surroundings, the creek, the chirps of birds, and the steady whirs and hums of insects added to his growing sense of well-being. All at once Otis was reminded of the tall yellow pines at the top of the Knownotten Forest. It made him homesick. He couldn't say when he'd missed his friends so much. Daisy especially, had been on his mind a lot since he'd come to his senses, and he had a feeling that it might be because she was thinking of him too.

He'd been attached to the young fawn since the day he'd pulled her from the flood waters in the Mountains of Scarford. Barely more than two hours past her birth, her parents had perished in the storm. Otis hadn't been able to do anything to save them, but Daisy was another matter. He'd picked her up in his talons and carried her all the way to Knownotten Castle.

King Kittle had been ruler of Knownotten Kingdom then. He loved all animals and Knownotten Castle was a safe haven for gentle creatures in need of a temporary home. In Daisy's case, the castle became her permanent dwelling. King Kittle couldn't bear to part with her, and it wasn't long before Daisy had the run of the castle and all its gardens. As far as King Kittle was concerned, the little fawn could do no wrong, even when she ate all the new buds on his favorite red roses.

A moment later and without any warning at all, a fleeting memory of Silvera's hypnotic song came floating back to him. Otis shuddered. His sudden movement startled the newt he'd been eyeing, and it disappeared under the plants that grew in the sandy soil beside the stream. Otis flicked his feathered ear tufts. The newt would have made a succulent treat. Nevertheless, he was grateful for the meal he'd had.

More than anything, he was glad to be on his way home again. He tried not to dwell on the increasing discomfort he felt in his left wing. But there was no use denying it, he'd have to slow down, and perhaps he'd need to rest more often. The missing feathers didn't help matters much either; their absence did hinder his air speed.

Refreshed after his meal and his short rest under the cool trees, Otis was anxious to take off again. The great owl spread his wings wide and lifted himself above the creek. His talons barely skimmed its surface while he looked for a break in the foliage. Once above the tops of the trees he climbed high in the cloudless blue sky and headed in the direction of Knownotten Kingdom.

Soon the sun would be setting, and Otis was determined to make the full journey home with as few delays as possible.

CHAPTER FOURTEEN

Otis took a few swallows from his tea cup and glanced at the faces around the table. He blinked several times, and his feathered tufts twitched. "Now you know why I couldn't get here any sooner."

"I knew something terrible must have happened to you to keep you away from us for so long." The whole time Otis had been telling his story Daisy had been looking him over, her soft hazel eyes filled with concern while she studied him. "What an awful place that was. I'm so glad you're home with us now." Daisy seemed to have taken in every detail of the great owl's scrawny, ragged appearance. She'd duly noting the missing feathers from his injured left wing as well. "I thought you were never coming back, Otis; I thought you'd been killed."

The great owl was perched on the back of a chair to Daisy's right, his usual place at the dining room table. He blinked in response to Daisy's comments. He was touched by her concern for him. "I very nearly didn't get back, Daisy." His throat was parched as well as tired from giving what he considered an overly long account of his whereabouts. He bent his head to peck at the fish cake Mallory had just placed on his plate.

"You were lucky to get away from that haunted place," Bozel spoke from his seat atop a pile of cushions on the chair to Daisy's left. "No one ever goes to Barren Island if they can keep from it."

Otis swallowed a beak full of warm tea and fishcake. "I was lucky, Bozel. But there's hundreds of bats living on that dreadful island, and they manage to come and go just as they please. Nothing seems to bother them, not even the osprey. Don't you think that's strange?"

"That is strange, indeed." Heak laid his fork down. His flabby jowls quivered a little when he looked from Otis to Bozel. "Do you think it is because they leave the island before the bird-creature comes out at night?"

"Since my mind has cleared, I've had a little time to think about that, but I really can't say for certain. It's true the bats are away while the creature is about. It's likely they've never heard the bird-creature's song, though it would appear the bats have lived there for some time."

"Weren't you afraid of the bats, Otis?" Bozel spread a lump of soft butter over his warm roll.

"Afraid of the bats? The bats have more reason to fear me. Some owls eat bats, especially the small brown ones. I, myself prefer fish or lizards or the occasional mouse."

"What about the Black Fisher Bats, weren't you at all afraid of them? They're so much bigger, and they have lots of pointy sharp teeth."

"I never gave it a thought until you mentioned it. Black bats would never harm you or me. As for those sharp teeth — they're used for eating raw fish. That's all they ever eat."

"I'm so glad you got home early," Daisy called out to Topaz when she saw him standing in the doorway of the dining room. She then nodded toward Otis. "Look who's here."

Topaz padded into the room and took his chair at the head of the table. "I was told you were back, Otis. What a narrow escape you had, too. I just left the kitchen, in case you're wondering how

I know about this already. Corra told me you nearly died on an island in the Slewnecky River."

"Corra and Mallory were the first two beings I saw when I got here. They found me in the courtyard and brought me inside. I intended to be here last night, but the wing slowed me down."

Mallory came into the room right behind Topaz with a basket of fresh baked rolls. "We thought you were dead when we first saw you. I don't know how you managed to fly all that way with a sore wing."

Otis' feathered ear tufts twitched, and his head swiveled to look at Mallory.

Mallory set the rolls on the table. "We were relieved to see you'd finally come home. You were gone so long Corra and I were beginning to wonder if someone should come looking for you."

"It's not likely anyone would have found me, Mallory, even if someone had come looking. No one goes to that island from what Bozel tells us. It's haunted, and it's the last place anyone would want to look."

"It seems that you and Bozel both had a narrow escape." Topaz's face became solemn. "I'd hate to think what might have happened to either of you if you hadn't been able to save yourselves. Bozel told us a story about an unfortunate fisherman from Cottersdamp Island who'd been stranded there. He didn't fare nearly as well."

"Is that so." Otis pretended to ruffle his feathers so no one would notice he'd shuddered.

The melody of the bewitching song sung by the bird-creature had come drifting back to him. This was not an uncommon occurrence since he'd left the island. It seemed to happen with even more frequency if he thought of the bird-creature. Almost any memory connected to her or the island was enough to cause such a thing. Otis wasn't altogether certain the creature didn't still hold some measure of power over him. *Will it never end?*

Daisy flicked her ears, and her forehead bunched a little. She hadn't missed the edge in the great owl's voice. "What else happened to you while you were on that awful island, Otis? Tell us more about the ghostly bird-creature."

147

"I'll tell you the whole story someday, Daisy, but I don't want to think too much about the island for now, especially the bird-creature."

It troubled Topaz to see Otis in such a scrawny unkempt condition. The great owl didn't look well at all. Topaz himself wanted to hear more about what had happened to Otis on that island, but he didn't want to call up any bad memories that would cause Otis to suffer all the more for the telling. Thinking he'd upset Otis by his mention of the ill-fated fisherman, Topaz was sorry to have brought it up. He felt the most important thing Otis needed now was good food and time to heal.

"I know you like to be on your own, Otis, but you're welcome to stay here at the castle until your strength returns and your wing has had time to mend properly."

Otis looked up from his fishcake and blinked. "I will stay, Topaz. I'd rather not be alone for a while. Not to change the subject, but where is Dooley? I haven't seen him since my return."

Topaz sat back in his chair, relieved that Otis had given in so easily. "I believe he may be visiting with Menna. Has anyone told you about the Spotted Gray Matoose?"

"Yes, I've heard the good news, and I look forward to seeing the chicks when they're ready to come out of their eggs."

Topaz licked a dab of melted butter from the tip of his nose. "Since poor Menna is all on her own, Dooley's looking out for her until the chicks are big enough to leave the nest and follow her about."

Otis shifted his grip on the back of the chair and ruffled his feathers. "Yes, I've heard how the Giant White Osprey slaughtered Menna's mate right in front of her." For a moment, a distant haunted look filled the great owl's golden eyes. His feathered tufts quivered, then stiffened.

PART THREE

Return to Cottersdamp Island

CHAPTER ONE

By the time Topaz stepped outside the kitchen door and into the evening's cool air, the daylight had begun to fade. Topaz sometimes liked to take a walk after dinner, and the back door of the castle was closest to the forest trail. Daisy would have come with him, but she had fallen asleep before the fire in the great-room.

Topaz wouldn't have liked to admit it, but he was glad Daisy hadn't come. At the moment, he didn't feel much like talking to anyone. His head ached from trying to think of a way to rescue the Green Fairies from Cottersdamp Island. When he wasn't worrying about the Green Fairies, his mind was on Otis.

He was disappointed that Otis had left the castle the next evening after his arrival. He worried Otis may be doing more damage to his injured wing by flying again too soon after his difficult journey back from Barren Island.

Looking back, Topaz realized he shouldn't have been too surprised when Otis insisted on returning to the forest. The great owl's behavior had been a bit peculiar during his short stay at Knownotten Castle. On several different occasions, Topaz had seen Otis sitting all alone in the great room, looking as if he might be preoccupied with some dreadful dark secret. Even when he wasn't alone, Otis' mind seemed to be elsewhere, and there were his long gloomy silences during mealtime.

Near the blackberry bushes, Topaz stopped to watch a garden snake glide smoothly across the path while he pulled a burr from the end of his tail. As soon as the distraction was past, his thoughts were right back on Otis again. He couldn't seem to help it. Otis had begun the conversation about leaving by talking about how much he missed his home in the tall pines and saying he didn't want to wear out his welcome at Knownotten Castle. Topaz believed this was probably true, but he suspected Otis had other motives for wanting to leave as well.

He wondered if perhaps Otis had tired of dodging his and Heak's questions about the haunted island. Topaz paused to scratch his ear. At the time, he truly didn't think he and Heak had been that much of a nuisance. But now he guessed they probably had.

There was nothing he or Heak could say or do to convince Otis to change his mind once the great owl had announced his intentions. Otis simply left, refusing to comment on anything either he or Heak had to say on the matter. Topaz felt Otis was being unreasonable; however, he'd kept his opinion to himself. Topaz sighed and flicked his tail. He truly regretted any part he or Heak might have had in driving Otis away.

At least Otis had managed to keep in touch since he'd left the castle, although, he'd spent more time with Bozel than with anyone else. Topaz couldn't imagine what they found to talk about. He sometimes wondered if they talked about Barren Island. *Do they ever mention the bird-creature?*

One disturbing thought after another seemed to tumble through his uneasy mind while he traveled down the long hill on his way to the forest. The nature of Otis' injury was another thing that troubled him. Thinking about it now, he believed one of the bones in the great owl's wing must be badly bruised if not cracked. It always took a long time for this sort of an injury to mend itself, and Topaz believed the injury pained Otis more than he let on.

Otis hadn't talked about his injury while he'd been staying at the castle, not unless he was asked. In fact, Otis hadn't talked much about anything during that time. All Topaz really knew about what had happened to Otis on the island, he'd learned from Mallory and Corra. That had been little enough. What he'd overheard that day outside the dining room certainly hadn't added much more.

Considering how dreadful Otis looked upon his return, Topaz felt sure there was a lot more to his story than anyone of them had been told. Whenever Topaz thought about Bozel's account of the old fisherman from Cottersdamp Island, it made him feel cold inside. It also made him wonder what, exactly, had happened to his old friend to change him so.

Once during one of their short chats, Otis had revealed a snippet of something new about the bird-creature and his unfortunate adventure. But for the most part, what had taken place on the curious Barren Island remained an irritating mystery. Topaz sometimes wondered if the attack by the osprey was in part responsible for Otis' unusual behavior.

The osprey had to have known about the creature who inhabited Barren Island and were themselves afraid to go there. Topaz believed that was the only reason they'd spared Otis, if their nest was anywhere nearby. Owls, in general, were notorious for stealing young nestlings to feed on. Not that Otis would; he much preferred to dine on mice and fish, or even frogs and lizards when living in the wild. *If not for the osprey, none of this would have happened to poor Otis, and Menna would still have her mate.*

Later, when Topaz paused to lap water from a pot hole, two startled rabbits scampered down the forest trail ahead of him. How simple their lives were in comparison to his own. Wishing he could rest his troubled mind, he tried to focus on the noise of the crickets. At times like these, their singing could be a soothing distraction. After a while, he had to give it up. This evening nothing seemed to stop the endless chatter and the stream of unsolved problems that beset him.

Since both Otis and Heak had left the castle, Topaz felt as if he had too much time to dwell on Otis and to worry about the fate of the Green Fairies. Yet for all the brooding he'd done over the little green beings and the mess they were in, he still hadn't come up with a way to rescue them from the island. Nevertheless, he could think of plenty of reasons why it couldn't be done.

The problem was, there were no waterways connecting Knownotten Kingdom to the Slewnecky River, and Topaz was at a loss for a way to get boats to Cottersdamp Island. Although he didn't want to believe it, he feared the Green Fairies may be doomed after all.

"H'hoooo, thought I might find you here," Otis hooted from above.

Topaz started and felt the hair on his back go up as Otis made his usual silent landing to settle on the path nearby. Bozel was with him.

Bozel slid to the ground before the great owl's wings folded. "We didn't mean to startle you, Topaz." He was looking at the broad row of spiked hair on Topaz's back.

"Not your fault, Bozel. Otis delights in catching me unawares and then frightening me out of my wits. That's the trouble with Great-Horned Owls. You never hear them coming, then they're right on top of you."

Otis fluffed his feathers and tried to sound offended. "I thought you liked that about me." When Topaz didn't comment Otis went on. "We were coming back from a visit with Menna when we saw you here all alone. We thought you might like some company."

It had been more than two days since Topaz had actually spoken to Otis, and he was glad to see that his friend had regained his sense of humor. "It's good to see you looking so well, Otis."

Otis flicked his feathered tufts and blinked to acknowledge the comment.

Topaz turned to Bozel. "How's Menna?"

"She's well."

"And the eggs?"

Bozel grinned. "They're beautiful. They're light gray and they have brown and black spots all over them."

"So she finally did let you see them?"

"Oh, yes. There's four eggs now, and they're almost as big as I am."

"I guess it won't be long before the chicks hatch."

"Menna says it will take two full moons before they'll be ready to come out of their shells."

"All is well then." Topaz scratched behind his ear with a hind foot. "Did you happen to see Dooley?"

"We didn't, but Menna told us he's moved himself into a new den."

"Dooley wants to be closer to Menna's burrow," Otis added. "He not only watches over her, he even brings her food."

"It's a relief to know Dooley's looking out for her. I'm glad they're getting on so well together." The corners of Topaz's mouth curled into a small smile. "Other raccoons in these parts wouldn't pass up the chance to rob Menna of one of those precious eggs if they thought they could get away with it."

"I'm sure that's true." Otis blinked. "Dooley can be quite considerate at times."

"Have you thought of a way to rescue the Green Fairies yet?" Bozel asked.

The end of Topaz's tail began to flicker. "I wish I could say I have. It wouldn't be so much of a problem if we could get boats to the Slewnecky River."

"Can't we bring them over the land?"

"I'm afraid not, Bozel. Even if we had enough boats it would be a hard journey over land, and it would take a long time. Too much time has been lost already."

Otis snapped up a moth and swallowed it. "I can't imagine how we're going to get the little folk off the island without boats. But if we're going to be of any help to them at all, we must do something right away."

Topaz was pleased to see how much improved Otis was since he'd seen him last. Apparently he'd been worried for nothing. If only this problem with the Green Fairies could be decided so quickly.

"I agree, Otis, but we need to come up with a plan that doesn't include boats. Can either of you think of a better way?"

Bozel bit his lower lip and shook his head. "No, but there's got to be."

Otis swiveled his head to look at Topaz. "Do you think the raven king would help us? I haven't been on good terms with him and his bunch as of late. But maybe if you were to ask...?"

While Topaz took a moment to think, Bozel filled the silence. "The Giant White Osprey will never let them fly over the river. They'll attack any birds that come near their fishing grounds whether they're fisher birds or not."

Otis blinked. "Can't say I'd blame the osprey for going after ravens. They're merciless when it comes to stealing eggs and nestlings too. That's why I think ravens might be the only birds bold enough to risk flying over the river. They wouldn't be afraid to provoke the osprey."

"The ravens may be merciless when it comes to stealing defenseless nestlings, Otis, but I'm not so sure they could hold their own in a battle with a pair of angry osprey parents. I've seen them back down when met head-on by much smaller birds." Topaz flicked his ears to discourage a mosquito. "It would be a mistake to rely on them for their help in this matter. I believe Bozel's right about the osprey. There's a good chance they'd attack ravens on sight."

Otis snapped up the mosquito buzzing around Topaz. "What will we do then? I doubt if there's another bird willing to risk a run-in with the osprey."

Topaz had an impulsive thought. He believed it could be the solution to their dilemma; however, he didn't intend to mention it until he'd had more time to think it through.

Otis stared at him for a long moment without blinking. "I know that look. Whenever your eyes begin to glow like that, you're up to something, Topaz. Have you come up with a plan to rescue the little green ones? If so, let's hear it."

"A thought did just come to me, but it's hardly a plan."

"Never mind about that Topaz, we'd like to hear it all the same."

"I'm afraid you and Bozel may not like it, but I see no other way."

Otis ruffled his feathers. "I'd say that's the best reason for telling us right now."

"There's a few things that need to be sorted out before I'll know if it's even possible."

"I'd still like to hear it, if you don't mind."

Topaz was annoyed with himself for admitting he had any sort of a plan at all. He knew how persistent Otis could be. Otis probably wouldn't stop pressing him until he knew everything.

"Come now, Topaz. We may be able to help."

"Well." Topaz sighed, wishing he didn't give in to Otis so easily. "I think we all agree the osprey are a danger to be avoided. There may be many more of them nesting in those parts than we know of. But there's no reason why we have to rely on birds of any kind to fly the Green Fairies off the island. You said it yourself the day you came back, Otis."

"I said...? What?"

"You said, *Nothing seems to bother them, not even the osprey.*"

"You're talking about the bats. How do you know what I said? You weren't even in the room at the time. Were you eavesdropping on our conversation before you came in?"

"Heak or Daisy must have told me," Topaz lied. "The point is, Otis, the bats fish those waters too, and from what you said that day, the bats aren't afraid of the bird-creature either. Don't you wonder about that?"

"Yes, Topaz, I do. I thought it might be because the bats weren't on the island when the bird-creature was up and stirring about. Heak and I both considered this as a possibility."

Topaz scratched the top of his head with a hind foot. "Could be there's another reason, one we haven't yet thought of."

All at once, Otis began to blink unceasingly. A nervous twitch, Topaz thought. He'd seen it happen one other time since Otis' return. He decided not to mention it.

"As for the osprey not attacking the bats." Otis swiveled his head to the side. Apparently, he too preferred to ignore the episode. "Perhaps they're simply too many of them to do battle with. Whatever the reason, you could be right, Topaz. The Black Fisher Bats might be the answer we've been looking for."

Topaz nodded, and the end of his tail flicked. "I only hope they'll be willing to help us."

"The Black Fisher Bats," Bozel blurted, his voice so shrill it caused Topaz to start. "How can they help? They'd sooner eat Green Fairies than help them."

"It makes perfect sense," Otis said, overlooking Bozel's outburst. "But how will you make contact with them? You can't go to Barren Island."

"I'll have to think about that. In the end, I may have no other choice." Topaz tried to visualize the Slewnecky River. He wondered how deep it was. He'd been to the lower end of the east branch, that part of the river below the rapids. But he'd never had to swim it.

Bozel paled to an ashy-green. "You can't mean that... No one goes to Barren Island on purpose. Besides, my folk will never do it anyway. They're scared to death of the Black Fisher Bats."

Topaz couldn't ignore the panic in Bozel's voice or the terror in his eyes. Even though Bozel's fear of the black bats was unfounded, that fear was real enough to Bozel, and it wasn't that hard for Topaz to understand it. His own fear of deep water still lived in his nightmares. Yet because he was too embarrassed to mention it to anyone, he'd kept it a secret for more than two hundred years. Even his closest friends didn't know.

In that way he guessed he was a lot like Otis; there were some things he too preferred not to talk about. Everyone was afraid of something.

"Those stories you told us you've heard about the Black Fisher Bats carrying Green Fairies off to feed to their young," Topaz lifted his chin. "They aren't true; they're simply tales."

"How do you know they're not true?"

"Because I know what bats eat, and they don't eat Green Fairies. You must trust me about this, or we won't be able to save your folk. It will be a scary thing for you to do, but your folk will be more likely to fly with a black bat if they see you do it first."

Bozel's brown eyes looked incredibly large in his small pale green face. "You want me to fly with a Black Fisher Bat?"

Topaz nodded. "This may be the only way to convince your folk that it's safe."

"I don't know if I can." Bozel's eyes filled with tears.

"I know you're afraid. I'd be the last one to fault you for that. The Black Fisher Bats are frightful looking. Even so, you must show your folk that you're not afraid to sit on the back of one of these harmless beings and fly with it."

Bozel shook his head. Despair had replaced the terror in his eyes. "I wish I could believe they're as harmless as you say they are. But even if I did fly to Cottersdamp Island on one of those creatures, my folk still may not do it."

Topaz tried again. "Think of it this way, when you return to Cottersdamp Island you'll already be a hero to the Green Fairies. Simply by returning with a plan to get them off the island you'll have earned their respect, and most of all, their trust. They will believe in you, and they'll be willing to do whatever you ask of them."

"But, what if they don't?"

"Now, Bozel, you and I both know you're making these excuses because you're afraid. But you see, the other Green Fairies don't have to know how you feel about this. They'll only be watching what you do. That's what's going to matter to them in the end. What they see you do is going to make all the difference."

Bozel kicked a rock and scuffed the toe of his boot in the dirt. "There has to be another way to get everyone off the island, there must be."

"What about your friend, Cazara?" Topaz purred lightly under his breath, hoping to calm Bozel. "She'll do it if you ask her to. And I'm sure you'll be able to convince your family to fly with the black bats. Your father will look up to you even more now."

Bozel sighed heavily and folded his arms over his chest. "I'm sorry to disappoint you. I feel like a lowly coward." He looked down at his boots. "But I can't help it. Even though you say the black bats are harmless, it doesn't help. Please believe me, I don't want to feel this way, but I'm scared to death of them."

Otis blinked. "Well, I think it's the osprey you should be worried about."

For a moment, Bozel was quiet. When he finally did speak, his lips trembled. "Please don't make me do this. I'm telling you right now, I know I can't go through with it. I would do anything to save my folk, but this is the one thing I'd rather die than do."

"You don't really mean that, Bozel. After all, you weren't afraid to fly with me, and you hadn't ever flown with an owl before."

"But that's because I'd had a chance to get used to flying when I had to fly with Menna, and I was never afraid of you, Otis."

"You were afraid of Topaz until you got to know him." Otis swiveled his head and fixed his golden eyes on Bozel. "I'm sure you would have been afraid of me too, if you hadn't gotten to know my friends first. There are many beings who have good reason to fear owls. They think of us as birds of prey, and not much different from the osprey.

Otis paused to watch an ant crawl over one of his talons. "I believe you're afraid because of all the terrible stories you've heard about the Black Fisher Bats since you were very small. Now you're being told that none of those awful stories were true. This is what you must believe if we're going to help you get your folk off the island."

Bozel folded his arms across his chest. "All the same, Otis, these bats have lots of sharp teeth. I saw them, and I saw them swoop down from the sky and grab living fish in their claws and carry them away."

"Many beings survive by eating fish. That doesn't mean they eat Green Fairies. You and I eat fish too. I understand that it's hard for you to believe these beings could become your friends. Yet, without their help, the Green Fairies have only two choices left to them, that of starving, or that of drowning."

CHAPTER TWO

While Topaz and Otis talked alone, Bozel sat by the creek to think. He knew what Otis had said about the Green Fairies having only two choices was true, and he hadn't come this far to fail his folk now. What if Otis and Topaz were right, and this was the only way to rescue them from the island? Would he really rather die than save his own folk?

He chucked a stone at the branch of a cherry tree that hung over the narrow creek, hearing the stone plunk as it landed in the shallow water. Rethinking his remark about dying rather than flying with a bat, he realized was probably the dumbest thing he'd ever heard himself say.

He'd only said it because he wanted Topaz and Otis to understand how afraid of the bats he truly was; he understood that now. But he was worried what his new friends must think of him for saying such a thing. *Maybe they'll even refuse to help me at all. What will I do then?*

Bozel slapped at a mosquito. He wondered if all Green Fairies really feared the bats as much as he did. Some of them had probably never even seen a bat before. He thought of his encounter with the Six Footed Sand Slank. The time he'd spent with the beast should have taught him something, like how wrong it was to judge a being by its appearance alone. As frightening as the slank looked, the creature had done him an unforgettable kindness in the end.

He wanted to believe what Topaz and Otis had said about the bats was true. Maybe the horrible stories he'd heard about them were nothing more than old fishermen's tales. Yet he knew his father believed in these tales too. Aside from his fear of the bats, there was a small part of him that felt sorry for the bats because they were so ugly. How they looked wasn't their fault, and it wasn't fair to judge them for that alone, or for eating fish, he reasoned.

Later that night, when Topaz returned to the castle, Otis was waiting for him. The great owl was perched in the small pear tree that grew outside the kitchen door.

"Thought you'd be out all night," Otis hooted.

"What are you doing here, Otis? It's late."

"Not for me it isn't. We have to sort this matter out tonight, Topaz. Bozel has finally agreed to fly to Cottersdamp Island with one of the black bats. He'll be full of questions about it by tomorrow. We need to go over the particulars beforehand."

"I knew he'd agree in the end, but I didn't expect him to make up his mind this soon."

Otis blinked. "Yes, as you say, it was quick. I thought he might need to sleep on it at least."

"I've been thinking about how I might be able to make contact with the black bats. It seems I'll have to go to Barren Island after all. It can't be avoided."

The great owl's feathered tufts twitched. "I get shudders whenever I think about that place."

"Who could blame you, Otis. You nearly met your end there."

Otis stared at his friend without blinking. "I don't think you ought to go to Barren Island either. It wouldn't be at all wise. Is there no other way?"

"I'm afraid not." Topaz sat on his haunches. "If there is, I hope I think of it before I get there."

The conjure cat's luminous eyes had taken on an eerie greenish cast in the darkness, giving him a somewhat monstrous appearance. This would have been unnerving for anyone else, but through the years, Otis had become accustomed to it.

"Do you think the bats really will help the Green Fairies? How will you speak to them; what will you say?"

"I've never had dealings with bats before, but I'm sure the words will come. There's plenty of time to figure that out before I reach the island."

"And you'll take Bozel with you?"

"No, not to Barren Island. It might be too much of a fright for him."

Otis snapped up a large mosquito that had drifted in front of his face. "I can fly him to Cottersdamp Island, if you like. You can meet up with us later, after you've spoken with the bats. It will give Bozel some time to talk with the other little green beings."

"Are you sure you're up to this, Otis? What about your injury? What about the osprey?"

"The wing will do if I stop for a rest now and again along the way. After sunset there won't be as much chance of running into the osprey. They'll probably be asleep by then. I'll glide in low over the water. They may not even notice me since I'll be coming from the mainland."

"As I recall, you were gliding over the river the first time you were attacked."

"It'll be safe enough after dark. I won't be anywhere near Barren Island."

"Neither was Menna's mate, from what Bozel told us."

The great owl began to blink. "You worry too much."

"If I do, you're to blame. The thing is, Otis, you'll still be over the Slewnecky River, and if you're that low they could take you for an intruder on their fishing grounds. It won't matter if it's Barren Island or if it's Cottersdamp Island, it's still their territory, and they may come after you."

Otis was quiet for a time. "You forget. It will be dark. Certainly they won't come after me at night."

"Day or night, do you think you should take that chance? Your wing is still healing and you'll have Bozel with you."

Otis blinked several times before answering. "Yes, I see what you're getting at. All the same, Bozel will be at risk no matter what, won't he? If I don't take him to Cottersdamp Island you'll have to swim there with him on your back. That means you'll have to swim to Cottersdamp Island and Barren Island. Those waters are pretty chilling at night. Not only that —there's quite a long distance between the two islands. You may have to travel all night to make it to Cottersdamp from Barren Island."

The great owl did have a point. Although Topaz hated to admit it, Bozel would probably be better off with Otis, considering his own fear of deep water, and the length of time it would take to travel over land from one island to the next. Otis didn't know about his fear of deep water, and Topaz saw no reason to mention it to him now.

Topaz stood up to stretch, then sat down again. "Take him then. I haven't decided if I shall need to go to Cottersdamp Island after all now that Bozel will be going there with you. I may, instead, wait on the mainland until it's time to swim to Barren Island and make contact with the bats. I'm not sure how long all of this is going to take. I'll know better after I'm there."

"Whatever you do, remember, Topaz, the bird-creature comes out as soon as the bats leave. You must be gone before dusk."

"Yes, I plan to be; I may go to the island as the bats are returning from a night of foraging."

Otis flicked his feathered tufts. "That may be the best way to go about it."

Topaz stood up and arched his tail. "I'll talk to Bozel early tomorrow morning, and I'll let Mallory and Corra know we'll be leaving the following day."

CHAPTER THREE

Bozel was up long before dawn on the morning they were to leave on their journey. With so much to think about, he'd hardly been able to sleep at all, or so it had seemed. Now that daylight was approaching, he refused to think about the fears that had haunted his dreams as well as his waking hours throughout the long night. Today he would only think about what it would be like to see his family and his friends again, especially Cazara. He was surprised to realize he thought about her more than he thought about his sisters, or even his parents.

Although Cazara had told him she could never forget him, he was beginning to have doubts. They hadn't spoken to one another for many days, and he couldn't help wondering if she'd still feel the same about him. There were plenty of other Green Fairies on the island close to her age. He knew of at least one who'd been more than happy to see him leave, and he was sure Fentzel would make the most of his absence.

"I couldn't sleep either," Daisy confided to Bozel when she found him alone in the dining room. "Are you worried about meeting the bats?"

Bozel had been standing in front of the open glass doors that looked out into the courtyard when Daisy had come into the room. He turned at the sound of her voice, pleased to see that she was up first. "That's one thing that kept me awake last night."

"Me and my friend Orange Blossom used to be afraid of bats, too. I still am a little, but I'm not sure why."

"Maybe it's because of the way they look?"

Daisy nodded. "Maybe. Anyway, I'm glad Topaz is letting me come with you, and I'm glad that we have this time to talk alone. I've wanted to tell you how sorry I am for the way I treated you when you were first brought here."

"What do you mean, Daisy? I thought you were nice to me. You and Corra made me feel less afraid about being here. You seemed to care about me more than any of the others did at first."

"I did care about you, and I still do." Daisy paused to look down at the stone floor, then lifted her eyes to look at Bozel again. "But, I was being selfish, too. I didn't think how scared or worried you might be. Topaz was right to tell me you were not a pet. 'Cause, that's the way I thought about you then. Now, I think of you as my friend."

Bozel smiled. "I think of you as my friend too, Daisy, and I'm happy my family will be coming here to live. I hope you'll want to be friends with them too."

Daisy nodded. "Sure I will. I want to be friends with all the Green Fairies, and Cazara too. She sounds nice the way you talk about her."

"Cazara is nice. I just hope she hasn't forgotten all about me."

"You two are up early." Corra came into the dining room with a tall stack of clean plates. "Couldn't help overhearing. I think your friend is going to be quite pleased to see you again, Bozel. Who could forget a brave Green Fairy like you? And one so good looking too."

Bozel felt his neck and face grow warm. He wasn't used to compliments. He gave Corra a shy smile. "I hope Cazara thinks like you do, Corra."

A moment later Mallory came in with a tray of warm scones and fresh strawberries. "We seem to be out of cream and honey this morning, Daisy. There's some goat's cheese in the pantry. Would you like some of that instead?"

"Yes, please, Mallory. This may be the last good meal we get for a long time."

Corra set the dishes on the table. "Even so, I bet you're glad to be leaving, at last."

Daisy nodded. "I've been looking forward to it. It will be the first time Topaz has ever let me come with him and Otis on a journey as long as this before."

"Will Dooley be coming with you?" Corra asked.

"Dooley's staying to watch over Menna. So, there will only be four of us going."

"Haven't you had your morning meal yet?" Topaz growled half under his breath from the hallway.

Daisy glanced at Bozel, and an uneasy expression flashed in her hazel eyes. "We were waiting for you and Otis. Is something wrong, Topaz?"

"Are you well this morning, Sire?" Corra asked when he didn't answer.

"I am well, Corra, concerned about Otis is all. Didn't mean to snap at you, Daisy."

Daisy's eyes widened. "Where is Otis? Is he all right? Is he going to fly ahead of us?"

Topaz stepped into the doorway. The corners of his mouth were curled, but he wasn't smiling. "No," he growled again. "Somehow, he's managed to reinjure that wing. He barely made it here this morning to tell me he won't be coming with us."

Topaz turned his attention to Mallory and Corra, his tone less angry. "Otis will be staying here at the castle while we're gone. Tillie is making up a room for him down here. He never should have left the castle in the first place. We tried to tell him it was too soon."

"Look, there's Otis, now." Bozel ran out into the courtyard, Topaz and Daisy right behind him.

Topaz stopped in front of Otis, his long tail twitching. "Otis, you told me you were going to stay inside and rest. You aren't fit enough to fly."

"Yes, Topaz. I know that, and I'm not so foolish as to attempt it. But, the least I can do is to show you the best trails to follow. It will save you some time and make your journey a bit easier, at least from here to the Slewnecky River. After that, you'll be following the river anyway. Barren Island should be easy to recognize, but I'll include some of the landmarks along the shore, all the same."

"In that case, I would be grateful for your help."

Topaz, Daisy, and Bozel watched as the great owl used his beak to sketch a map in the earth, there in the courtyard.

"It would be wise for all three of us to study this map," Topaz told Daisy and Bozel. "Should any one of us get lost or if we become separated from one another, we'll all end up in the same place sooner or later if we stick to the same trails."

When Otis was about finished, Bozel pointed to what looked like a tiny islet in the lower part of the eastern branch of the Slewnecky River. "Is that the Isle of Samoway?"

Otis looked up, his golden eyes blinking. "That's where a large colony of Spotted Gray Matoose used to live. But I never knew the name of it."

"That's it then. That's where Menna came from. Over here looks like the rocky beach, the place where I should have beached the boat."

Daisy inched closer to the map. "Where did you meet the scary sand slank?"

"It might have been about here." Bozel pointed to a place across from the Islet of Samoway "I wish I'd had the chance to thank him for sending Menna to find me."

"You might get to see him on this journey."

"Maybe, Daisy, but it doesn't look like we'll be going anywhere near those awful rocks this time, so I doubt that I will."

Daisy shook her head to discourage a bee from landing on her nose. "And this time you won't have to walk, you'll be riding on my back."

"That's kind of you, Daisy, but I couldn't do that; I wouldn't want to weigh you down."

Daisy made a funny noise in her throat, her version of a laugh. "I don't see how that could happen, you couldn't weigh any more than a small goose. I know you can run fast, but if you try to walk all that way and keep up with me and Topaz, you'll tire out soon enough."

"Then I shall be most happy to ride. Thank you, Daisy."

Topaz arched his tail. "It's time we left. We have a long way to travel before nightfall. If you and Daisy have had enough time to study Otis' map we'd better be on our way."

Bozel looked at the map again. "It would help if I could make a drawing of the map so I can take it with me."

Topaz nodded. "Corra has some scraps of parchment in the kitchen. Why don't you ask her for a piece of it and something proper to write with."

When Bozel returned to the courtyard with the parchment and a stick of pressed charcoal, Corra was with him. She was carrying a large cloth sack.

"What's all that?" Daisy asked.

"Food and a couple of blankets, my dears; you didn't think I'd let you leave without anything to eat did you? After all, you didn't even have your morning meal."

Topaz's whiskers stiffened slightly "That's thoughtful of you Corra, hope my ill temper didn't offend you this morning."

Corra smiled. "Never, Sire."

"I'll be happy to carry it." Daisy bent her forelegs beneath her in order to lower herself for Cora's convenience. "Bozel, do you think you'll be able to keep the sack from falling off if Corra can hoist it onto my back?"

"I'll do my best."

Once she'd gotten the sack hoisted onto Daisy's back, Corra gave it a long studied look. "Hmm."

Daisy looked over her shoulder. "What's the matter?"

"I'm afraid that if this sack goes down, Bozel will go down right along with it. I'd better try to balance the food so the heavier things are on either end of it. Maybe that will keep the sack from sliding around and slipping off."

Daisy bobbed her head. "Thanks, Corra, you seem to think of everything."

As soon as Bozel finished making a quick sketch of the map, he climbed onto Daisy's back. Corra secured the sack by tying a long cord around it and Daisy too. She then gave the ends of the cord to Bozel. "When you're riding, it does help to have something to hold on to."

It was time for everyone to say their goodbyes.

CHAPTER FOUR

The sun was up before they reached the trail that lead to the river. His walk being more of a trot, Topaz naturally traveled at a faster pace than Daisy. There were times when she had trouble keeping up with his long-legged strides. Had the conjure cat been on his own, there would have been fewer stops, if any, for food or rest that day.

The stops were much too short anyway as far as Daisy was concerned. After they crossed the log bridge over the west fork, they settled down to supper. The sun had set, and the fireflies had begun to emerge from everywhere all at once. Their tiny winged lights flashed like bits of gold in the approaching darkness.

Topaz intended to move on after they'd eaten; however, he took pity on Daisy and Bozel when they fell asleep during their meal. He allowed them to sleep for a while longer before he woke them. They traveled until they came to the end of the woodland trail between the west and east branches of the Slewnecky River, finally stopping at the waterfall on the east fork. This one was quite small compared to the falls farther up.

This close to the river, Topaz, Daisy, and Bozel could feel the fine cool spray of water coming off the falls as they traveled along the river's edge. The noise of the rushing water was loud and constant.

"Wait here," Topaz shouted to them, "and do not wander. There's something I must look into."

Upon his return, a short time later, Topaz lead Daisy through the slippery mud and under a huge rocky arch beneath the falls.

"Watch your step here, Daisy, this part drops down."

Beneath the rocky arch, Daisy followed Topaz through a black hole and into a small cave. Though the air was cooler here, the inside of the cave was surprisingly dry, and the sound of the water much quieter.

Topaz sat on his haunches. "I wanted to make sure the cave was empty before I brought you inside. Brown Bears and Shaggy Red Buckwetchers like to sleep in the caves around these parts. This one smells as if it hasn't been used for some time though. I think we can spend the night here without worrying about any unwanted visitors."

Daisy crouched down to allow Bozel to climb off.

"It's so dark in here. I can barely see my hand in front of my face." Bozel remarked as he untied the rope that secured the sack, relieving Daisy of her burden. "How did you know about this place, Topaz?"

"I discovered this cave long ago. I was on a mission for the kingdom at the time."

Daisy's ears straightened. "That must have been when King Kittle still ruled."

"Yes, Daisy, it was, and long before you were born."

Daisy looked around the cave. Her large bright eyes scanned the ceiling first, then the cave's deeply shadowed corners. "My eyes are still adjusting to lack of light, but I can see a bit better now. If the moon weren't half-full, I probably wouldn't be able to see anything at all in here." She lifted her head and sniffed the fusty air.

"There are no bats, Daisy. I inspected the cave for bats, too, before bringing you and Bozel inside."

Hearing that, Daisy relaxed. She curled her front legs in toward her body and lay her head down. "I was more concerned about Bozel. I'm not as scared of them as I used to be. How long can we stay here?"

"I won't wake you again until sunrise."

Daisy released a small sigh and fell asleep almost at once.

Bozel pulled the blankets from the sack and spread one of them over Daisy, though it was hardly big enough to cover her by half. He wrapped himself up in the other one, and rested his head against a corner of the food sack.

Topaz slid his paws out in front of him to rest on his belly. He glanced around the cave, remembering that long ago mission and the first night he'd slept here. He'd been alone, even though he and King Kittle had planned on making this journey together. As the king's companion, Topaz almost always accompanied the king on his missions, unless he was off on an adventure of his own.

However, the morning they'd planned on leaving, King Kittle had awakened feeling poorly. It was only natural that he should send Topaz in his place, giving him permission to act on his behalf should the need arise.

This visit to Jakester Hamlet was meant to be nothing more than a good will visit from a neighboring kingdom. Nevertheless, during the gathering a minor dispute between two other rival kingdoms erupted. Had such matters been left unresolved, they would have festered into a much greater problem later on, perhaps even war.

Dealing with these matters was never simple or easy. Even so, Topaz did manage to bring both kingdoms to a mutual understanding before his visit ended. He'd done this by using the skills he'd learned from watching King Kittle in years past. Topaz had learned a great deal from the king about the art of peacekeeping. The king always strived to do the right thing, and he was careful not to offend anyone, no matter how unimportant they seemed to be.

As King Kittle's confidence in Topaz grew, the king came to rely on Topaz even more. It wasn't long before Topaz became the kings Personal Advisor as well as his Liaison. Topaz was honored to hold these posts, and he did enjoy his missions for the kingdom. All the same, he had no desire to become anything more, least of all King. Nevertheless, the decision had not been up to him. King Kittle had wished it so for the good of the kingdom. Having no royal successor to rule after him, King Kittle insisted Topaz should be the one to wear the crown when he was gone.

By now, Topaz had become used to the responsibilities of the kingship, and he'd even become happy in his new life. In the beginning, when he'd thought about what being king would mean, he wasn't sure he could live up to his vision of the kind of king he should be. Now, he believed his former king would be pleased. Knownotten Kingdom remained a peaceful happy land, and the inhabitants continued to thrive.

On the following day, Topaz was in less of a hurry. He allowed Daisy and Bozel to nap during the day so they could travel at night when the air was cooler. They ate their last meal of the day late in the afternoon. After another short sleep they set out again in the dark of night. Topaz kept to the trail along the river and traveled at a slower pace.

For Topaz, whose nocturnal vision was far superior to that of most other beings, the trail wasn't at all hard to follow. The half-moon helped to light their way and Daisy had no trouble keeping up. She didn't begin to fall behind until the river trail started its long steep climb along the cliffs.

When the terrain did level off, the river was some distance below them, and to their right, a deep forest of hemlock and spruce. Topaz stopped to give Daisy a rest, but was on the move again before anyone had time to become too comfortable. He didn't want to have to rouse them out of a sound sleep.

"Something's watching us," Bozel whispered to Daisy a short while later.

"More than one something," Daisy answered in a soft tone, seeing that there were several sets of eyes peering at them from the darkness on their right.

Topaz glanced at the forest. "Never mind, Daisy. Better to watch where you're going."

"What if they're wolves? They might be following us."

"It's just as likely to be a herd of elk or deer. If those eyes do belong to wolves they will take less of an interest in us if we don't look back at them."

Although Daisy and Bozel said no more about it, that wasn't the last time they saw pairs of eyes staring out from some distant wooded place. Whether or not they belonged to a herd of harmless creatures or a pack of starving wolves, they were never close enough to know for certain, and they never heard a wolf's howl.

The next day, they followed the same plan. Daisy and Bozel didn't mind traveling at night. They liked getting up to the noise of the crickets and the fireflies' golden lights. There was something comforting about hearing the croaks of the frogs and the buzzing sounds of the night insects, even though some of them turned out to be hungry mosquitoes.

As the night wore on, the trail made a gradual descent until it was nearly level with the river. The trees thinned, and for a long while, the woods disappeared altogether. Toward first light, the woods appeared again. This wood however, was a good deal thinner than the one they'd left behind.

Just before dawn Bozel spotted the eerie outline of Barren Island off in the distance. The familiar and ominous land mass lay about midway from the shore. Even from as far away as the mainland, Barren Island looked menacing. The tall spires of its charred trees pierced the rising fog like giant black spikes.

Nevertheless, Topaz sounded doubtful. "Are you sure this is Barren Island?"

Bozel nodded. "It has to be. There's only one island below Cottersdamp, and as you can see, its trees have been badly burned."

Topaz looked around. "Hmmm, that's strange."

"What is?" Bozel asked.

"I seem to remember you saying there were high cliffs on both sides of the shore when you passed this way before, and I'm certain you said there were no trees?"

"That's right, there weren't any trees, and the cliffs were high. But Sezel's map was altogether different. The map showed trees and no cliffs."

"Do you mind if I have a look at that map?"

"It got ruined, so I didn't keep it. But I remember it clearly. That's why I thought Sezel had made a mistake."

The end of Topaz's tail began to twitch. "That would be the reasonable explanation."

The tone in which Topaz had spoken made Bozel wonder what he meant by that. "Is there an unreasonable explanation?"

"Yes. Barren Island floats."

Bozel's eyes widened. "I wondered about that."

"What about Otis' map?" Daisy asked.

"Wish I'd paid more attention to his landmarks along the river," Topaz mused.

Bozel pulled the rolled parchment out of his shirt pocket and opened it out on Daisy's back in front of him. Although it was a little hard to see in the dim light of the early dawn, the map showed high cliffs without trees just as Bozel had seen it on his journey by boat. This was enough to confirm their suspicions about the nature of this haunted island.

Topaz left Daisy and Bozel on the path, and walked down to the river's gritty edge. For several long moments, he stood there looking out over the water, observing the flow of the current. On the surface, the current didn't appear to be moving fast at all. Yet Bozel had said Barren Island possessed a pull of its own, a pull strong enough to draw a fisherman's boat to its shores.

"Are you going to talk to the bats now?" Bozel came up beside him along with Daisy.

Topaz turned to meet Bozel's eyes before he answered. "The bats will be returning to the island soon, if they haven't already. We couldn't have arrived at a better time."

Daisy pawed the wet sand with her front hoof. "But aren't you going to sleep a little first, Topaz? We've been traveling all night."

"There'll be plenty of time for sleep when I get back, Daisy. I won't be there long."

"Some of them are coming back now." Bozel was looking north toward Cottersdamp Island.

It surprised Topaz to hear the eagerness in Bozel's voice. It seemed to him that the Green Fairy was beginning to make peace with his fear of the bats. The bats flew over the river, Barren Island directly in their path. As they drew closer, it became clear that these were the large Black Fisher Bats.

A few moments later, the smaller Brown Bats came fluttering in from all directions. Their numbers uncountable, their masses spread out across the sky for miles. Bozel and Daisy watched the sky in silence. Then Bozel remembered something he thought might be important. When he turned to tell Topaz, he was astonished to discover the conjure cat had slipped away unnoticed.

CHAPTER FIVE

Never before had Topaz been given a reason to speak with bats. This visit to Barren Island would be an experiment. If he did indeed manage to communicate with them successfully, there was still the chance the bats would refuse to help. Why should they trouble themselves with an isolated community of beings they'd never had dealings with before?

If it turned out the bats were agreeable, Topaz hoped they wouldn't mind taking the Green Fairies all the way to Knownottten Kingdom. Nevertheless, it would be enough if they were willing to carry them only as far as the mainland.

The cold water was bearable. Several feet from the shore the mild pull of the current began to tug at him. The current's pull was like a gentle invitation, encouraging him to venture out a bit farther and then a little more, and that's what he had done. In the few moments that followed, he'd felt himself being drawn farther and farther out into the river. When he looked back at the shore, he could see that well over half the distance to Barren Island was already behind him.

At this point the current grew noticeably stronger. It carried him as though his body were weightless. He knew the river was too deep for his feet to touch its bottom, yet he hadn't had time to dwell on it or to be afraid. With practically no effort on his part, he was soon stepping onto the beach of Barren Island. It had been almost too easy. He wondered how easy it would be on the swim back to the mainland when the current's strong pull would be working against him.

Barren island was just as Otis had described it, a desolate ruin of scorched lifeless trees, many of them without branches. The charred spires and twisted blackened shapes of what had once been a verdant forest, appeared to float in the ghostly morning fog.

The fire had been so long ago that no scent of the burned wood remained. There was another smell, however: the overpowering stench of bat guano choked the humid air. Thousands of bats had made their homes in the burned out rubble of what remained.

Fortunately for Otis, he hadn't been affected by the odor. Being an owl, Otis didn't have a good sense of smell, many birds didn't. Topaz guessed that was why some birds could feast on carrion. As for him and his heightened sense of smell, the stench was strong enough to make his eyes water.

With dawn quickly approaching, most of the Black Fisher Bats had already returned to the island, and the smaller Brown Bats were arriving in greater numbers. So far, the bats appeared to have taken no notice of him.

As soon as the bats reached the island they settled into their burned out stumps and hollows. Except for some occasional chatter amongst them, the island was quiet. There was no sign of the dreaded bird-creature, and Topaz didn't expect her to make an appearance any time before nightfall. So there was no pressing need for him to hurry.

All the same, he'd been traveling throughout the night and he wanted to keep this meeting brief. He intended to make contact with the black bats and sort everything out within the hour. That is, if the bats were willing to help. Afterward he'd return to the mainland for a long sleep.

Yellow Conjure Cats were born with a natural ability to send thought messages to other members of their breed. Some conjure cats — like Topaz — were even capable of transmitting their thoughts over long distances. Their parents began their training in the use of thought transmission at an early age. It actually began with their mothers before they were birthed into the physical world. Communicating with other beings in this manner was not so common.

Over time, and with regular practice, Topaz had learned to use this skill well. He'd spoken to other beings in just this way on many different occasions. This form of communication was most useful when ordinary means of making contact weren't practical.

By transmitting his thoughts to the bats in this quiet way, Topaz hoped to make his message clear to all of them at the same time. Then it would be up to the bats to decide amongst themselves if they wanted to help him rescue the Green Fairies.

Bats didn't mingle with other beings, and this was a concern to Topaz. He didn't want to be thought of as a trespasser. Yet he was here, and planning to intrude further by asking them for their help. He wasn't at all sure what these reclusive creatures would make of his actions. They may be offended by his presence here. Worse, they may even feel threatened. The last thing he wanted to do was to frighten them off the island.

When it looked as if all the black bats had returned to the island and things had settled down, Topaz began to focus on directing his thoughts to them. His first message was simple. He told them who he was and what he was. Then he waited for a response. A clatter of loud squeaks arose from the bats with a startling abruptness. This went on for some time before it became quiet again, and Topaz received a direct message in return.

The bats wanted to know why he'd come to their desolate island. Topaz was quick to come to the point of his visit. He told them he'd come because he was in need of a kindness from them. The bats responded by asking what sort of a kindness.

Afraid he might express something that would discourage the bats from helping him, Topaz was a bit hesitant to explain too quickly. Instead, he ask the bats if they knew about the storms that still raged over Cottersdamp Island. Immediately, another clamor of squeaks rose up from the black bats who seemed to be in residence all over the island. Understandably, they made quite a racket. Once they settled down again, Topaz received his answer.

The bats did indeed know of the storms over Cottersdamp Island. From the skies, they had witnessed how small the island had become as more of it was washed away by the heavy rains. All the same, the bats didn't understand what this had to do with a request for kindness.

Topaz was pleased by the response he'd received from the black bats so far, and this encouraged him to be somewhat bolder. *The inhabitants of the island are in grave danger*, he transmitted.

Before he could finish the message, another loud clamor of squeaks and shrieks began to echo from the hollows of the charred trees. Topaz was patient as he listened to what sounded to him like meaningless chatter, while the bats finished their lengthy discussion. When all was quiet, he received a message. *We now understand what you want of us, but we can do nothing.*

Topaz was stunned. *You may be the only hope they have.*

Even if that's true, we cannot give the help you seek.

But, why...? I don't understand.

Once again, there was a roar of chatter. Then the reply came. *Didn't you know? They're afraid of us.*

Yes, I did know. I suppose I should have told you that right away, but I thought it would be best if you could meet one of their folk first. He's come looking for your help and he wants to show all the others that they have nothing to fear from you.

As Topaz and the black bats continued to exchange thoughts, he learned that the bats had tried to help the Green Fairies a number of times in the past few days. Nevertheless, each time a few of them attempted to approach the island, the Green Fairies would run away and hide. Finally, the bats had given up on trying to make contact with them.

If the rains continued as they had, Cottersdamp Island was destined to vanish into the Slewnecky River. The bats had come to accept this with certain resignation, and they believed it would happen quite soon. Topaz stiffened and his tail flicked. This was alarming news. Conditions on Cottersdamp Island were much worse than he'd imagined.

After another uproarious discussion and some hesitation, the bats agreed to meet with Bozel. It was decided that Topaz would bring Bozel to Barren Island after all. The meeting was to take place just before dusk. This was the usual time the bats awoke to leave the island and forage for food. If all went well, by tonight, Bozel would be making the flight from Barren Island to Cottersdamp on the back of a large Black Fisher Bat.

The responsibility for getting the Green Fairies to cooperate with the black bats would be Bozel's. He alone would have to convince his folk to accept their help. If the Green Fairies were in agreement, the black bats were prepared to fly them off the island and take them to a safe place. Knownotten Kingdom was not out of the question if the Green Fairies were willing to make the long flight.

A rush of relief poured over Topaz when his communications with the black bats had finally been concluded. The exchange between them had gone much better than he'd expected. Now that he knew he could count on them to help the Green Fairies, he believed everything else would work itself out. Topaz felt a thrill of excitement when he thought about sharing this good news with Daisy, and especially Bozel.

The exchange had taken longer than he'd imagined it would. For some reason, which he didn't quite understand, he'd been feeling a slow drain on his energy, and by the end of it all, he was quite exhausted. He sent another message to the bats, telling them this, and saying that he'd like to stay on the island a while longer and have a short nap before attempting the long swim back to the mainland.

The black bats were strongly against this, and they cautioned him not to do it. *It's not safe for you to linger here any longer, Topaz. You may not be tired for the reasons you think. Should you fall asleep here, your mind will be left unguarded. Asleep, your thoughts and intentions will be at risk. Beware of the Ghostbird,* they warned. *She is a dark spirit who feeds on the life-force of all living things, plants as well as animals. That is why nothing can grow here anymore.*

How is it that you're not affected? Topaz asked the black bats.

We are as one being, the bats replied in thought. *Our minds are linked and we have ways to block her. Together, we are too powerful for the dark spirit to overcome. She cannot influence our thoughts or draw off our life-force. She has tried and failed.*

I see, Topaz responded. *Then I will go now.*

Go quickly, Topaz!

Topaz was surprised by how much the bats knew about the Ghostbird, as they called her. He was glad he'd sent them that last message instead of just going off to sleep. With his mind now set on leaving the island, Topaz intended to go right away. Nevertheless, when he tried to stand up, he discovered his back legs weren't working.

After several more attempts of struggling to push himself up, he did manage to get all four of his legs beneath him. Even so, to place one wobbly paw in front of another and move forward without collapsing turned out to be quite a feat. In spite of his slow clumsy gait, Topaz did reach the edge of the shore. Once there, he plunged himself into river.

He expected the cold water to revive him and give him the surge of energy he needed to make it back to the mainland; however, it didn't happen as easily as all that. Not only was the current against him now, its pull was much stronger here, so close to the island. He shuddered and his pulse quickened. *Is this the power of the Ghostbird? Can she keep me from leaving this island?*

Topaz waded in deeper and began to paddle, alarmed by the effort it took. The muscles of his legs so weak, that despite all he was putting into it, he couldn't make any real progress. Not until now did he begin to understand the difficulty Otis had been up against. Only now was he able to grasp why it had taken Otis so long to escape from this haunted place.

Desperate to gain some distance from Barren Island, his sluggish limbs churned in the water until exhaustion claimed him. Helpless, he crumpled into a heap against the shore.

"We should go look for Topaz." Bozel threw a small piece of driftwood into the river. "He's been gone a long time, much too long, I think."

Daisy stood up and shook off the wet sand. "Look where? I've been watching for Topaz all this time, and I'm sure I would have seen him swimming in the river if he was on his way back to the mainland."

"Do you think he might have fallen asleep on the island, Daisy?"

Daisy stared across the river, her large hazel eyes filling with tears. "I knew he shouldn't have gone before he rested. What's going to happen to him when it gets dark? What if he can't get back to us?"

CHAPTER SIX

The rain was lighter that afternoon, giving Hirsol and Sezel an opportunity to salvage some of the wood from Sezel's old one room cottage. Two days earlier, the whole thing had collapsed into a huge pile of wet splintered boards. Fortunately, Sezel hadn't been there. Reza had invited him over to their place for an early supper.

The demise of the cottage was expected. The old place had been falling apart, piece by piece, for years, ever since the death of Sezel's wife. With Suezy gone, Sezel had lost interest in the upkeep of the cottage and had spent more time fishing downriver than staying at home. That is, until the unceasing storms and the long rainy seasons had made fishing dangerous and impossible.

Hirsol and Reza had been trying to get Sezel to abandon the old place and move in with them, even before Bozel's room was empty. Nevertheless, each time, Sezel had refused to budge on his resolve to remain there until he died. His excuses for staying had always been the same. "I thank you for your concern, Hirsol. But I can't leave my home. I been living here most of my life. If I was to leave this little cottage, I might forget all the good memories I have. I collected all those good memories whilst I been living here."

Sezel's cottage wasn't the only one that had been destroyed since Bozel had left the island. Many families were now living together under the same roof in homes everywhere on Cottersdamp Island. Those who hadn't lost their homes to the storms and the mud slides were obliged to open their doors to neighbors who had. Living on this small isolated island, they had no one else to turn to except each other.

Everyone knew it wouldn't be long before everything on the island would be in total ruin. The earth was saturated with rain, and the foundation of every home there was in jeopardy. The lives of the Green Fairies had become a matter of surviving from one day to the next. Those who had a little more than their neighbors shared whatever they could spare.

The inhabitants of Cottersdamp Island did what they could to salvage anything that might be useful from the ruined houses. Many of them had tried to build boats and barges from the salvaged wood. The problem was, the wood was water-logged and impossible to work with. The wooden pegs they usually used to join sections of wood together simply wouldn't hold properly.

Hirsol reached for the board Sezel held out to him. "If only we had a few days of sunshine to dry out some of this wood."

He and Sezel planned to make a raft without the need of wooden pegs. They were taking the wood from Sezel's fallen cottage and lashing the pieces together with thin strips of old cloth, which had been braided to make it stronger.

Sezel handed Hirsol another long board. "This looks like a good piece. See if this one will do any better."

Hirsol took the board.

"Do you really believe this raft is gonna work, Hirsol?"

Hirsol wiped his damp forehead on his shirtsleeve, smearing mud. "Well, it might hold together long enough for us to get to the mainland, if we're lucky. I don't give it much hope beyond that."

On Cottersdamp island, Green Fairies had always made their boats from gourds. They had never had to rely on wood for that purpose. Wood was used for building houses and furniture, or for fuel to supply heat, or cook food. The idea of using wood to make boats was unheard of, and the Green Fairies had no skill for it.

Sezel rubbed his muddy hands against his trousers. "I think Bozel will be back soon."

"I wish I could be as certain about that as you seem to be, Sezel."

"It's true, you'll see."

"What makes you so sure?"

"I feel it, is all; I feel it in my being, and I'm never wrong about those things."

Hirsol looked up from his work. "You know, Sezel, I had a strange dream about Bozel last night."

"Is that right? What was it about?"

"Well, it was... I don't think I ought to talk about it."

Topaz was annoyed with himself for having slept this late, and he didn't understand why he was lying in wet sand. The position of the sun told him it was late afternoon. *Why have Daisy and Bozel let me sleep so long?* Still weak, he raised his head to look around expecting to see one, or both of them somewhere nearby. What he saw instead were the charred remains of Barren Island.

The realization came to him like a thunderous blow to his breast. Nevertheless, the shock wasn't enough to bring him to his feet and get him moving.

CHAPTER SEVEN

"Something awful must have happened to Topaz," Daisy whimpered. "It's going to be dark soon. What are we going to do?"

"I don't know, Daisy. I'm scared for Topaz too. The bird-creature will be waking up as soon as the daylight's gone."

"What if Topaz is lost? He could have left from the other side of the island and swam to the wrong side of the mainland. If he did that, I wouldn't have seen him leave Barren Island."

"Daisy, Topaz is too smart to get lost, he wouldn't swim to the other side; he'd know better."

"What if he's drowned?"

Bozel kicked a pebble into the water. "I don't believe he's drowned either."

"Why do you think he isn't here?"

"I don't think Topaz ever left the haunted island. I think he got stuck there, like Otis did, but I don't know what we can do about it."

"I wish Otis was here. He'd know what to do."

"We should try to find help while there's still some light left. Somebody must live around here." Bozel thought about the Six Footed Sand Slank, hoping they might find a kindly creature willing to help them.

"Let's take a look in there." Daisy lifted her chin to suggest the small woods several yards behind them.

A thick layer of fog had spread over the island by the time Topaz awoke again. He rolled onto his belly and stretched his huge paws out in front of him. The bats had left some time ago. He'd heard them fluttering over him, and he'd done nothing to stop them from going. Not that he could have; he hadn't the strength to open his eyes. How foolish he'd been to underestimate the power of the Ghostbird.

He groaned inwardly. The chance to rescue the Green Fairies from Cottersdamp Island had been lost, for this night anyway. There was nothing he could do about it until the bats returned to the island at dawn. Above all, he had to get back to the mainland. It troubled him to think what Daisy and Bozel must be going through, not to know what had become of him, or if he'd even return.

When he'd left them that morning, he never imagined the two of them would be there alone after dark. The footprints he'd seen in the soft soil on the trail above the beach that morning troubled him more now than it had then. The only reason he hadn't mentioned it was because he didn't want to upset Daisy.

The footprints were old. The beast had come and gone. So what would be the point of giving her something to worry about just before he was about to leave them all alone. Now he was having second thoughts about that decision. What if the beast did come back that way? Topaz stood up on trembling legs, and tried to walk. After a few steps, his limbs buckled beneath him.

While he lay there in a heap on the wet sand, a soft tinkling sound came to him from somewhere out of the fog. His ears pricked. *The wordless song of the Ghostbird.* From what Otis had told him during one or their more recent chats, shutting out her song might be the only way to resist her cunning influence.

Nevertheless, Topaz suspected her power over him had begun the moment he'd stepped onto the island. Through dazed, half-lidded eyes, he watched her dazzling form materialize out of the fog and move smoothly toward him. He strained to keep his eyes open, fearful he might lose sight of her. Why, he wasn't quite sure. *What's she going to do?*

In the next instant, her silvery image was adrift in front of him, frail and shiny in the moonlight. She glowed with a light that must have been her own, one that burned from within.

He stared up at her, taking in the details of her shimmering gown and her odd bird-like features. Although she was an alluring figure, Topaz found her presence chilling. When she sang to him, her voice was like a thousand tiny bells tinkling in a gentle wind. It might even have been the way Otis had described it; he couldn't seem to remember clearly. Unlike Otis, Topaz did not find her charming or enchanting. Her tinkling bell-like voice served as more of a sinister forewarning since he already knew who and what she was.

When the singing stopped she called him by name. The sound of it so soft and light. It echoed through his head.

"How is it that you know my name?"

"Your thoughts came to me while I slept. My dreams have told me why you are here. I have been waiting for the darkness to come so I could bring my song to you."

Her words struck him like blows. The black bats weren't the only ones to receive his messages that morning. He wondered how much more she knew. He dare not ask for he knew full well what this creature was up to. Her attempt to keep him talking was a deliberate distraction, a way to prevent him from attempting to leave the island and a clever way to gain even more control over him.

Even though he was well aware of her wicked motives, he was tempted to engage in conversation with her simply for the sake of his own curiosity. He didn't doubt she knew this. The Ghostbird was a cunning creature indeed, for the spell she was so busily weaving seemed to be working on him quite well.

He was beginning to understand how Otis had fallen under her spell and why the great owl had lost track of so much time. Had the bats not warned him about guarding his thoughts and his intentions from her he may have been beyond all hope by now.

Still he'd already fallen asleep here. There probably wasn't much she didn't know about his mission and his presence here on the island. Worse, this creature had gained an influence over him he would not have thought possible, considering this was their first meeting and the first time he'd heard her bewitching song.

Losing control of his body frightened him; however, he felt fortunate the creature had not yet taken over his mind. His only means of defense against her was his ability to reason and to use his conjure power. If that were taken from him he would indeed be powerless.

Since he'd dropped out of the conversation, the Ghostbird had taken up her song again. Topaz ignored her, making every effort to focus inward. Whether his conjure power would protect him against the Ghostbird's influence, he couldn't be certain. Nevertheless, he was about to find out. If nothing else, it would serve to weaken the strength of her spell.

With this in mind, Topaz closed his eyes and began to purr. He purred softly at first, then a bit louder. Gradually, he increased the volume until the shrill rhythm of his purr vibrated throughout his being and the Ghostbird's song became lost in its steady rumble. Sometime passed before Topaz opened his eyes again. When he did, his first sight of the Ghostbird forced him to gulp his next breath.

The Ghostbird did not appear to him now as she had when he'd first seen her. Until this moment, Topaz was certain his mind hadn't been affected by her power. All at once, he could see he'd been wrong. Apparently this creature had been deceiving him all along. By calling on his conjure power, Topaz had just destroyed a vital part of the deceptive illusions she'd been using to enchant him.

The proof was right in front of him. Gone were the fine silvery feathers that had adorned her lashes and her slender, graceful wings. Gone too, the silver beak and the long shimmering gown. Her ghostly image, no longer lovely, had become that of a wraith, a deathly spirit clothed in rags and covered with filth.

The once delicate bird-like features had altered to resemble those of a hungry vulture. Topaz shriveled from the sight of her. Seeing her as she truly was, he hated her beyond measure. Even more loathsome than her vile appearance was what he sensed about her wicked soul.

Her malicious spirit, cloaked in the dark aura of evil, smelled of a corpse long buried. The stench was unbearable and Topaz began to gag. This was the worst thing that could happen. The more he gagged, the less he purred.

Somehow, he had to get control of himself. Purring was vital. It's what he did to activate and sustain his conjure power. Without it, the Ghostbird would destroy him.

He got to his feet, surprised to discover that most of his physical strength had returned. He bounded into the water and began to paddle, knowing he had to get away while his conjure power was still strong enough to protect him.

Away from the Ghostbird, he no longer suffered from her evil smell. He took up his purring again. Even though the current was now against him, he made considerable progress in distancing himself from the island. In the moon's subtle light, he could see the shores of the mainland in the distance.

Nevertheless, something suddenly changed. The current renewed itself. It became stronger. More powerful. It sucked at his limbs and pulled him back again and again. Topaz couldn't understand why. He was certain he'd gone well beyond the boundaries of Barren Island's malevolent current before he'd allowed his conjure power to lapse. Yet he couldn't have been more wrong.

Once again, he'd misjudged the Ghostbird and the extent of her reach. He'd let his guard down, believing himself in safe waters.

He tried to focus on his purring even while he paddled against the vile current. This time, it seemed that no matter how hard he tried he couldn't break away from its powerful magnetic pull.

The endless battle against the current left him breathless and panting. His energy waned. He lost the vigor for purring and his conjure power suffered for it. At this low ebb, he could no longer protect himself against the influence of the Ghostbird.

Weak and exhausted, Topaz felt himself slip beneath the surface of the river. Water filled his nares before he could close them off and jerk his head up. He tried not think about the deep water or how far away he was from the mainland while he choked and sputtered and fought for every breath.

After several moments of struggling for air, he gave it up and began to relax in the water. It came as no surprise to him that he was dying. He could feel his life-force being drawn from him. Thoughts of the present drifted away. Darkness hovered over him.

Moments later, he was running through the ancient Knownotten Forest, dazed and confused. The colossal velvety green columns towered above him as he sped over a cushion of wet moss. Its softness crushed beneath his weight as he bounded along.

"Keep moving, Topaz." His father's deep voice shattered the silence. "You're always lagging behind."

Topaz pushed on. With all his being, he tried to catch up to his father while his chest heaved and he strained for a lung full of air. His breath came in fast painful bursts, and his aching limbs felt heavy and awkward.

Next he could smell the moist earthy fragrance of the forest, and it filled him with a fierce longing to be with his cousins again and to see the rest of his family.

Bits of blue sky peaked through the canopy of green leaves that loomed far above him. The sun's bright golden rays streamed down through the tops of the trees to dance in the air all around him.

Nevertheless, Topaz felt chilly and wet. The thick layer of downy soft fur that was meant to protect his skin against the rain and the cold was saturated with water.

"Father, why am I so wet?"

"There's no time to worry about that now, Topaz. We mustn't keep the others waiting."

CHAPTER EIGHT

"It gets dark here so fast." Daisy tromped through the weedy undergrowth, Bozel rode on her back. "By now the bats have already left Barren Island."

"Keep your voice down," Bozel whispered next to Daisy's ear. "I think I hear something scratching around over there."

Daisy stopped in her tracks. Her ears pricked. She spoke in a hushed voice. "I can hear it now, too. What do you think it is?"

From where Bozel sat on Daisy's back, he had the advantage of being able to see over the tops of the dense shrubs that otherwise would have hindered his view. "I don't know, but I just got a glimpse of something big. No, huge...and shaggy looking with horns, and it has thick nasty looking claws. Whatever it is, I don't think it's a being we'd want to meet up with."

"I think I should run," Daisy whispered, picking up the creature's odious scent. Her legs trembled with indecision as her natural instincts for self-preservation began to take over.

"Oh, no, Daisy. Don't do that. If it hears your hoofs pounding through the brush it might come after us, and you may not be able to outrun it."

"Can you still see it?"

"I can, but it would help if the moon were a little brighter. It's over there between those two thin trees.

"What's it doing?"

"It seems to be ripping something. Oh, good grief - it's got another animal in its claws, and it's tearing it apart with its teeth."

Daisy stuck her head through a small gap in the shrubs. At last, she was able to get a look at the creature. She glimpsed its broad snout and long yellowed teeth when it rose up and sniffed the air. She pulled her head back right away and turned her face toward Bozel. "I saw it; I just saw it stand up on its hind legs."

Even as she spoke, Daisy began to move backward. Trying hard not to make any noise, she placed one delicate hoof carefully behind the other and backed away from the scene.

Bozel felt a tremor run through her. Her body began to quiver. Not wanting to spook her, he didn't say anything until they were on the beach again. Then he leaned forward and spoke to her in a gentle voice. "Daisy, are you all right?"

"No, and I won't be until we get away from here."

"But what about Topaz? What if he comes back and we're not here?"

"We can't worry about that now." Daisy's words were clipped and snappish.

Bozel was surprised by the change in Daisy's voice. She sounded nothing like herself. "What kind of a creature was that? Have you ever seen one before?"

"No, But I saw what it was eating."

"What was it?"

"A deer, and that's why we have to leave now."

Bozel stroked Daisy's neck. "I'm sorry you had to see that, Daisy. No wonder you're shaking. I should look for our blankets before the fog covers everything. I'll put them over you, warm you up a little."

"We go now, Bozel, and you stay put. I'm not going to take a chance on losing you in this fog."

"Go where? We can't leave without Topaz."

"Don't you remember what Topaz said we should do if we get split up?"

"He said to stay on the trail, and follow the map. But, this is different. If we leave here, we may never see Topaz again."

Daisy moved into a gallop. "We're going to do it anyway, Bozel, so hang on."

Bozel was plunged forward as Daisy took off down the beach. He did all he could to hold onto Daisy's neck.

It was a long time before either of them spoke again. Bozel was too preoccupied with not falling off, and Daisy was more concerned about putting some distance behind her.

They were miles away before Daisy slowed down. "Look up there, what is that?"

Bozel strained to see through the thickening fog. "What? Where are you looking?"

"There." Daisy motioned with her head, tilting it toward the river. "Part of it looks like it might be in the water."

"Hard to say from here, Daisy. Could be a bunch of boulders."

"I think it's Topaz," Daisy shouted, picking up speed.

When they were several yards closer Bozel spoke close to Daisy's ear. "You're right, Daisy, it is Topaz. I can see his stripes."

Daisy's speed increased again without warning. Her small hoofs pounded against the wet sand while Bozel bounced wildly around on her back. Less than half the size of a Knownotten Fairy, Bozel's small arms were barely long enough to reach around her broad neck, yet he managed to hang on all the same.

The moment Daisy reached Topaz she skidded to a stop. Her front legs buckled beneath her, and she went down beside him. Bozel rolled off Daisy's back to stand next to her. He stared at the limp furry body sprawled in the wet sand. All at once he felt as if he could hear his heart beating in his ears as the edges of his vision blurred.

CHAPTER NINE

This wasn't the first time Bozel had seen an unconscious being on the beach. He and his father had found more than one drowned fishermen on the shores of Cottersdamp Island. Usually it happened after an unexpected storm had come up and capsized their boats. Sometimes it had been impossible to revive them. But, this was Topaz, his hero. Somehow, he had to save him.

Once the numbness of finding Topaz unconscious and drowning was past, Bozel fell to his knees next to the conjure cat's chest. He then placed both his small hands on the cat's ribs and leaned forward. He pushed with all his strength. Water barely trickled from Topaz's nose and mouth. Bozel pushed again to try and expel more water.

"He's so cold, Bozel. Is he going to be all right?"

Tears streamed down Bozel's cheeks as he worked. "I wish I knew, Daisy. I wish my dada was here to help me push the water from his chest. I'm pushing as hard as I can, and I'm afraid it's just not enough."

Daisy's head dropped to her chest, her eyes closed briefly. Bozel thought she might have been saying a small prayer. She then began to sob.

Bozel's arms were losing strength. He knew his pushes weren't as effective as they'd been in the beginning, and he worried he wouldn't be able to keep going. Yet he pushed several more times after that. Even so, he couldn't force any more of the water from Topaz's chest. So he used both hand to message the cat's throat instead. All at once, Topaz coughed and his belly heaved. Water gushed from his nose and mouth.

Topaz tried to lift his head. Nevertheless, he was just too weak and he simply lay there.

"Please, Topaz. Please," Daisy begged between sobs. "Open your eyes and look at me, Topaz."

When Topaz didn't respond, Daisy began to lick the sand from his face with her long narrow tongue.

Bozel leaned forward to place his hand in front of Topaz's pink nose to feel for his breath. That's when he heard a soft rumbling sound in the conjure cat's throat. "He's purring, Daisy, can you hear it? He knows we're here."

Daisy did know. The strange luminous eyes were finally open and staring right at her, their greenish glow as eerie as ever in the darkness.

Bozel wiped the water from his face. It was a futile gesture in light of the heavy downpour. Angry storm clouds hovered above them, slashing the sky with broad streaks of dark gray and black. "It's still quite a long way from here," he shouted over the noise of the wind and the rain.

Daisy's stomach grumbled from hunger. She wanted to shake the wetness from her coat, but Bozel was sitting on her back. They'd been traveling for hours, ever since they'd found Topaz. As soon as he could stand, Topaz was set on leaving despite his unsteadiness. Daisy tried to convince him to rest a while longer, but it hadn't done any good.

Worried about the time they'd already lost, Topaz insisted he'd had more than enough rest already. Against all evidence to the contrary, he declared himself fit and able to cope with whatever lay ahead. Daisy herself was tired, but she didn't dare complain, though she'd been without sleep for nearly two days.

When Daisy and Bozel asked Topaz how he happened to end up so far up the beach, he was purposely sketchy about the details. He told them all about his meeting with the Black Fisher Bats; however, little was said in regard to the Ghostbird, as he now called her. He saw no need to frighten them. Daisy and Bozel had enough to think about for the time being. They could hear the rest of the tale later, when they were safe at home in Knownotten Kingdom.

Bozel patted Daisy's neck. "You must be tired, Daisy. Would you like me to get off and walk for a while?"

"I am tired, but not because of you. You might as well ride. You'll only get stuck in the muck if you try to walk."

Overhearing their conversation, Topaz turned to peer at Daisy and Bozel over his shoulder. "We should all take a rest and find something to eat. It's about time I tried to make contact with the black bats, anyway. It's nearly dawn. By now, they will have begun to return to Barren Island."

"Will they be able to hear your thoughts from so far away?" Bozel asked.

"I'll know soon, Bozel. You and Daisy might want to stay close by until I learn something. We could be on the move again.

Daisy watched Topaz lap water from the edge of the river. Afterward, he sat on his haunches facing Barren Island and curled his long tail neatly around his paws. His luminous eyes appeared to glaze over, taking on a bizarre and unfamiliar look Daisy had never before seen. Instead of their normal topaz color or the eerie greenish glow she'd grown accustomed to seeing in low light, they had become a dark smoldering amber.

Once Topaz focused on making contact with the black bats, he didn't have to wait long.

We hear you, Topaz; why haven't you been back to the island?

Topaz explained what had happened. Under the circumstances, the black bats agreed that it would be unwise for him to come to Barren Island ever again. They had another solution; however, first, they would need to rest.

Only a little food remained in the sack Corra had packed for them. All the same, they had to leave it behind with the blankets. Daisy munched on the tender new plants she found growing near an outcropping of granite boulders.

Topaz waded into the river and caught a fish. He shared it with Bozel. Since they had no way to cook it, they ate it raw. For Bozel, eating raw fish would become one more memorable experience of his return journey to Cottersdamp Island. Since sleeping in the pouring rain didn't appeal to anyone, they continued along their way up the beach.

"That's it," Bozel shouted through the downpour after they'd been traveling for the better part of the day. "That's Cottersdamp Island." He pointed to a dark land mass, almost invisible beneath a fog bank that lay in the middle of the river.

"What happens now?" Daisy asked Topaz.

"Now we wait for the Black Fisher Bats."

There was no shelter from the rain on the rock strewn beach, and the woods behind them offered none as well. All things considered, Topaz thought it best if they remained out in the open. He wanted to be certain the bats could find them when they came looking for them at dusk. In the meantime, they snuggled close together and tried to sleep in spite of the wet weather.

For a long time Bozel lay sleepless and shivering in the rain, listening to the deep rhythmic breathing of his companions. He thought about his family and tried to remember Cazara's pretty face, her curly brown hair, and round hazel eyes. *What will I say to her when I see her again?*

CHAPTER TEN

Reza and Hirzol were awakened by a loud crash followed by an even louder cracking sound. They felt their bed slide sideways as the floor tilted beneath them. "The house is going," Hirsol shouted. He grabbed Reza's arm, and in one powerful motion, yanked her from the bed. "We have to get Sezel and the girls to safety."

"Is this the end?" Reza cried. She ran out into the hallway along with her husband. "Good Spirit, save us; the whole house is moving."

Hirsol staggered and turned toward the back of the house and the other two sleeping rooms.

"We're sliding." Hirsol and Reza heard Sezel yell.

A long and drawn-out ear splitting crack exploded above their heads when the large sycamore tree beside the house uprooted and crashed through the roof over the back rooms. One of the tree's huge limbs struck the main crossbeam that supported the roof and snapped it in half. Sezel stood up just in time to be struck down by the falling beam. The blow knocked him unconscious.

"Momma, Dada." Reza and Hirsol could hear the terror in Itza and Izzie's young voices as they cried out to them for help, but their own response was drowned out by the noise of yet another thunderous crack when the house itself heaved a massive shudder and broke in two.

Reza screamed when she felt the back of the house drop, the sudden impact jarred every tooth and bone in her body. The deafening clatter of boards and beams followed when the roof over the back rooms gave way and collapsed altogether.

CHAPTER ELEVEN

When sleep finally came, Bozel dreamed of a strange dark kingdom, steeped in shadow. Besides him, a huge flock of sinister black birds were its only other inhabitants. Bozel feared the birds, and he tried to get away from them, but they followed him everywhere. They seemed to be trying to tell him something important.

Even so, Bozel didn't want to hear what the birds were saying. He wished they'd simply go away and let him sleep. Nevertheless, these creatures were as relentless as the rain. They were tweeting so loud now that Bozel thought his ears would break and he'd never be able to hear anything again.

Topaz, Daisy and Bozel stared into the black mass of chirping pinched faces. Dozens of Black Fisher Bats were huddled all around them. With dusk approaching, what little light there had been began to fade rapidly, and the rain was still coming down rather hard.

Topaz felt Bozel stiffen. The Green Fairies small back pressed against his side. "Topaz, what do they want?" he stammered.

Topaz suppressed a yawn. "They want to know if you're ready to go to Cottersdamp Island."

Bozel shivered. "What should I do?"

Before Topaz could answer, he received a message from the bats.

We know the Green Fairy fears us, Topaz, and we do understand. You may tell the Green Fairy we only wish to help. No harm will come to him or to any of the other Green Fairies.

As Topaz processed this compassionate message from the black bats, a new plan began to take form in his mind. He asked the bats if they would go along with him. The bats agreed without question.

"The bats know you're afraid of them," he said to Bozel.

Bozel gave another shudder. "They do?"

"Many of those here now are just as frightened of Green Fairies, so they understand how you feel."

Bozel turned to look at Topaz. His eyes widened. "The Black Fisher Bats are afraid of us?"

Topaz nodded. "Those that are afraid would prefer not to be among the first group of the bats to go to Cottersdamp Island. But they agree to come later if they're truly needed."

"What do the black bats have to fear from Green Fairies?"

"They say it's because of your green faces; they're so unpleasant to look upon."

Bozel straightened, his head jerked and his eyes widened even more than they had before. "Our faces?"

"Not only that, they've also heard scary stories from injured bats who have tried to land on your island seeking refuge."

"What kind of scary stories?"

"They say the Green Fairies wouldn't let them rest there. They say rocks were thrown at them to make them go away."

Bozel's face tightened. "I've never heard that before. I'm sure no Green Fairy would throw rocks at an injured being."

"What if a Green Fairy thought he might be in danger of an attack? Can you see how he'd want to do all he could to keep that from happening? Sometimes our fear of something can cause us to imagine things that may never happen at all. And when it does, we often behave badly."

Bozel was quiet for a moment. Topaz wondered if he might be thinking about his frightening encounter with the sand slank.

"I suppose it could have been like that." Bozel's color darkened. "Please tell the bats I'm sorry to hear that happened to them. It was a heartless thing for my folk to do."

Topaz pretended to channel Bozel's message to the bats. He waited as if to hear a message from the bats in return. "The bats believe you're sincere, Bozel, and they hold no ill will against you or your folk. But they're worried about their safety on your island."

Bozel's face was solemn, his eyes glazed with tears. "I'll talk to my folk. I'll make them understand that the bats are our friends. I'll tell them the bats would never do anything to harm us."

Turning once more to the black bats, Topaz appeared to repeat the process with Bozel's last message. Afterward, he turned back to Bozel. "The Green Fairies might be less afraid if they knew that no more than two or three of the bats would be coming to the island at any one time. At least until your folk have had time to get used to the bats and accept them as friends."

Bozel nodded. "That would be best. Seeing so many big black bats all at once would be too scary."

So far, Topaz was relieved by Bozel's responses. "It would be better if you went to Cottersdamp Island alone the first time, Bozel. Just you and one of the black bats. This will give you time to explain everything we've been talking about to the Green Fairies."

Bozel stood up and ran his fingers through his soaking wet hair. "In the beginning, I didn't think my folk would be willing to let the bats come anywhere near them. I guess that's because I was so scared of them myself, but now that I understand how they feel and what they think, I believe this plan can work."

Topaz looked at one of the black bats and nodded. "It will, Bozel, and I'm glad we both can finally agree on this. If you're ready to leave, Gee is waiting to take you."

The nod from Topaz to Gee was a prearranged signal Topaz and the bats had agreed upon in their earlier communication. Following through with the plan, the black bat in front of Bozel moved forward. The bat's wings quivered slightly as it bowed its head toward him. Then the bat pulled its wings in close to its body and waited.

For a moment, Bozel stared at the Black Fisher Bat. Then his gaze shifted back to Topaz, his color somewhat paler. "What does he want, Topaz?"

Topaz sat up on his haunches. "This is Gee. He's a bit nervous about doing this, but he wants to help the Green Fairies, so he's willing to be the first of his kind to allow a Green Fairy to sit on his back and fly with him."

Bozel took a step forward. "Hello, Gee," he stammered through chattering teeth. "My name is Bozel. I - "

"He probably doesn't understand what you're saying to him, Bozel. But he does understand how you feel."

"I see." After a short pause, Bozel went on. "What should I do then?"

"Gee is waiting for you to climb onto his back."

Bozel did as he was expected without another moment's hesitation. His movements were stiff and awkward, and he didn't appear to be at all sure as to how he should go about it.

Topaz waited until Bozel was seated on the black bat's back before instructing him further. "You'll need to hold on, Bozel. So get a grip on that tuft of hair you see on the back of his neck. One more thing, you'll want to lean forward so you don't get blown off while he's in flight."

Again, Bozel did as he was told, except for grabbing onto Gee's hair.

Just as Topaz was about to say something more to urge Bozel to hold on, Bozel sprang upright. "When are you coming, Topaz?"

"I'll come a little later. In the meantime, you'll need to convince your folk that the black bats want to help them escape from Cottersdamp Island before it's too late."

Bozel nodded.

"Tell them the bats are waiting here on the mainland, and that they're ready to take them all the way to Knownotten Kingdom. It will save them a long hard journey over the land without food and other supplies. After they've had time for that bit to settle, Gee will send a message back here that it's safe for more bats to land. You'll have to trust Gee's good judgment on this. He'll know when the time is right. Then two or three more of the bats will come."

Again, Bozel nodded his understanding.

"Once your folk feel safe enough to begin flying with the bats, you can tell them about me. I think it would be wiser to let them get used to the bats before another unfamiliar being comes to the island."

"I didn't think about that. I'm so used to you I hardly think how you look anymore. I'll tell them about you and about the Land of Knownotten, too."

With that, Bozel leaned forward and took hold of the tuft of longish hair that stuck out from behind Gee's head. "So I should lean forward, and hold on to his hair like this? Won't that hurt him?"

"Well, you'll only be holding onto him, Bozel. Just be careful not to yank it."

Seeing how rigid Bozel sat on Gee's back and the look of near panic that still shone from his eyes, Topaz felt a rush of tenderness for the small green being. He then spoke to Bozel in a softer, gentler tone. "You mustn't be afraid to hold on tight with both hands, Bozel; it really won't hurt him. In fact, he'd like you to know that he intends to take great care to see that you arrive safely."

This was the reassurance Bozel needed, and Topaz was glad to see that his grip tightened without hesitation. As soon as it did Gee's wings opened, and the large Black Fisher Bat was in the air before Bozel could take another breath or change his mind.

"I didn't even get to say goodbye."

Topaz started when he heard Daisy's small voice beside him. He'd been so focused on Bozel and the bats he'd forgotten she was even there. "Neither did I, Daisy. But we'll both see him again soon."

"Was what you told Bozel really true?"

"Was what true?"

"You know, about the bats being afraid of Green Fairies, and the part about the Green Fairies throwing rocks at the bats who tried to land on their island... Did the bats really tell you all that?"

Topaz hadn't counted on being questioned about this. His whiskers twitched while he tried to come up with a believable explanation that would satisfy Daisy. "The truth is, the bats know the Green Fairies are frightened of them."

Daisy rolled her large hazel eyes at Topaz. "Hmm. But what about all that other stuff you said about the rocks?"

When Topaz didn't answer right away Daisy made a small noise in the back of her throat.

Topaz recognized it as a sign of her disapproval. The end of his tail began to flicker. "Well... what would you have done, Daisy?"

Daisy paused a moment before giving Topaz her answer. "You don't have to worry, Topaz."

"What do you mean; worry about what?"

"About Bozel finding out the truth; I've just decided not to tell on you after all."

CHAPTER TWELVE

"I've got to go to Cottersdamp Island." Topaz spoke as if the thought had just occurred to him.

"What? Right now?" Daisy's eyes seemed to grow as she stared at him.

"Yes, now. The Green Fairies need my help."

"How do you know? Did you just get a message from Gee?"

Topaz nodded. "I'm afraid it can't be helped, Daisy, but I'll have to leave you here."

"Why do you have to go?"

"There's been a mud slide. Another house collapsed. This time some youngsters got trapped inside. From what Gee's telling me, the youngsters may even be Bozel's sisters."

Daisy's head dropped. "Oh, no."

Topaz stood up and shook. He arched his tail, about to leave. The rain wasn't quite as heavy as it had been. "You won't mind staying here alone with the bats, will you?"

Daisy shook her head. "I'm beginning to get used to them, and I know they won't bother me. Poor Bozel, will you be able to save his sisters?"

"I'll know soon enough," Topaz told her over his shoulder as he waded into the Slewnecky River. A shiver run through him when he felt the first splashes of cold water against his already wet belly. "I hope Bozel has had enough time to warn them about me. I hope they know I'm coming."

When Topaz reached the storm-torn island, a group of Green Fairies were waiting for him on the sandy shore. All of them carried some sort of a lantern. Apparently, Bozel had had time to convince his folk they had nothing to fear from the huge, striped, furry creature with four legs and luminous eyes.

Topaz was conscious of a mild uneasiness amongst them, though he may have mistaken their nervous disquiet for curiosity. Or perhaps they were anxious about leaving the island and having to sit on the back of a flying black bat. No matter, Topaz tried not to stare at the Green Fairies. He was well aware of the effect his extraordinary eyes had on other beings who had never seen a Yellow Conjure Cat before.

At first he thought it odd, seeing so many small green beings in one place at the same time. Even though he hadn't thought about it before, it surprised him that no two of them looked alike. Some were taller or thinner or had bigger noses or more hair than others, and they were even different shades of green.

One of the older Green Fairies stepped forward. "Bozel told us to expect you. I'm to show you the way there."

Topaz was relieved the old one had no objections to riding on his back. It helped to save time.

Further inland, the wet sand gave way to slick mud. Topaz had to test the ground in some places before trusting it to bear his full weight without him sinking in too deep. The climb up the washed out mountain trail was long and hazardous, not only slippery with mud and full of holes, but strewn with every manner of forest debris.

Hirsol and Reza smiled through their tears as they greeted him. They told him how their house had been reduced to a pile of rubble within moments, trapping their two young daughters and their friend, Sezel, inside. All of this had happened only a short time before Bozel's arrival.

While Topaz stood looking at the twisted heap of collapsed boards that lay beneath the uprooted tree, he wondered how anyone could have survived such a disaster.

"We've been calling to them, but we get no answer," Hirsol said.

"They may not be able to hear you," Topaz offered, hoping what he said was true. "Can you show me what part of the house they were in?"

Hirsol nodded. "I'll take you there, or where I believe it is."

Topaz followed Hirsol through the muck and around to the rear of the ruined house.

"This is about where Itza and Izzie's room should be and down here..." Hirsol tromped through a few more feet of mud then stopped. "This is where Sezel was sleeping."

As unlikely as it seemed, Topaz wanted to believe they were all still alive and that no one was hurt too badly.

The ground around what had once been Hirsol's home, was a soft sea of mud, not much different from the rest of Cottersdamp Island. Thankfully the rain had slowed to a light drizzle. Nevertheless, that could change quick enough, and another long hard downpour could cause more disasters like this one.

"Do you think I should start moving some of this rubble?" Hirsol asked.

"It's best if I take a look around first. Moving anything now will be risky."

Hirsol pushed his sopping hair back from his face with a muddied hand. "That's what I thought too. I was afraid that if I moved something, and it happened to be the wrong thing, this whole mess could go sliding right down the mountain and into the river. That's about the time Bozel showed up. After we talked with him, I thought it best to wait till you came."

Topaz studied the mass of rubble before them. "It's a good thing you did, Hirsol. From the looks of things, it would be just as easy to cause another cave-in."

Hirsol creased his lips and nodded.

"It's going to take time to do this properly, Hirsol, but in the end, we will get them out."

Hirsol wiped his broad forehead with the sleeve of his shirt, adding more dirt to the worry lines etched there. "What can I do?"

"I may need your help later on, but for now I'd better work alone."

"Guess I'll come back later then, see how things are going. In the meantime, I'll make sure folks are getting off this mountain and they know where to go and wait for the bats."

Hirsol put up a brave front. Even so, Topaz could hear the anguish in his voice. He knew how hard it must be for Hirsol to walk away and leave the life of his friend and, most of all, that of his two daughters to a strange being he'd never seen before.

Topaz walked around the wreckage again. The large cross beams that had once supported the roof had been hewn from logs. They looked heavy. He wondered how the small green beings had been able to raise them to such a great height. They must have had to use pulleys and strong rope.

He circled the site yet again, Topaz stopped where Hirsol believed the bed chambers were located. He wondered if they actually were in the same place. Everything was in such turmoil.

"Can you get my sisters and Sezel out of there, Topaz?" Bozel had come up behind him. "Do you think they're even still alive?"

Topaz took in the Green Fairy's small tearstained face. "Sometimes we don't know how something's going to turn out, Bozel. But we must never give up, or think the cause is lost. If you believe the best, more times than not, everything will come out all right."

"That's what my dada would say. He says we should never think the worst until it happens, and that to speak the worst is to make it real. That's what all Green Fairies believe. I guess that's why we've stayed so long on Cottersdamp Island. No one wanted to believe it would ever come to this."

Topaz flicked his tail. "It may be best that we don't always know what will happen in the days to come. If we did, we would give up without trying to make a difference. Sometimes, if we refuse to give up, we really can change things. The hard thing is to know what cannot be changed."

"I don't want to give up, Topaz. It's just that we haven't heard a sound from them, and I'm afraid the worst has already happened."

"They could be under so much rubble that it's impossible to hear their voices. There may be other reasons too."

"You mean, they could be knocked out?"

Topaz gave a shrug.

"How will you get them out?"

"It's going to take time, but I'll do everything I can."

Bozel's face looked grave, his head was cocked to one side. "Will you have to use your special power?"

"What makes you think I have special power?"

"Daisy told me, and then I saw how you called the bats and how you talked to them."

"What did Daisy tell you about my special power?"

"She said Yellow Conjure Cats can do anything."

For a moment Topaz was silent. His eyes softened and he gave Bozel a wan smile. "Conjure cats can do many things, but not just anything. Our power does have limits. All the same, you must believe I will use whatever power I have to find your sisters and your friend, and get them out safely."

"How can I help?"

"I know you want to help Sezel and your sisters, but this you must leave to me. Your help is needed elsewhere right now. The lives of many still depend on you, and you can make sure they get off the island before more slides like this one happen."

Bozel's face darkened, and his head dropped a little. "I know I should be helping the other folk, but I've been so worried about Itza and Izzie... I'll see to it now, Topaz. Will the bats take everyone to the castle?"

"The bats are willing to do just that. But remember, Bozel, the bats have a long flight ahead of them, and they don't see as well in the daylight. So your folk must leave the island as quick as they can."

Bozel turned to go. "I'll start by getting everyone down to the beach right away, and I'll be sure they know what to do when they get there."

"One more thing, Bozel. Once you're there in Knownotten, it will to be up to you to see that your folk are properly looked after. They're going to need food and water and a place to sleep until they can build their own lodgings. You'll have to see to it that Corra and Mallory know what to do for them, and that they have enough help to take care of these things."

Bozel looked at Topaz and nodded. "I'll make sure they have plenty of help, and I'll help too. All will be well, Topaz."

Topaz gave Bozel a cattish grin. "I believe it will, Bozel."

CHAPTER THIRTEEN

Relieved to be alone at last, Topaz stared at the mountain of muddy boards and sticks that loomed before him. He studied the pile for a good long while. Where was he supposed to begin looking for Sezel and the girls in all this wreckage? There wasn't enough time to search through every bit of it.

His biggest concern was how to prevent a cave-in. That would be an even bigger disaster. Yet, he had to get them out of there as quick as he could, before something else went wrong. The fastest and safest way to do this was to find out where they were before he began moving anything at all.

Thought messages had worked quite well with the bats, and Topaz was of a mind to use a similar method to make contact with the Green Fairies. After some consideration, he finally settled on a seldom used method that would allow him to learn the exact whereabouts of each one of them, the mind's-eye, as the Elders had called it. This too would take time, but not as much time as moving this mountain of debris only to discover he'd wasted a lot of time by looking in the wrong place.

There were two important differences between locating the Green Fairies and sending thought messages to the bats. In the case of the Green Fairies, he'd have to connect with each one of them separately. The other difference was more complicated. It involved putting himself into a much deeper conjure state.

This method would allow him to find them, one at a time, by honing in on their heart beat or their breathing. By tracking any one of these, he'd find out precisely where they were, no matter how deep in the rubble they might be buried.

Topaz had never been taught this particular method of making contact with another being. What conjure training he'd had along these lines was limited; however, he'd heard the Elders speak of this method often enough. The mind's-eye had been used by his great grandfather, Amber Tiger, when one of Topaz's cousins had gotten himself lost in the forest as a cub.

There was a good reason why making contact with other beings in this manner had been so rarely used. The Elders considered this conjure state to be one of the most dangerous. Even for a conjure cat with superior skills, it was only considered as a last resort.

What made this practice so unsafe was the effect it had on a conjure cat's sense of time. Had Topaz known of any other way to discover the whereabouts of Sezel and the youngsters in a timely manner, he wouldn't think of relying on such desperate measures.

To suspend time was a common practice among conjure cats when entering into a trance, and it was often necessary. But, to lose track of time altogether for an indefinite amount of time was extremely hazardous. The drain on the conjure cat's life-force could be fatal.

What he was about to do might have been considered reckless or foolish had any of the Elders been here to judge his actions. Aside from that, to put his own life in peril again so soon after his encounter with the Ghostbird was to trifle with death itself.

Even so, he had made the decision. Topaz readied himself as he always did when intending to call upon his conjure power. He sat on his haunches, curled his tail around his great paws, and began to purr. Purring was not only a way to activate and sustain his conjure power, but it also helped him to clear his mind and keep it focused on his breathing.

With every breath he drew, Topaz imagined that breath flowing through his heart. He didn't know what Sezel or the youngsters looked like, other than the fact that they were small and green. Nevertheless, he kept an image in his heart and in the inner eye of his mind – the mind's-eye.

Each deep breath was a slow and deliberate act that pulled him deeper and deeper into the well of his own being until he began to sense the vague essence of another being's presence. With his mind's-eye as his guide, he sought after this essence until he felt it become stronger. Whoever he happened to be after at the moment, whether it be Sezel or one of the sisters, he knew he was close to where they were.

How long it would take to track all of them he couldn't be sure. Time could not have mattered less to him now, and this was the danger. Time had already been forgotten. For time did not exist in this extraordinary other dimension where Topaz now resided. There was no need of it here.

There was only this breath, and this breath was all there was until the next breath came, and then the next one. His entire being had come down to no more than one breath at a time. All sense of who or what he was or might have been was of no importance in this timeless void, and he was destined to wander here until he found what he'd come searching for.

CHAPTER FOURTEEN

Darkness engulfed him, darkness and the grime-filled musty air. He coughed and tried to move, but something heavy bit into his left shoulder as if it meant to crush it. Yet his shoulder didn't hurt nearly as much as his head. He reached up with his free hand to finger the huge lump on the left side of his skull. It was sticky with the blood that trickled from a large gash. Although he was still groggy, he remembered being struck down.

Sezel, I know where you are.

Sezel rolled his eyes, trying to look around. *This knock on the head has got me hearing voices.*

The voice in your head is real, Sezel. I'm sending my thoughts to you, and I can hear your thoughts in return.

You can hear what I'm thinking? How can you do that? "Who are you?" Sezel said aloud.

When Topaz heard Sezel's actual voice, he spoke aloud as well. "My name is Topaz, I'm a friend of Bozel's. Now that I know where you are, I can get you out of there."

Topaz had been able to track Sezel through his breathing. Still in the trance, he'd groped his way around the outskirts of the rubble until he was nearest the place where the old one was trapped. He visualized the space Sezel was in, and he could see the large beam that appeared to be resting on Sezel's shoulder. Beyond that, he had no way of knowing what to expect until he began to remove the layers of wreckage.

"Where is Bozel?" Sezel asked.

"He's helping the other folk get off the island... Tell me, Sezel, are you badly hurt?"

"Something's got me pinned down. The pain's not too bad as long as I can keep still."

"One more question, Sezel. Do you happen to know how Itza and Izzie are?"

Sezel coughed. A small moan followed. "Oh, no. Are the little ones trapped in here too? What about Hirsol and Reza?"

"Hirsol and Reza are safe. But I've yet to find out where Itza and Izzie are."

"See to them first, then. I'm in a tight place in here. It's so dark I can't see a thing, but I believe one of those large beams has me pinned down. It could be a good long while before you'll be able to get me out of here."

"You may be right, Sezel. When Itza and Izzie are safe, I'll come back for you."

Guided by the mind's-eye, his inner vision began to move through the debris once again. It maneuvered its way under and around the rubble that had fallen in on the short hallway between Sezel's sleeping chamber and that of the two sisters. Topaz continued his search in this manner, hoping to feel another's heart beating deep within his own. Or perhaps he'd begin to sense the closeness of another being's breath as he had when he'd felt Sezel's breath.

After that, only moments had passed before he'd begun to hear Sezel's thoughts. Could he be so fortunate as to find Itza and Izzie alive as well?

He moved on, his travels took him through dark hidden spaces inside the rubble and through long twisting passageways like tunnels. The tunnels were filled with rocks, mud, and ragged plants that had been torn from the hillside during the slide. The shattered limbs of trees jutted in every direction as did the broken wreckage of the crumbling house.

Sometime later, Topaz entered into another collapsed chamber trashed with muddy clothes, bedding, and splintered furniture. This small concealed space, packed with debris, was not where he might have expected to find the sisters' sleeping chamber.

At first he believed the mind's-eye had somehow been misguided. But here in this isolated pile of ruin he finally began to sense the essence of another living being and to feel the hammering of a small frightened heart within his own.

When he stopped to listen he could hear the sounds of a young voice crying as she spoke aloud to her sister.

"Please, Itza, say something so I'll know you're alright."

He heard a groan and then a whimper. "Izzie, can you help me?"

In the moments that followed, Topaz felt his own heart thump hard in his chest, his skin prickle, and his breathing return to normal. His search for Itza and Izzie finally over, he'd been thrust back into the world of time.

"I have you now," he said aloud, feeling his spirits rise. "I know exactly where you are, and I'm going to get you out of there as quick as I can."

"What did you say, Izzie?"

"It wasn't me talking, but I heard someone mumbling. It sounded like, *I'm going to get you out of there.*"

Topaz spoke louder. "How badly are you hurt, Itza? I'm here to help."

"Izzie, someone really is talking to me."

"This time I could hear it better," Izzie said.

When Topaz realized the sisters had trouble hearing what he said clearly, he spoke even louder. "My name is Topaz. I'm a friend of your brother, Bozel."

"You know Bozel? Where is he? Is he here on the island?" a young feminine voice asked.

"Yes, he's here. Right now, he's helping your folk leave the island. In the meantime, I'm going to get you out from under this pile of rubble before it slides down the mountain. So, we're going to have to work fast."

As an afterthought, Topaz wished he hadn't said the part about *"sliding down the mountain"*. He didn't want Itza and Izzie to panic.

"Is our mum and our dada trapped in here too? What about Sezel?" Izzie asked.

Topaz was relieved that Itza and Izzie hadn't noticed his thoughtless remark. "Your parents are helping Bozel, they weren't caught in the cave-in, but Sezel is trapped beneath something heavy and he may be badly hurt."

"Can you help Sezel too?" Izzie asked.

"Yes, I will get him out as soon as both of you are safe. Sezel has asked me to see to the two of you first."

From what Sezel had told him about his being pinned, Topaz suspected any attempt to rescue Sezel before finding the sisters could cause a great many things to shift. More than likely, it would result in another cave-in, or worse.

Sezel must have suspected this as well. That must be why he'd wanted Topaz to find the youngsters first. Nevertheless, this wasn't something Itza and Izzie needed to know, not right now anyway.

"Are either of you hurt?"

"My arm hurts a lot, but it's not bleeding," Izzie said.

Itza tried to move. "I'm not hurt. At least, I don't have a pain anywhere. But my foot is stuck under something heavy, and I can't pull it out."

"Is there an opening anywhere where you are? Can you see the moon or feel the rain?"

"No," Izzie said, "but there's cool air coming in from somewhere. There's crawly things in here too. Something just ran across my forehead."

"Oh no," Itza said, a small shudder in her voice. "I hope that wasn't a spider. I don't like spiders. They're creepy, and sometimes they bite."

"I wish you hadn't said that, Itza. Now I feel like there's things crawling all over me. How long will it take to get us out of here, Topaz?"

"I'll know better once I begin to move some of this rubble. I don't believe either of you are buried too deep in there. I can hear your voices well enough. Now that I know your whereabouts, it shouldn't take me long to get to you. It's better if you don't move around too much in the meantime, though. More stuff might fall in on you if you do."

Topaz hoped he was right about Itza and Izzie not being too deep beneath the rubble. The fact that he could hear them as well as he could didn't prove it was so. His sense of hearing was more acute than that of ordinary beings. Yet he wondered how well they could hear him. So far, they seemed to have heard everything he'd said since their conversation had begun. But he'd been speaking much louder than usual.

Now that Topaz had been released from the trance, he was no longer able to rely on the mind's-eye for visual guidance. It had served its purpose; he'd found Sezel and the sisters. Beyond that, its uses were limited anyway. He scanned the huge stack of debris until he found a small opening. He peered inside. Nevertheless, the hole, situated as it was, made it impossible for the moon's light to penetrate.

Topaz scanned the pile again, looking for a place to begin. He'd start by removing the larger pieces of timber at the top of the pile. This was the tricky part. Move the wrong thing and he could cause an avalanche of debris that would bury Itza and Izzie alive in the mud if it didn't crush them to death first.

He took a slow deep breath and pushed the dreaded thought from his mind. Centering his attention on the mound of rubble before him, he made a study of how each piece of debris lay in relation to the other. This whole mess was akin to a giant puzzle.

Every piece of rubble must be chosen with care and removed without disturbing what lay beneath it. Topaz didn't want to risk upsetting even the smallest object if he could prevent it. If one thing fell, others would be likely to follow, and who knew where it would all end. In his mind's eye Topaz had been able to visualize the small compact space Itza and Izzie were in. He knew they were close together, and he was glad of it. It would help to save time.

He grasped the first large piece of timber between his jaws, careful to lift it so as not to upset the rest of the pile. He lay it over to one side and took another, then another until he heard Izzie's voice shouting up to him.

"I can feel the rain on my legs."

"Me too," Itza said. "I feel rain on my face, and I can see two green lanterns shining in the darkness."

"Those would be my eyes," Topaz admitted.

"Your eyes," one of the sisters repeated.

"Yes," Topaz answered, without bothering to explain. "There are only a few more boards left to move. After that, I should be able to see what's keeping you from pulling your foot loose. Whose foot is it that's stuck?"

"It's Itza's foot," Izzie said.

"As soon as Itza's foot is free, I will pick both of you up and carry you to a safe place. Once the two of you are out of harm's way, I'll go help Sezel."

Topaz was about to say more, but he hesitated to consider how he should phrase his words before he spoke again. "There's something I ought to tell you before you see me. Some beings have been startled by my appearance at first sight. I only mention this because I don't want you to be afraid of me."

"Did you come from the Land of Knownotten?" One of the sisters asked.

"Yes, but I'm not a Fairy or an Elf. I'm a Yellow Conjure Cat."

"A Yellow Conjure Cat? What do you look like?" Itza asked.

Topaz had just picked up another board. He set the board aside before he tried to answer. "Well, as you know cats have four legs, and I'm a rather large cat - "

"Four legs? Why do you need so many?"

"What's a cat?" Izzie asked.

"Never mind, I think it might be better if I don't try to describe myself to you after all. Just believe that in spite of how I look, please trust that I won't harm you."

"We do trust you, Topaz," Izzie said.

"I don't think Bozel would have asked you for help if he didn't trust you, and if our brother trusts you, we have no reason not to. So you see," Itza said, "it doesn't really matter what you look like. We won't be afraid of you, even if you are a big ugly beast."

"Well..." Topaz cleared his throat. "I have nothing to worry about then."

For a cat the size of Topaz, removing the rubble that covered Itza and Izzie didn't require a great deal of physical strength. Nevertheless, the work was slow and dirty, and after a while, his jaws did begin to ache. Small bits of wood and grit got into his nose and mouth, and some of it even lodged between his teeth.

It was Itza who saw Topaz first. "The green lights really are your eyes." She sounded surprised.

"I hope they didn't frighten you."

"Your eyes are strange, Topaz, and a bit spooky, too. But you're not at all ugly. I think you're the most beautiful being I've ever seen."

"It's kind of you to say so." Topaz purred lightly under his breath.

"I want to see you too, Topaz," Izzie said.

"You will as soon as these last few pieces of timber are out of the way. The problem is, there's a lot of dirt and other stuff from the trees scattered all over them. It could get into your eyes unless you keep them closed until I'm done moving things around."

Topaz grabbed another long piece of timber between his jaws and set it to the side. With this last piece out of the way he was finally able to get a good look inside the space where Itza and Izzie were trapped. He let out a long breath and smiled down on the sisters. "There you are at last."

"It's true," Izzie said, when she got her first good look at Topaz, "You are beautiful. I couldn't think what a being with four legs would look like. We've never seen beings with more than two, except for lizards and frogs."

"Spiders," Itza said. "You forgot about spiders, Izzie."

"Your eyes are scary though, Topaz. It seems as if you're looking right through me. Are you?"

Topaz couldn't help but smile again. He'd gotten this same question from Daisy when she was much younger. "I can't see through you. But you're not the first to think such a thing."

Now with the rubble out of the way, Topaz could see why Itza was unable to free her foot. It was mired in mud up to her ankle, and a large chest-of-drawers was sitting on top of it.

Topaz was silent for a long time while he studied the chest. He knew he could move it. That wasn't the problem. What worried him was the mass of debris stacked up behind it. The chest-of-drawers was the only thing holding back the avalanche of mud and timber that threatened to break loose and bury them both.

Had it not been for the huge chest-of-drawers sitting exactly where it was, he had no doubt that Itza and Izzie would have been buried alive beneath a wall of mud before he could have found them. That was still a possibility.

"I'm going to get you both out soon. In the meantime, I'll move those pieces of rubble between you so you'll be able to see each other."

Even with the light from the half moon it was still pretty dark inside the deep cavity where the sisters were. They were not as close to the surface as Topaz had imagined them to be. When he removed the broken headboard and the rest of the trash between them, it did open the space up enough to allow a bit more of the moonlight to filter in. Itza and Izzie's spirits seemed to brighten once they could see each other, although Itza's back was to Izzie.

What now, he wondered. His mind whirled. He could use his conjure power to hold back the landslide of mud and timber from crashing down on Itza and Izzie, but someone would have to help Itza pull her foot out of the mud and then take the two of them to a safe place while he kept his focus on holding back the debris.

The chest had already begun to inch forward, pushing Itza's tiny foot even deeper into the soft mud. Topaz reasoned that if the chest was raised up and out of the way, Izzie might have the strength to pull her younger sister from the mud. That is, if her arm was not too badly injured.

Nevertheless, it would be impossible for them to scramble over all that rubble and climb to safety on their own without causing other things to shift and slide. Even the smallest disturbance to that heap of debris that surrounded them could start an avalanche of trash moving in any direction.

A sudden ear splitting scream from Itza and Izzie caused Topaz to start. Just as he turned to look in the direction of the sisters' stares, Otis settled down beside him without a sound.

"For heaven's sakes, Otis. Make some noise the next time you do that. You nearly scared us all to death."

Otis appeared unperturbed by the conjure cat's flare-up. He merely blinked and rotated his feathered head to look at him. "Thought you might need help."

Topaz glared at him briefly. "Well, I must say your entrance was timely." He returned his attention to Itza and Izzie. "This is my old friend, Otis. He's come to help me get you out of there."

Itza and Izzie appeared to relax somewhat, their color had returned to near normal. "Are you a bird?" Itza asked.

"I'm a Great-Horned Owl. Haven't you ever seen an owl before?"

The sisters shook their heads.

Otis' large disk-like eyes flashed in the darkness like two golden moons. "Well, I guess that's not so unusual. I've never seen Green Fairies before either, that is, not until I met Bozel."

The sisters giggled.

"You know our brother?" Izzie asked.

"I do, and what are your names?"

"I'm Izzie and this is my little sister Itza."

"I'm happy to finally meet you both. You wouldn't believe how many times your brother has mentioned the two of you in our conversations together."

Topaz kept his voice low. "Excuse me for interrupting, Otis, but this whole mountain of mud and rock is about to come down on us."

Otis' head swiveled back to Topaz. He spoke only loud enough for the conjure cat to hear. "Yes, I wondered if you realized that everything here looks to be moving, or it's about to. But not so much as to cause anyone to take much notice unless they happen to be paying close attention. I will see to the little green ones if you can hold back the mess for a while. Then we had all better get off this island. The back side of it has already gone into the river."

The end of Topaz's tail quivered. "I'd like to do just that, Otis, sooner than later. But there's another Green Fairy buried beneath a mountain of rubble over there. Topaz pointed his chin in the direction where Sezel was trapped. I hope what happens here won't put him in even more danger."

Otis' eyes flashed again. "We'll have to work fast then."

"Besides holding back the mess, I have to raise that chest-of-drawers. Itza's foot is stuck fast in the mud beneath it."

"I see." Otis blinked. "So, I'll have to pull the little green one out as soon as you move that thing."

"Think you can do it?"

A long moment of silence passed before Otis finally spoke. "That space may be too small for me to get into... If I'm to get them out of there at all, I'll have to grab them by their shirts to do it. I don't see any other way, Topaz. Unless, you think you have the time to remove more of the rubble."

"I'm afraid it would be too risky to remove anything more. We'd better make the most of the time we have. If you think you can do this, Otis, take Izzie first."

Otis uttered a low-pitched sound to signify he agreed with Topaz, and he was ready to do his bit.

Topaz glanced at the owl and nodded. He then spoke to Itza and Izzie. "Otis is going to fly in and fetch you now, Izzie."

"Fetch me how? What's he going to do?"

"He only needs to grab hold of your collar with his toes so he can lift you out of there and carry you to a safe place." Topaz purred softly under his breath, thinking this might help to calm and reassure Izzie.

Izzie's gaze shifted to stare at the great owl's feet. "His nails look awful long and sharp."

"Otis isn't going to scratch you, Izzie. He's done this sort of thing before. All you need to do to help Otis out is to stand up tall."

Izzie's bottom lip began to quiver. "Can't he take Itza first?"

"Otis has to take you first, Izzie. There's no other way. Only then can I free your sister. You must go now. Are you ready?"

Izzie's small head bobbed in silence.

CHAPTER FIFTEEN

Otis spread his huge wings, and lifted himself to hover above the deeper end of the small trench where Izzie waited. Her petite form stood hunched and cringing below him. Otis wouldn't have been able to grab her at all had she not been standing.

The great owl's wing span was so wide that even with his toes extended, he could barely reach far enough to grab Izzie's collar. She shied away from him as soon as he made a pass to get hold of her. Otis swung round and glided back to hover over the space again.

"I know you're afraid, Little Green One. But you must not hinder me. I need your help if I'm going to lift you out of there safely."

Still cringing, Izzie moaned as if she suffered from a terrible stomachache.

"The best way to do this is to make yourself as tall as you can, then hold a piece of your collar straight up. That way I can grab onto it. At the same time you must think of how happy your family is going to be when they see that you and your little sister are safe."

On the next pass Otis found Izzie standing on her toes with her eyes squeezed shut. She held up the collar of her shirt just as Otis had suggested.

Otis snatched her up in one quick sweep and carried her through the air. He set her down again before she even had time to finish her scream.

"You'll be safe here for now," Otis told her. "Stay put while I go and get your sister."

He left her on a broad strip of timber that rested on a fairly level place in the mud. The ground here didn't appear to be in any real danger of sliding. Not for the moment, at least.

When Otis returned for Itza, he found Topaz sitting on his haunches. The conjure cat appeared to stare into the deep hollowed space where Itza lay trapped beneath the heavy chest. He wore an intense expression on his striped yellow face, and his purr was steady and shrill.

Otis had seen his friend in a conjure trance before, and he could never tell how long one would last. He guessed it would depend on what Topaz needed to do. But Otis had learned from experience to stay clear of him.

With that in mind, Otis perched on the limb of the fallen tree that stuck out of the rubble a few feet away from where Topaz sat. While he waited for Topaz to lift the chest, he preened the feathers on his breast. Moments later the chest-of-drawers began to move. It rocked back and forth in the mud.

Otis' first thought was for Itza. He worried she'd be terrified, having no idea of what to expect next. She may even think the chest, or some of its drawers were about to fall on top of her. Otis himself wasn't quite sure that wouldn't happen.

When he swiveled his head to look again at Itza, he had no doubt that his instincts about what she had on her mind was justified. Itza squirmed nervously, and her eyes were brimmed with tears.

All at once the small Green Fairy became absolutely still, and so did the chest-of-drawers. As for Topaz, in all this time, he hadn't moved a hair. Otis had already stopped his preening, but he couldn't have moved if he'd wanted to.

Otis realized he'd settled too close to Topaz after all. As a result, he was also locked into this peculiar dreamlike space along with Itza and everything around her. Both of them were captives in a changeless void where nothing moved. This couldn't have been more unsettling for Otis, especially since his experience on Barren Island. The last thing he wanted to feel was powerlessness.

At long last, the chest, all of its drawers intact, broke free of the mud with a loud sucking thunk and began to rise, only to stop inches above the place where it had been stuck.

When Otis saw the tears start to roll down Itza's dirty little green face, he realized that both of them had been released from the conjure spell, and they were free to move about once again. Not so for Topaz; he could have been fashioned from stone for the look of him. This was such an oddity. Otis couldn't help but stare at his friend, if just for one moment longer before he sprang into action.

His feathered head swiveled back to the chest-of-drawers. The chest remained suspended as if it had been frozen in place, as Otis was sure Topaz intended it should. For the time being, the chest continued to serve as a barrier to the refuse that was piled up behind it.

This was the opportunity the great owl had been waiting for. Not knowing how much time he had, he flew off the limb and glided over the trench. He swooped down as low as he dared with his talons extended and grabbed Itza by the collar. But when he attempted to fly away with her, he could not budge her. Her foot was stuck fast in the mud.

Otis pulled harder. When he did, he felt the stretchy fabric of her collar rip. A chilling fear streaked through him when he realized that Itza's foot was still stuck and quite firmly so. Not knowing what else he could do to get her out, Otis tugged on the collar even harder. The more he yanked on it the more the collar tore.

"Let me go, let me go, you big dumb bird," Itza screamed at him through her tears. "Can't you see I'm stuck? If you really want to help, give me something to dig with."

Against his better judgment, Otis released her and flew off to do her bidding. He grabbed the first small pointed stick he saw and dropped it down to her. "Hurry," he screeched while he hovered on the air above her, watching a huge mound of mud ooze downhill from another direction.

He shot a quick glance at Izzie. For the time being, she was safe. However, the hillside above her looked more and more unstable. Conditions here were likely to change for the worst at a moment's notice, or no notice at all.

This wasn't the first time Otis had witnessed mud slides. He'd seen them during some of the bigger storms in the Mountains of Scarford and in the Tom-Tom Forest as well. He feared Itza and Izzie were one small breath away from mortal danger.

Meanwhile, Itza was busy frantically scooping the mud out from around her buried foot with both hands. After jabbing herself a number of times, she'd thrown the pointed stick away.

Yet it seemed to Otis that no matter how fast Itza worked, she couldn't stay ahead of the mud. The mud, already deeper, oozed in faster than Itza could ever hope to scoop it out.

This is taking too much time. Otis didn't want to think about what might happen if he waited any longer. Beside himself with concern for Itza's well being, Otis lunged in and seized her by the collar without warning, ignoring her screams of protest. He pulled on the collar with such a fierceness that Itza was yanked free within seconds, doing even more damage to the already torn collar.

His heart pounding, he swung her tiny body up into the night sky. He felt the collar rip even more as he flew. His thoughts churned with dread. *If the collar tears away completely... If she should fall...*

As soon as Izzie saw that Otis was near enough, she reached up and grabbed Itza around the legs and eased her into a soft landing. The sisters sobbed aloud as they embraced each other. Otis dropped onto the plank of wood beside them, Itza's ripped collar and a piece of her shirt still tangled in his talons.

He looked the girls over. A few scratches and bruises were the only injuries he could see at a glance. Most of Itza's wounds had been self-inflicted by the pointed stick.

"Get your mum to clean those right away," he told her.

Itza nodded to acknowledge she'd heard, but kept her eyes downcast. "I'm sorry I called you a dumb bird, Otis. I don't know why I said that..."

Otis' feathered ear tufts twitched. "You were scared. Had I been in your place, I might have behaved the same."

As if by magic, Reza and Hirsol appeared.

Reza enfolded Itza and Izzie into her arms at once. "Thank goodness the two of you are alive."

The great owl introduced himself. "My name is Otis."

"We know." Hirsol bowed his head in an expression of his gratitude. "Our son, Bozel, told us who you were. He saw you flying over the island. We didn't want to get in the way, so when we got here, we stood back there to watch." Hirsol used his thumb to jab the air behind him. "Our family and all of the other Green Fairies want you and Topaz to know how grateful we are for everything you're doing for us and for all you're about to do. We may never be able to repay this kindness, but we hope to live our lives in such a way as to be worthy of your bravery and the risks you're taking on our behalf."

CHAPTER SIXTEEN

At the end of the trance Topaz felt weak and somewhat shaky. He yawned, then stood up to take a long stretch. Several moments passed before he had his bearings. As soon as he saw Otis and Hirsol talking he went to join them.

He'd heard most of what Hirsol had to say, and he wanted to let them know how he felt about Bozel. "Your son is brave as well, Hirsol. He's had much to overcome on the journey to Knownotten and again on his return to Cottersdamp Island. Were it not for Bozel, I might have drowned. I'll tell you all about it someday."

Hirsol bowed his head again to acknowledge the honor Topaz had bestowed on his son. "He's a good son, and I'm proud of him. I'll tell him that when we have time to talk. But I'm sure he must already know how I feel about what he's done to help our folk." Hirsol shook his head. "When Bozel left here, I doubted we would ever see one another again. Even though it's against my beliefs to give into such thoughts, I've been having lots of doubts lately. I doubted you'd be able to find our daughters in all of this rubble. I'm glad I was wrong. I was wrong about the black bats too, it seems."

Topaz watched the slow beginnings of yet another small slide as he listened to Hirsol talk. "I'm afraid the ground we're standing on may not be safe for much longer, Hirsol. It would be best for you and your family to get off the island as soon as you can."

"I'd like to see my family off. Itza and Izzie can leave now with Bozel and their mother, but I don't see how I can. I'll stay here on the island until all our folk have left and until I know Sezel is safe."

Topaz's whiskers stiffened. "You must do as you feel best, Hirsol."

Hirsol nodded to Topaz, then squeezed Itza's hand. "Time to get you all off this island," he told her.

In the few moments he and Hirsol had stood there talking, Topaz couldn't help noticing how much momentum the small slide had gained. Not only was the slide moving faster, it had grown in size. When it broke, it would take everything in its path along with it. That included a small portion of the house that still remained standing. If that happened, Topaz feared they would never find Sezel alive.

He turned toward the wreckage. "I must see to Sezel."

"If you can spare me, I'll take Hirsol and his family down to the beach," Otis called after him. "Even if it takes two or three trips it will still be faster than leaving them to travel down the mountain on foot."

"Safer too," Topaz added over his shoulder. "And since Hirsol is staying, I've decided I may need his help after all, and a few of the other Green Fairies as well. They'll be useful when it comes time to pull Sezel out and carry him to safety."

Otis stretched his wings. "I'll see to it that he gets back here in time. Are you going to need me too?"

"I believe you're most needed to get folks down to the beach. You can spot the stragglers, especially if they're stuck somewhere on the mountain."

Otis gave Topaz a throaty reply before he sailed after Hirsol and his family.

Large puddles of muddy rainwater had accumulated around the site. Nevertheless, the pile of rubble on top of the place where Sezel was trapped looked about the same. Topaz called out to the old fisherman while he sloshed his way through one of the deeper puddles, nearly the size of a small pond.

"Thank the Good Spirit you've come back, Topaz. Did you find Itza and Izzie? Are they all right?"

"Both of them are safe. By now, they're probably on their way to Knownotten Kingdom along with Reza and Bozel."

"That's good to hear. I was beginning to worry that something awful might have happened to them."

"Thought you might be thinking you'd been forgotten and left behind."

"Can't say it didn't cross my mind, but deep down, I believed you'd come back for me, sometime. Neither of them was hurt then?"

"Some scratches I think, that's all."

"That's a relief, but I didn't hear you mention Hirsol. Is he all right? Didn't he go with his family?"

"Hirsol is well, but he refuses to leave until he knows that you're out of that hole and everyone's off this island." Topaz glanced back at the small slide, measuring its progression. "I'm going to start moving this rubble out of the way now. Some bits of wood and mud may slide off and fall through the cracks, but I'll try to be careful. Watch it doesn't get into your eyes. Cover them if you can."

"I'll do that," Sezel cleared his throat. "How did Hirzol get his family off the island? Did you bring boats over the mainland?"

Topaz paused, a huge piece of timber balanced between his teeth. He didn't quite know how to tell Sezel about the black bats. It might be better not to answer the question directly, he decided. He set the piece of timber off to the side.

"Hirzol should be here soon. Then he can tell you all about it."

Sezel coughed to clear the dust from his throat. "I hear purring. Did you bring a cat with you?"

When Topaz wasn't conversing with Sezel, he purred lightly under his breath. It was a habit; it helped him to stay calm and keep his mind focused while he dealt with the task in front of him. "I am the cat, Sezel."

Sezel gave a short laugh. "Did I hear you right? Did you say you're a cat?"

"A Yellow Conjure Cat, that is."

"You're a real Yellow Conjure Cat?"

Topaz could hear the smile in Sezel's voice.

"Begging your pardon, Topaz, but I didn't think there were any conjure cats left in this world. I sure didn't expect to ever meet one. Been to Knownotten a few times, long time ago that was, but I never did see a conjure cat when I was there."

"You should be seeing me soon. There's a few more boards to get out of the way before you do though."

"I want you to know I'm grateful you come back to help me, Topaz. But while you were helping Itza and Izzie I started thinking... I can't see how you're gonna get me out of here... This beam, pinning my shoulder, it's got to be the big broad one that was holding up the roof."

Topaz spit out a small splinter of wood. "I believe you're right about that."

"Well, the thing is, this beam...it's big and it's heavy, I don't think it can be moved...not even by a conjure cat."

"I am going to move it, and when Hirsol gets back with more help, they're going to bring you out of there." Topaz picked up another board and laid it aside. "Everyone is leaving this island tonight."

"I'd like nothing better, Topaz. I know I shouldn't be thinking it can't be done. Hirsol would give me a scolding if he heard the things I've been saying to you."

"A scolding about what, Sezel?" Hirsol had just made his way around a huge puddle too deep to wade through, the same one Topaz had come through earlier. Three other Green Fairies followed him. They carried lanterns and a fishing net of finely woven mesh. Two of them shared the awkward burden of the net.

"It's best I don't say, Hirsol. I don't want you getting mad at me. I'm too glad to hear your voice and know that you and all your family are safe."

"The Good Spirit is watching over us, and as soon as you're out of there, we'll all be on our way to Knownotten Kingdom."

Topaz worked on in silence, while Sezel and the others talked back and forth.

"As always, it's still raining," Sezel said. "I can feel it now, and I can see your big green eyes shining down on me through the darkness. They're as bright as a new moon."

"I can see you too, Sezel. With a few more pieces of timber out of way, I'll be able to get a good look at what's keeping you pinned in there, and I'll know how to free you without causing something else to fall in on you."

Once the remaining boards and the rest of the debris were out of the way, Topaz crouched down and peered into the space where Sezel was trapped. The large beam resting on Sezel's left shoulder leaned at an angle. It was supported by a smaller crossbeam. Another small crossbeam was wedged against it. It looked impossible to move. Topaz straightened and stepped back, careful to balance his weight on the loose boards to prevent them from sliding.

Topaz studied the larger beam again. Had the board not been positioned as it was, Sezel's shoulder probably would have been crushed by the weight of the it. More than likely, Topaz figured, Sezel would lose the use of that arm anyway; nevertheless, his life could be saved if their good fortune held.

Now that Topaz could see the details of Sezel's predicament more clearly, he now knew what he needed to do.

Topaz turned to Hirsol and the others. "Sezel's in a bad place. If I move the large crossbeam, the smaller ones will fall in on him.

Because of the way the beams are propped against one another, I'll have to lift more than one beam at a time. It may take a while to raise all three of them, but once they're out of the way you'll all be able to go in and carry Sezel out of there."

Hirsol glanced at his companions, then looked back at Topaz, and nodded. "That's gonna be a bit rough on Sezel, ain't it?"

The end of Topaz's tail twitched several times. "I have to agree with you, Hirsol. I'm sorry for your friend, but he will suffer great pain when he's moved."

The Green Fairies exchanged wary glances and moved their feet restlessly in the mud.

Hirsol pointed to a narrow passageway in the rubble. He'd seen Topaz clearing it while he and the other Green Fairies stood talking to Sezel. "Is that the way you'd have us go in and out?"

"Yes, but you'll need to be careful. There's a few boards sticking out at the bottom. So it might be a little tricky going through there. It's best if you don't knock against anything on the way in or out."

"I can see some of those boards from here. We'll watch out for 'em, and we'll be careful, Topaz."

The other Green Fairies nodded in agreement.

Hirsol rubbed his chin. His eyes shifted away from his companions and back to Topaz. "We're ready to go in as soon as you give us the word."

"That's the other thing I need to tell you." Topaz's whiskers twitched. "I won't be able to speak to you again until this is over. When you see that the beams have stopped moving, you'll know it's safe to go in and get Sezel. But you mustn't take too long to bring him out of there."

The Green Fairies shared a few nervous looks, knowing what would happen if another slide broke loose, or Topaz had to relinquish his hold on the beams before they all got out in time.

CHAPTER SEVENTEEN

T opaz sat on his haunches and curled his tail around his
paws in the usual manner before he called on his conjure
power. Then he began to purr as a means of focusing his concen-
tration. His attention seemed to be centered on the place where the
larger beam and the two smaller ones intersected with one another.
In any case, that's how it appeared to the onlookers.

Inside his conjure cat's mind, something quite different took
place. His mental energy was actually focused inward. The image
of the wooden beams, their position in relation to one another,
and how that would affect the outcome was already fixed in his
mind. All other thought had been suspended. This was important,
because the key to accessing and directing this powerful source of
energy, the supreme force, depended on his ability to remain atten-
tive to the task above all else.

Topaz could feel the power of the supreme force surging
through him. It coursed through his brain and his body like small
bolts of lightning, its energy drawn directly from his life-force.
Unfortunately, Topaz had pushed himself far beyond the limits any
conjure cat should expect himself to endure in so short a time.

In so doing, he'd broken the basic laws of his Code. Still weak from his near-death experience with the Ghostbird, he'd placed yet another burdensome strain on his life-force. This he'd done intentionally by summoning the supreme force again and again with little regard for the consequences. In this instance, the consequences were likely to be fatal. This power had its price.

Nevertheless, it was too late for second thoughts. The point at which he could have turned back had past. This mission was as much of a commitment to him now as his next breath. With every successive breath he took he could feel the power within him growing stronger. Painfully stronger. Pain was a warning. A signal that something was about to go wrong. And, Topaz knew exactly what that was.

CHAPTER EIGHTEEN

The large beam began to shudder and shake loose the lumps of mud, small rocks and other debris. Sezel cried out in pain as soon as the large beam moved. The weight of it ground into his injured shoulder. A few long boards were disturbed. They slid and tumbled in all directions as all three of the beams began to rise at once. But for some reason that no one present was able to comprehend, not one of them fell on Sezel.

The large beam and the smaller cross beams that had become wedged beneath it were the only three pieces of timber that supported the ruined wall behind them, and with the rise of those beams, the ruined wall was weakened further. As this wall began to crumble, the mess behind it erupted into an explosive spray of mud, sticks, and rocks with the force of a small volcano.

The instantaneous burst of noise and flying debris caused Hirsol and the other Green Fairies to duck for cover. Then the two smaller beams suddenly crashed down. The boards knocked against one another as they fell into a heap onto the passageway that had recently been cleared for the Green Fairies.

When the chaos ended, Hirsol was on his feet right away. "Sezel, are you all right?"

"I'm all right," Sezel yelled back while he tried to suppress a cough. "But I don't know if you'll still be able to get in here and get me out."

"We're coming in now, Sezel, and we're gonna get you out no matter what."

Hirsol looked around for his companions. The other Green Fairies had just come out of hiding. They brushed the dirt from their faces.

The Green Fairy called Ponsel spoke first, his voice shaky. "I thought all of us were going to be buried alive in this mountain." Ponsel was also the first to notice Topaz. "We seem to have come out of it all right, but I'm not so sure about him, Hirsol."

The worry lines in Hirsol's forehead bunched. "He looks the same as he did before. Doesn't he?"

Ponsel stared at Topaz a while longer. "This is the first time I've ever seen a conjure cat, but I think he looks different. I just can't say exactly how."

Hirsol sloshed his way over to Topaz. He reached out a hand, about to place it on the conjure cat's brow, but hesitated. "I wanted to see if he felt too cold or too hot, but I don't think I ought to touch him while he's like this. I might cause something awful to happen. Let's get Sezel out of there first, then I'll get word to Otis. I hope he will know what to do for Topaz if there's something wrong."

Hirsol and the others hurried along the designated path. They pushed aside the small pieces of debris that had fallen during the chaos. At the end of the path, they had no choice but to slow down as the two smaller beams that had fallen barred their way.

It took some time for the Green Fairies to climb up and over the beams, dragging the fishing net with them. Hirsol was the first to make it to the top with a little help from Ponsel.

"How much time do you think we have?" Ponsel asked in a quiet voice, not wanting to alarm the other two Green Fairies.

"I don't know, but we better not waste any of it. It's gonna take longer to carry Sezel out."

Sezel appeared to be no worse off, only dirtier.

"How's your shoulder?" Hirsol asked him.

Sezel spoke through tight jaws. "It might be broke. It hurts bad, and I ain't been able to move this arm, even a bit."

Hirsol pulled a long strip of cloth from inside his shirt. "I need to bind that arm to your body before we move you."

Sezel coughed and wiped at the dirt on his withered face with his good hand. His eyes were bright with the increased pain brought on by the movement of the beams as they were lifted. The chaos that followed along with his jarring cough had only added to his discomfort. "There might be another cave-in. I wish you wouldn't take the time to do that before you get me out of here."

"All right, Sezel, I won't. But I do need you to bend your knees and lift your backside so we can get this fishing net under you. We're going to use it to carry you."

"No need for that. I can walk. My legs ain't hurt, just my shoulder and my head where that beam struck me and knocked me down."

"Sezel, I know you like to do things your own way, but this time you need to trust my judgment. We can get out of here faster if you let us carry you. You might be too wonky to get up and start walking around."

"Hirsol's right, Sezel," Ponsel said. "There's a couple of beams blocking the path, and I don't think you should try to climb over them. Let us carry you."

Sezel waved a hand in the air. "I'll do what you say then." His pale brown eyes filled with tears as he took in the wall of green faces gathered around him. "I don't mean to make trouble. I'm truly grateful to all of you for staying behind to look after a useless old fisherman like me."

CHAPTER NINETEEN

No sooner had they gotten Sezel inside the passageway than they heard a tremendous noise behind them as the last beam, the largest of them all, crashed onto the path with a thunderous boom. As soon as that happened, the pit where Sezel had been trapped began to collapse in on itself. Boards clattered together as they fell on top of one another to create a massive dirt storm that filled the air around them with all sorts of flying rubble.

Stunned by the sudden unexpected upheaval, the group halted for an instant to assess what had just taken place.

"We've got to get Sezel over that barricade before we're all trapped," Hirsol shouted. He referred to the two beams that blocked the passageway.

Hirsol and Ponsel climbed up on top of the beams. They hoisted the fishing net with Sezel in it along with them. The other Green Fairies helped push Sezel up and on top of the beams, then climbed up themselves. It took equally as long to hoist him down on the other side; however, once they had, they all ran. Sezel howled in pain as he was jostled and jiggled about. The rain had stopped some time ago, but they'd all been too busy to notice.

By the time they were clear of the passageway, the tumult was at an end. When they stopped to rest a safe distance away, Hirsol and Ponsel exchanged looks, both of them had the same thought at once.

The Yellow Conjure Cat lay on his side in the muck with his eyes closed.

Hirsol stood over Topaz and shook his head. "I'm afraid I don't know what to do for him. I hoped Otis would have come back by now."

"I'll go look for him," Ponsel offered. "Where should I start?"

"I thought we might catch a glimpse of him flying over the mountain. But I haven't seen him since he took my family down to the beach. Most likely he's still on the beach getting folks lined up to fly with the bats."

As soon as Ponsel turned to go, Hirsol called after him. "Hold on, Ponsel, maybe there is something we can do. Let's try to revive him ourselves. I'm afraid to waste any more time looking around for more help " Hirsol knelt down beside Topaz and began to rub the conjure cat's face and head vigorously with his small hands while he called Topaz by name.

The first thing Ponsel did was to place three of his fingers on Topaz's nose. "I knew something was wrong with him," he huffed. "His nose is as dry as an old bone, and it's warm too."

"Is that bad, Ponsel? What's it mean?"

"All I know is, all four-legged beings are supposed to have wet noses, and their noses ought to be cold. I spent some time around some of them when I used to travel up north on the river. If their noses get warm and dry, it's usually 'cause they're sick."

"He's not gonna die is he?"

Ponsel leaned over and placed a hand on the conjure cat's furry chest. "Well, he's still breathing and I can feel his heart beating under my hand. As long as his heart beats, there's still hope."

On an impulse, Ponsel began to massage Topaz's chest and then his throat.

When he opened his eyes Topaz was taken aback to discover Hirsol and Ponsel kneeling over him. He ached in every muscle and every joint, and his head pounded.

"What's happened?" he asked, when he saw himself covered in mud and pieces of trash.

Hirsol's voice sounded small and frightened. "You've been unconscious, Topaz. Are you all right now? Or would you like one of us to go and fetch Otis?"

Topaz sat up and shook his head to clear it, but the sudden motion made it hurt even worse.

Hirsol shifted his weight from one foot to the other. "I didn't know how long we should let you be before we tried to find your friend, Otis." Hirsol paused, his eyes stole uneasy glances around the mountain. But now that you're awake, we'd better get out of here, quick."

When Topaz stood up he felt as if the whole mountain was spinning. A few moments passed before he could steady himself and recall what he'd been doing before he'd passed out. Just then he remembered Sezel. He looked around for the pit.

"What's happened here? where's Sezel?" Topaz shouted, when he saw the pit had caved in.

Ponsel pointed across the way. "Sezel's waiting for us over there with the others."

Topaz looked to where Hirsol's companion pointed. He was a little surprised to see Sezel on his feet. A sling supported his injured shoulder. The left side of his head was caked with dried blood and the gash in his temple still oozed. Sezel's almost white hair was filled with dirt and bits of other rubble. It stuck out around his head like a ragged halo. The rest of him looked no better.

"You look dreadful," Topaz said.

Sezel grinned. His pale brown eyes danced with good humor. "Guess you ain't seen yourself lately." He tried to laugh, but it turned to coughing instead.

Topaz was about to shake the mud and grit from his fur, but thought better of it when he realized Hirsol and his companion would bear the brunt of his actions. As he looked around, he noticed the steady streams of muddy rainwater that ran down the face of the mountain above them.

In the moon's subtle light Topaz could see several new and extremely deep crevices in the soil. The mountain itself had turned to sludge. Huge sections of it had already broken apart and fallen. It bought large trees, massive rocks, and what was left of the vegetation down with it.

Topaz turned to Hirsol and Ponsel. "We'd better get to the beach as soon as we can." He crouched down to allow the Green Fairies to climb onto his back. "I can take all of you down the mountain at once if you'll scrunch yourselves together."

Regardless of all he'd put himself through in the past few hours, he'd managed to survive one more critical drain on his life-force. Without a doubt, this crisis would shorten his life by several years. He counted himself fortunate to have survived at all. Yet there was nothing else he could have done. Sezel and Bozel's sisters were safe, and that meant a lot.

Miserable aching wretch that he was, he had to get these folk off the mountain before the next slide came bearing down on them all.

The mud beneath his feet was soft and slick, causing him to skid and stagger with nearly every step. The journey down the mountain was a new adventure in uncertainty for all of them. If the Green Fairies hadn't troubled to wrap the long ends of the fishing net around Topaz to secure Sezel on his back, the old fisherman would have fallen into the muck more than once.

As it was, Sezel was bounced and bumped about a great deal. Topaz was sorry for having to put him through what must have been a horribly painful ordeal; nevertheless, it was the best he could do. There was no time to take the care he would have liked for the sake of Sezel's comfort.

The other Green Fairies held onto his thick fur with both hands while Topaz slipped and slid in his race to stay ahead of the slide that threatened to overcome them. Should it gain any more momentum, they'd all be doomed.

Even when Topaz reached the bottom of the mountain, he couldn't keep from losing his footing. *This is like trying to walk through slime.* He looked around the cluttered beach. It was an endless quagmire of muck and wreckage. Uprooted trees, broken limbs, heaps of vegetation along with rocks of all sizes, and parts of trashed houses littered nearly every foot of the beach that wasn't under water. Topaz attempted to pick his way around and over these obstacles. But he became stuck in the mud many times over. The load he carried on his back added to the difficulty.

At long last, Hirsol spoke up. "Sezel is the only one of us who really needs to ride."

"You're right, Hirsol," Ponsel said. "The rest of us can walk."

Inwardly, Topaz gave a sigh of relief. With his load a great deal lighter, he managed to avoid becoming stuck more than once or twice before he reached the firm wet sand on the edge of the river.

CHAPTER TWENTY

Bozel and Cazara stood on the littered beach clinging to one another. The rain had stopped at long last, and the first light of day had begun to brighten the sky over Cottersdamp Island. It was brighter now than either of them could remember since before the Great Hurricane.

Cazara laughed through her tears. "I was worried I'd never see you again, Bozel. I was so afraid you'd been drowned."

"I'm glad you at least thought about me," Bozel teased, trying not to grin too broadly. "I worried you'd be wed to the candle-maker's son by the time I saw you again."

Cazara laughed and gave Bozel a soft punch on the shoulder. She stopped laughing when she saw his face become somber. "Bozel...? What is it?"

"Nothing... Just that while I was away, I kept wondering if Cottersdamp Island would still be here when I got back."

"You may have gotten back to us just in time. I heard about your house. My dada said your sisters were trapped inside with Sezel when it fell."

Before Bozel could respond to Cazara's remark, he saw his father struggling through the mud, making his way toward them.

"You should have left by now, Bozel," Hirsol called out, skirting the edges of the trash that lay between them. "You promised you'd leave as soon as you found Cazara. Why are the two of you still here?"

Without waiting for an answer, Hirsol stopped and turned to Cazara. "Haven't your folks left the island by now?"

Cazara nodded. "They have," she stammered.

Bozel wanted to explain that he and Cazara had only found each other a few moments ago. But seeing the strain in his father's face, he was certain his father didn't care to listen to explanations. Whatever he had to say could wait until later. "We'll go now, Dada."

"Well, what are you waiting for, Bozel? Find the bats before that mountain comes rolling down on top of us."

Bozel and Cazara followed Hirsol's glance as he looked into the distance at the mountains behind them. There could be no doubt that what Hirsol said was actually beginning to take place.

One massive section of the mountain had broken away and fallen apart in several places all at once. A part of it was headed in their direction. It roared down the mountain, bringing trees, ruined houses, and huge boulders along with it.

"Run!" Hirsol screamed.

"We're going, Dada." Bozel, still holding onto Cazara's hand, pulled her along with him. They slipped, skidded and even fell a few times as they careened through the muck together. They ran as fast as they could pick up their mud caked feet and put them down again. Together they hurtled rocks, broken limbs, and pieces of ruined furniture; some of it looked familiar.

Hirsol was right behind them. He shouted above the rumblings of yet another vast slide, "Keep going, you two. Faster! For heaven's sake, don't look back."

Bozel and Cazara halted just in time to avoid a collision with a massive bolder that had tumbled down the mountain and hurled itself in front of them. Bozel steered Cazara around a pile of rock-filled mud and an uprooted tree before they caught sight of the bats. A group of them were about to land farther down the beach.

Still holding hands, they leapt over a small log that lay in their path. This maneuver helped to shorten the distance ahead of them as they pushed on.

"Can we stay together?" Cazara shouted as they neared the bats. "I'm too scared to do this by myself."

CHAPTER TWENTY ONE

Four other Green Fairies stood waiting, Sezel among them. Topaz lay in the wet sandy soil at their feet, so covered in mud and sand he might have been a part of the landscape. He could easily have gone unnoticed.

As soon as he caught sight of Bozel, Cazara, and Hirsol he got to his feet and bounded toward them. "We're the last to leave the island," he told them. "Everyone that survived has been accounted for."

When Hirsol looked up at Topaz, there were tears in his eyes. "I'm grateful for all you've done for us, Topaz, and for all you're willing to do to help us get settled again. I know we'll have a good life in the Land of Knownotten. We'll work hard to make sure of that."

Topaz began to purr. "It will be a good life, Hirsol. It's going to take me some time to get back, so I won't be there to greet you when you arrive. But, please know that you're all welcome, and that this will be cause for a great celebration shortly after I return."

While Topaz and Hirsol talked, the remainder of the Green Fairies prepared to fly off the island. Bozel had already seated himself on the back of a black bat with Cazara tucked neatly in front of him, looking pale and giddy.

In the background, Cottersdamp Island continued to self destruct. For the time being, they were in no immediate danger of being buried alive. Even so, the ground did shake and shudder beneath their feet as they watched the mountain crumble. It was a compelling sight, and they couldn't help but stare at it.

"What will you do now, Topaz?" Hirsol asked. "Earlier, Bozel told me you have a friend waiting for you on the mainland. Would that be the little being called Daisy?"

Topaz nodded. "As soon as all of you have gone I'll be on my way back to the mainland. Daisy and I will make the journey back home to Knownotten together."

Hirsol bowed his head. "A good journey to you then, Topaz. I hope we'll see each other again soon."

Even after the last bat had flown away, taking Hirsol and Sezel with him, Topaz continued to linger on the beach of the forsaken island. He had stayed not only to rest, but to watch the final devastation of the island unfold. The mountains had already vanished, and the island was half the size it had been when he'd first come ashore.

Not until he felt the ground begin to drop away beneath him did he get up to leave. The time to brave the cold deep waters of the wide Slewnecky River had come once again for what he thought would probably be the last time.

Before he left, Topaz reminded himself that upon his return to Knownotten Kingdom there would be a Ceremony of Remembrance. The ceremony would honor all the Green Fairies who had lost their lives to this devastating disaster.

The Ghostbird had no power over the river's current in the waters this far to the north. The swim back to the mainland was uneventful though long and tiring. Topaz was only a few yards from the shore when he realized he no longer feared swimming in deep water. Last night, he hadn't even given it a thought on his way to Cottersdamp Island. At the time, he'd been too worried about Bozel's sisters to think of anything else.

CHAPTER TWENTY TWO

Daisy was asleep on the dry sand, her head rested on a pile of soft grasses. She was not alone. Otis stood on top of a granite boulder a few feet away. He held a large fish down with one of his talons while he tore off small chunks of it with his beak. "There's enough for the two of us if you're hungry."

Topaz shook the river from his coat before he stretched out on the sand close to Daisy. "I think I'd just like to sleep for a while." He yawned. "How's your wing?"

"It will do well enough. I'm in no hurry to get back to Knownotten though. So I'll probably arrive there at about the same time as you and Daisy. How are you, old friend?"

"A little tired... I hope you won't mind if we finish this conversation later,..."

The loud screech of an owl and Daisy's cries for help woke him. At first the terror in her voice paralyzed him. In another instant he was on his feet. He bounded toward her screams, thrashing through the dense brush and the tall thin trees that grew above the beach. Not only were her cries born of fear, they were steeped in pain and the anguish of hopelessness.

Topaz knew this because he could feel it too. It was as if Daisy was a part of him, or he a part of her. Her pain was his pain. When the pain's sharpness subsided, a burning ache followed. The ache mingled with a weakness so complete it nearly overcame him. *She will be gone before I can reach her.*

His heart cried out for her. *Oh Daisy, how could I let this danger befall you? This is not a death you deserve. I never should have brought you with me.*

He was deep in the woods before he caught sight of the hairy horned beast that had her. It disappeared from view moments before her cries stopped. A trail of blood spatters guided his way. The sight of Daisy's blood soaking into the earth beneath his paws was more than he could bear. Waves of mindless rage streaked through him. This torment was soon replaced by vicious thoughts, and the intense desire to rip this shaggy creature into many small pieces.

Otis suddenly appeared from nowhere, flapping helplessly above him. "It's a mangy buckwetcher," he shrieked. "The beast took her in there - behind those brambles, and I can't get through them."

Long tufts of reddish brown hair were caught on the thorns. On the leaves, there were smears of blood. With a jerk of his head, Topaz motioned for Otis to move away.

He crept closer to the immense thicket of thorns that grew over the cave's invisible opening. He sniffed at the smears of blood, Daisy's blood. The stench of animal waste and rotting hides wafted out to meet him when he pushed his head through the thorny thicket. He forced his way through it and into the cave, unmindful of the biting thorns.

Inside the cave's foul and gloomy interior, the remnants of chewed bones and vacant skulls lay scattered about the dusty floor. But there was no sign of Daisy or the thing he hunted, and no sound echoed from the cave's limestone walls. Topaz circled around inside in a half crouch. Sniffing. As he moved alongside the wall, he glanced over his shoulder a time or two to watch his back in case another beast was lying in wait.

Toward the extreme rear of the cave, Topaz discovered two openings in the rocky wall. *Tunnels.* The scent of Daisy's blood and the stink of the Shaggy Red Buckwetcher filled his nostrils. The odors were much stronger at the mouth of the second tunnel. He padded inside and kept to the right of the wall for guidance.

This far away from the cave's entrance there was barely enough light to see where he was going. He was but a few feet inside the tunnel when he found himself in total darkness. Even for a conjure cat, it was impossible to know what lay ahead.

After he'd gone a few yards, the floor of the tunnel took an abrupt slant downhill. Topaz felt a gentle wind blowing against his back. Sometime later, the air inside the tunnel changed again. This time the wind blew at him from the opposite direction. The gentle airflow continued on in this manner, a weird phenomena that made it seem as if the tunnel itself was alive and breathing.

A strange occurrence, but not the first time Topaz had witnessed such a happening inside the tunnel of a cave. Experience had taught him to expect another opening of some kind at the tunnel's other end. The utter darkness warned him that the opening was not to be found anytime soon.

The air exchange and the long trek through the tunnel in the inky darkness added to his sense of having been swallowed up by a mammoth-sized monster. The sensation played with his imagination, and it gave the air around him a sinister feeling of foreboding. Next Topaz felt the tunnel plunge deeper into the rocky earth. It wound its way around sharp crooked corners and through slits of rock so narrow he had to squeeze himself though them.

It was hard to imagine how a creature the size of a buckwetcher was able to pass this way. Yet he knew his sense of smell did not lie. The creature had come through this tunnel, and it had Daisy. Topaz never doubted he'd catch up to the buckwetcher. He knew he had to. But would Daisy still be alive? Why had her cries stopped? Was it because the buckwetcher had already broken her neck?

Topaz traveled for what seemed like miles through the absolute darkness with only the sound of his own breathing to comfort him. The tunnel burrowed deeper into the rock, curling around two more curves before he saw a faint shaft of light and heard the soft sounds of water dripping. Around another short bend a broad cavernous space opened before him.

High above the cavern's rocky floor a wide fissure in the limestone ceiling allowed the light of day to enter. Only a small portion of the cavern was illuminated, but enough of it to show off a section of its colorful walls. Subtle shades of oranges, pinks, and purples stood out in the badly lit interior. The rest of the cavern remained cloaked in deep shadow, hidden by the twists and bends of the cavern walls and their secret chambers. Long lumps of limestone appeared to drip from the cave's high ceiling; several others jutted up from its angled uneven floor.

The Shaggy Red Buckwetcher stood hunched and drinking from the large sinkhole in the floor beneath the fissure, its back to the tunnel. The animals long reddish-brown hair was matted and streaked with gray. Daisy's body lay on the stone floor a few feet away. Blood pooled from the puncture wounds in her neck.

Topaz crept into the shadowy chamber, his ears pressed flat against his head. His long tail twitched. In a crouch, he inched forward on the balls of his feet until he stood directly behind the ragged beast. Without warning, he leapt forward and onto the buckwetcher's back. His unsheathed claws dug deep into the beast's thick shaggy hair until he found its flesh.

The beast roared out in painful surprise. It turned its broad muzzle toward Topaz and growled, its jaws snapping. Before the buckwetcher's teeth could find a target, Topaz pulled back. He sank his own teeth into the creature's other shoulder. He hit bone right away, astonished by how little flesh there was on the beast despite its enormous bulk.

Blood trickled from the jagged wound in the buckwetchers torn flesh. Topaz bit in again. This time he clamped his jaws on the side of its neck. The buckwetcher's deafening roars echoed from the cavern walls, and it tumbled onto the stone floor of the cave, taking Topaz with it.

Topaz broke his hold on the beast and leapt to his feet before it had the chance to roll over on top of him. He hissed and his lips curled away from his teeth, as he felt the hair on his arched back rise. A deep growl rolled in his throat.

Slowed by the injury to his right shoulder, the buckwetcher took a great deal of time to get to its feet. At first, it tried to put weight on the right foreleg, but it seemed it couldn't bear the pain. Finally, the buckwetcher tucked the limb beneath it and hobbled forward on three legs. The long hair on its shoulder where the flesh had been torn was matted and dripping with blood. The wound in its neck bled more freely.

The buckwetcher snarled at Topaz and shook its broad snout. Throwing its head back, it roared again and showed its teeth. Tarnished fang-like incisors protruded from the front of its crowded mouth. It continued to limp toward him still on three legs. Its face bore the scars of many battles.

Topaz stared into the intense black eyes and saw rage and the glint of the buckwetcher's intent to kill him. He took a quick step back to get out of the way just as it lunged for him, its open mouth dripped with long ropes of saliva. The creature's teeth missed his face by only a few hairs.

When Topaz caught a whiff of the buckwetcher's hot, rotten breath, he shook his head. The beast turned and lunged again without pause. This time its fangish incisors ripped through the hide on the his flank and drew blood. Topaz made a loud shrill noise akin to a scream and slashed the air with one of his open-clawed paws.

The buckwetcher stood up on its hind legs, the useless right foreleg dangled in front of it. Blood flowed heavily from the deep jagged wound in its shoulder. Even so, the creature was ready to resume the battle. It began by making a quick broad swipe with the mammoth-sized claws of its uninjured forepaw. It aimed for its opponent's luminous eyes.

The unforeseen blow opened three painful gashes across the top of Topaz's head slightly above his eyes. Topaz lashed out with his other paw this time. He made contact but did no damage. The buckwetcher's hairy coat was too thick for the blow to matter.

Still upright, the beast stumbled forward, ready to slash Topaz again. But it fell to the floor of the cave before it could come within range. Blood pumped from the wound on the side of its neck and spread rapidly across the stone.

CHAPTER TWENTY THREE

Daisy moaned as she opened her eyes. Her long lashes fluttered nervously when she looked around the cavern. She tried to place something familiar. Her breath caught in her throat when she spotted the buckwetcher. Then seeing all the blood, she realized the beast had been slain. Eventually, her eyes came to rest on Topaz.

As soon as Daisy saw him she tried to get to her feet. Yet each time she made the effort, she slid forward. Her front hooves scraped helplessly against the stone floor of the cave. Topaz quickly crossed the distance between them and came to stand beside her. The battle with the buckwetcher had ended only a moment ago.

Daisy, still half dazed, lifted her face to gaze into the conjure cat's luminous eyes. They held a trace of green in the dim light that filtered through the fissure above them.

Her voice was weak. "Topaz... I knew you'd come for me."

"How did you find us?" Topaz asked Otis.

"I was circling overhead when I heard the mangy beast's roars through a long crack in the ground. That's how I knew there was another way to get inside the cave."

Daisy winced as Topaz's raspy tongue cleaned the blood from the wounds the buckwetcher's teeth had made in her neck.

When Topaz stopped licking, Otis inspected the wounds. "That will do, Topaz. You should look after yourself now, your flank is beginning to bleed again. You're fortunate that wound wasn't any deeper, more fortunate still that you weren't blinded. His claws almost got your eye."

"I'm glad there's a bright side to all this, Otis."

Otis flicked his feathered tufts and leaned forward to stuff a few wads of spider's web into Daisy's wounds with his beak to stanch the bleeding.

"Owwww. That hurts, Otis."

The great owl's feathered ear tufts twitched again. "Didn't mean to be so rough, Daisy, but I have to plug these awful holes in your neck. I'll look for some brown moss on the way home. It will keep the wounds from festering." Otis pushed another wad of the sticky web into the wound for good measure. "You'll bleed less if you can keep still for a while."

"But I want to drink water."

Otis blinked. "Good, and you should. You've lost quite a bit of blood, you know."

Topaz stopped licking his wound to look at Daisy. "Will you be able to walk to the sinkhole? It isn't all that far, but you can lean against me if you think it will help."

"Let me try to do it on my own first." Daisy made several attempts to stand, but her hoofs were unable to gain enough traction on the slippery stone. After a gentle nudge from Topaz, she finally pushed her hindquarters up and got her forelegs to straighten beneath her. Her first few steps were wobbly on the cave's uneven floor. Nevertheless, Daisy made it to the sinkhole before her legs gave way beneath her.

By the time she'd gotten there and begun to drink, Otis was back with more spider's web.

"I'm sure this will be enough, Daisy. But you really should stay put for a while." He pushed the rest of the sticky web into a part of the wound that had begun to bleed again. Daisy was too thirsty to cry out in pain this time, but the skin on her back shuddered, creating small ripples, and she trembled ever so slightly.

Otis turned his attention to Topaz. "How did you ever manage to take down a Shaggy Red Buckwetcher? The beast is at least six times your size."

"It wasn't a fair fight," Topaz admitted. "I jumped him from behind."

"Really, Topaz, it was better than he deserved, grabbing our Daisy the way he did. Even so, you could have been killed."

Topaz's whiskers twitched. "Besides that the beast was old, Otis. He was slow for a buckwetcher, even though his claws got me more than once. From the look of him, he was half starved as well. There wasn't much more to him than hair and bone."

Otis swiveled his head to look at the body of the slain buck-wetcher. "Still, buckwetchers are dangerous beasts. The battle almost always goes in their favor. Few beings have ever come out of it alive. I hate to think what would have happened to our Daisy if you hadn't caught up with the beast when you did."

Daisy lifted her chin to look up at Topaz. "He would have eaten me soon enough. I owe you my life, Topaz."

The corners of Topaz's mouth curved into an uneasy smile, and a meek expression appeared to overshadow his luminous eyes. "I'm honored that you should think so, little friend. But it was I who brought you here... I should have protected you better."

CHAPTER TWENTY FOUR

D aisy slept for the rest of the day. Topaz napped beside her, curled in a ball, his head resting on his front paws, much like an ordinary cat. Toward evening, Otis left the cave through the overhead fissure to gather some nuts and wild flowers for Daisy's supper. Later, he caught a fat bass to share with Topaz.

"Did you see any osprey while you were fishing?" Topaz asked, between mouthfuls, as he devoured his share of the fish.

"No, and no buckwetchers either, but that's not to say there aren't any prowling about. They blend in all too well with the trunks of the trees and the woody shrubs that grow in these parts, especially at this time of the day."

Daisy looked up from the sinkhole where she'd been drinking. "How's your wing, Otis? Does it still pain you?"

"It's not so bad anymore, Daisy. What about you? Does your neck hurt as much as it did?"

"It's sore. I suppose it will be for a while, but I'm feeling a lot stronger now. It helped to eat something."

His meal finished, Topaz stood up and lapped water from the sinkhole. He then sat back down on his haunches next to Daisy.

"It's good to hear you're regaining your strength, Daisy. We need to leave this place as soon as you feel you're ready. It's best if we don't linger here too long. From the looks of this cave, more than one buckwetcher likes to use it."

Daisy and Topaz watched the great owl take his leave through the wide fissure in the roof of the cavern. Daisy just couldn't help it; she stared at the dead buckwetcher as she and Topaz passed by it on their way to the tunnel. The memory of the scene she'd witnessed with Bozel in the woods two days before flashed before her. she shuddered.

Topaz noticed. "What's wrong, Daisy. Are you alright?"

Daisy wagged her head. "I saw one of these being before."

Moments later, she and Topaz were sheathed in darkness inside the long tunnel. Without truly wanting to talk about it, or even believing she ever could, the story of the buckwetcher feeding on the flesh of the deer it had slain poured out of her.

Had she not lost consciousness before this buckwetcher carried her into the cave, Daisy believed she would have died of fright before the beast had had the chance to eat her. Somehow, talking about it now helped her to cope with the darkness, and it made the trip through the tunnel seem a lot less long.

At Dawn Topaz and Daisy caught their first glimpse of the Black Fisher Bats away in the distance.

"Look, Topaz, the bats... They're coming back from Knownotten."

Topaz gave Daisy a cattish grin. We're not that far from home ourselves now, Daisy."

CHAPTER TWENTY FIVE

Heak craned forward to examine the scars on either side of Daisy's neck. "You have done a fine job of caring for young Daisy's wounds, Otis. They are healing quite well. It seems you did not need my advice after all. But I am glad you flew to Gista-La and told us what had happened to poor Daisy and Topaz."

Otis flicked his feathered tufts to acknowledge Heak's remark.

Heak returned to his place, next to his cousin Tad. He looked across the table at Otis. "Gnomes have always used brown moss to treat wounds such as these. How did you come to learn of it?"

The great owl blinked. "It's something I remember seeing my mother do."

Daisy looked up from her plate. "I'm so glad you were there, Otis."

Tad stirred a teaspoon of honey into his mint tea. "Thank the Good Spirit you and Topaz are on the mend, Daisy."

Daisy's long dark lashes fluttered. "I was lucky Topaz got there when he did. How's your knee? We weren't sure if you'd be able to walk here for the Welcoming Celebration. Gista-La is so far away."

Tad set his cup down and placed a long arm around Heak's shoulder. "My cousin takes good care of me. His new ointment worked like magic on my swollen knee."

Dooley smeared soft butter on a gooey cinnamon bun. "How's the plants in your forest, Heak? Did you treat them with the poison from the raccoonberries?"

"Thank you for asking, Dooley. The solution worked well for most of the plants." Heak heaved a sigh. "But alas, we could not stop the plague altogether until we burned out a large patch of plants."

Tad finished chewing a bite of his sandwich and swallowed. "The patch we burned was badly infested. It must have been the place where the plague started to begin with."

Topaz only half listened to the conversation that went on at his table. His wounds were still healing, yet he suffered no pain. He nibbled on cheese and sipped tea while he watched the Green Fairies from Cottersdamp Island mingle with the Knownotten Fairies and Elves. The rose garden was more crowded today than it had ever been, and he enjoyed the activity of those around him. All of Knownotten Kingdom had come for the celebration, and everyone had brought a favorite dish to share.

Reza patted Hirsol's arm as she rose from the table. "Think I'll go and see what Itza and Izzie are up to while the two of you talk."

Hirsol nodded to Reza and washed down another bite of his nut-butter roll with a slurp of cold tea. "How's your cottage coming along, Sezel?" Now that the Green Fairies had begun to build their own homes, they'd left Knownotten Castle and gone to live amongst the forest folk.

Sezel leaned forward and placed his elbows on the table. "It's coming along. The Knownotten Fairies done most of the work, though. The windows are about all that needs doing now. I'd of had em' in myself, but this old shoulder still ain't acting right."

He lifted his arm up and down a few times and then rubbed his shoulder where the bone had been crushed. "I been bathing it in the creek every day since we came, But you know how it is with the old ones."

Hirsol bobbed his head. He knew Sezel's arm would never be half as good as it once was. A Green Fairy's magical ability to heal themselves did diminish with age. Topaz and Otis were quite surprised to learn Sezel could use the arm at all.

Sezel looked out over the forest. "Gonna start a little garden next week. Finally got Ponsel to part with a few of those gourd seeds his missus brought along. I can spare some if you think you can use em'"

Hirsol's eyes began to sparkle. Well, well. In that case, I'd better make a set of carving tools for Bozel's next birthday.

Menna left the rose garden to stroll through the petunia patch in search of her favorite plump green worms. Her fluffy brown chicks followed close behind her. Barely a fortnight had passed since they'd hatched. When Menna and her four chicks came to a standstill, Itza and Izzie squatted on the ground close by and beckoned for the chicks to come to them.

Itza lay the back of her hand on the ground. She giggled when the chick's tiny sharp nailed feet stepped into her open palm. "It tickles, Menna."

"That's Willow," Menna dipped her head. "It was his father's name."

"And this one?" Izzie held the chick out for Menna to see. Her hands were cupped protectively around it.

"I call her Knowa...in honor of the Knownottten Forest - our first real home. Knowa was the first of my chicks to break through her shell."

Itza touched a finger to the top of Willow's head and caressed his silken feathers. "How do you manage to tell them all apart?"

"A mother knows, Itza. But if you will look at each of the chicks closely, you will see that their feathers all have a slightly different pattern. Doola has a dark spot on the top of her head. And then there's Bozel - he's just a little smaller, and his feathers are a bit lighter than any of the others."

Cazara grabbed Bozel by the hand. "Let's try the apple tarts. Quick, before the music starts up again. I wouldn't want to miss the next dance."

Bozel grinned and reached for a tart. "Not even for the pleasure of eating? I have yet to taste the spinach soup or Corra's triple berry pie."

"Oh, no, the music's starting already. Hurry, Bozel."

Bozel laughed as he allowed Cazara to pull him back into the ring of dancing Fairies and Elves.

Daisy stretched her neck to reach for the last cinnamon bun. When she noticed Dooley watching, she decided not to take it after all. "Why don't you eat that one, Dooley?... I'm stuffed anyway."

Dooley's bushy tail swished, and his eyes brightened. He picked up his butter knife. "We could share it. Would you like a little butter on your half?"

Heak smiled and glanced down the table at Topaz. The conjure cat looked on in silence, his eyes wide with amusement. He was wearing one of his cattish grins.

―END ̄OF ᗷOOK

Sneak Preview of Topaz and the Evil Wizard

CHAPTER ONE

The young Fairy called Orange Blossom stood in her open doorway and stared out into the forest. The sun had already set and the sky had begun to darken. She released a heavy sigh and whispered aloud, "Where's Thistle? He should have come home by now." Thistle was always home before dusk. He would never leave her alone at night to worry about him. He'd certainly never do this with their mum and dad out of town. Besides, Thistle loved to eat. It wasn't like him to miss a meal, most of all his supper.

From somewhere in a more distant part of the forest, she heard an owl hoot. Orange Blossom sighed again and felt the gloom of night begin to wrap itself around her.

All at once a cold blustering wind swept through the forest. It rattled the branches of the trees near her family's small stone cottage. An icy chill ran through her. Orange Blossom hugged her arms and watched the evening shadows change shape in front of her. They spread across the ground bringing eerie images that made her feel lonely and afraid.

She turned and stepped inside, closing the door behind her much harder than she'd intended. A rush of tears blurred her vision. "Where are you, Thistle?" She moaned. "It's almost dark. Please, Brother, come home."

Orange Blossom went to the fireplace and stuck a long reed into the fire. She caught a flame to light another candle. This one

1

she placed in the front window, a beacon of light for Thistle to find his way home in the darkness.

There was only one explanation to account for her brother's curious behavior. Something terrible must have happened to him. He could be hurt and lying somewhere in the forest half-dead and unable to get help. Or maybe he'd drowned while swimming alone in the lake that sat in the middle of the meadow.

All sorts of dreadful thoughts came to mind. It was as if her imagination had taken off on a wild goose chase of horrors. With so much time alone to think, she began to recall every scary tale she'd ever heard about missing children. Everyone who lived in the Kingdom of Knownotten was familiar with these old legends. They had been told and retold many times over to entertain and frighten each new generation of Fairy and Elf children.

Even so, Orange Blossom reminded herself, these legends really were true. Although these awful things had taken place hundreds of years ago, it didn't make the tales any less frightening. it was a time, their father told them, when many dark forces hovered over the land.

Orange Blossom tidied the kitchen and swept the floor. Afterward, she sat by the fire and tried to concentrate on her knitting. But some of these stories continued to play in her head. She'd heard them so many times she remembered most of them exactly as her father always told them.

She laid her knitting in her lap and rubbed her eyes. It was hours past her bedtime, and she was extremely tired. Yet she hated to go off to bed before Thistle came home. But, try as she may, she couldn't keep her eyes open.

Finally, she decided to turn in for the night. She left the door to her room half open. That way she might hear Thistle if he came home later that night. Thistle's supper had been left on the table, a moist towel over it to keep it from drying out. Not bothering to change into her nightdress, she lay on top of the quilts. She pulled a light blanket she always kept at the foot of her bed up over herself.

After a long restless night of too little sleep, the dawn finally came. As soon as Orange Blossom awoke she threw off the blanket and ran to Thistle's room. She didn't really expect to find him there. But, when she looked into the room and saw his bed was still empty, feelings of fear and disappointment swept over her, nevertheless. Her brother had never done anything like this before, nor would he. Something was wrong, something terrible. Orange Blossom knew she had to go out and look for him. Once again, the meadow came to mind. Thistle was friends with lots of the animals who lived there. When his chores were done, the meadow was where he spent most of his time.

With no thought for a morning meal, Orange Blossom left the cottage wearing the same dress she'd slept in. Two separate woodland trails branched out from her front yard. Either one of them would have taken her to the meadow. The lower trail was the one most traveled, the one Thistle usually took, because it happened to be the shortest.

The trail farther up the hillside meandered through the mountains. This trail fed into several others. Most of these trails were now overgrown; they had been for many years. Some of them wound their way into the deeper, darker, and more ancient parts of the Knownotten Forest. Long, long ago that ancient forest had been the ancestral home of the Yellow Conjure Cats.

Hundreds of years earlier, those large cats had roamed the mountains and the forest to protect it. They'd kept it safe from wicked beings who would have invaded the kingdom and taken it over.

Orange Blossom pushed the thought away. This early in the morning, parts of the forest were still in deep shadow. This was especially true in places where the trees had grown close together. Dark thoughts about unhappy times wasn't something she wanted to recall whilst walking alone in the forest. Better to recite the names of the trees and the wildflowers aloud to keep from thinking anything bad.

Even though the lower path was by far the quickest way to reach the meadow, it was still a long walk from her cottage. Orange Blossom was only half way there when she ran out of trees and plants to name, so she kept up her spirits by singing. If *Thistle is someplace close by, he'll hear me, sooner or later.* Orange Blossom wanted to believe it was possible to meet up with her brother somewhere along the way.

Nevertheless, she saw no sign of him anywhere on the trail through the forest, and by the time she reached the meadow, she was about to cry. The only footprints she'd seen were those of the animals.

As she walked through the meadow, a plump white opossum called down to her from the limb of a cherry tree. "Good morning, Orange Blossom. What brings you to the meadow so early?"

Orange Blossom took a few steps back and looked up. "I'm looking for my brother. Have you seen him, Nilla?"

Grabbing onto the next lowest branch, Nilla eased herself down to it. She was careful to balance the weight of her six youngsters that rested on her back. "Thistle? Gosh, no. He never comes here before noon."

"Did you happen to see him yesterday?"

"He was here yesterday. I saw him playing hide and seek with a badger and two young bucks. He didn't stay long, though. I remember, because he wanted to go swimming. I overheard him complain to his friends that the water was too cold."

Nilla inched forward on the branch. The branch was thin; it began to bend and creak under the opossum's weight. Orange Blossom held her breath as she watched the branch dip even lower when Nilla moved closer to the end of it.

The opossum didn't appear to show any concern that she and her youngsters might be headed for disaster. The branch swayed up and down while Nilla steadied herself and eyed the cluster of ripe cherries that grew just beyond her reach. "I didn't see him after that. I thought he might have gone home early."

"Well he didn't, Nilla. He didn't come home all night."

Before stepping onto the next lowest limb, Nilla nosed one of her young opossum back into place. "Maybe he decided to sleep in the forest with some of his woodland friends. The two young bucks left early too."

Orange Blossom wiped at a tear and shook her head. "I wish that were so, but Thistle never stays out all night. Even if he had, I'm sure I would have seen him on my way here this morning."

Nilla's whiskers twitched. She made an odd clicking sound. "I see why you're worried. What will you do now, Orange Blossom?"

Orange Blossom pushed a wisp of her fair hair away from her face. "I'm not sure, really. Maybe I should walk up to the lake. Someone there might have seen where he went."

"If I see him again, I'll let him know you're looking for him. I do hope you find him soon. He's bound to be somewhere here in the meadow."

There was no sign of Thistle at the lake, not even a footprint. At a loss for what to do next, Orange Blossom sat on a large boulder to think while she fought back the tears and the panic she felt. She'd already talked to several other animals who lived near the lake. No one had seen Thistle in days.

Otis, a Great-Horned Owl, made a low sweeping glide over the meadow. He was looking for a tasty tidbit to top off his morning meal before heading home. He lived in the tall yellow pines at the top of the forest. When he spotted Orange Blossom, he hooted a greeting. Orange Blossom waved to Otis in return, but there was no cheery smile as usual.

Otis wondered about this. *How come she's in the meadow at such and early hour? And all alone.* He'd never seen her here without her brother. Besides that, she looked upset, dazed, like someone lost or afraid. Believing something must be amiss, Otis dropped to the ground beside her and folded his great wings.

"Where's Thistle?" he hooted.

"Thistle —" The words stopped in Orange Blossom's throat. A series of loud sobs burst out instead.

Otis' golden eyes blinked. "Has something happened to Thistle?" He waited for her to gain control of her crying.

"I don't know." She sobbed again.

Otis cocked his head to one side. *Well, that's a strange answer.* "When did you see him last?"

"He didn't come home all night." Orange Blossom sniffled. "And now, I can't find him."

When the great owl heard this, his feathered ear tufts began to twitch. "No wonder you're upset. That's not at all like Thistle. What do your folks think about this; are they out looking for him too?"

Orange Blossom began to cry again. This time Otis thought she'd never stop. Between sobs, he learned that both their mum and their dad had gone off to Boarsbreek to help her grandfather make some repairs on his cottage and begin his new garden. It seemed likely they'd be gone for a few days more, at least. Not knowing what else he could do to console her, Otis stayed by her side until she was all cried out.

"I've no place else to look, Otis. What am I to do?"

Otis blinked several times before he answered. "I believe you've done all you can for the time being. Why don't you leave this matter to me for now. I think this is something your elders ought to look in to.

In the meantime, it might be best if you stay here in the meadow where you'll be amongst friends. It's never good to be alone when you're worried and upset. I'll come and find you the moment I have any news."

Orange Blossom dried her face on the hem of her dress. "How long will you be gone, Otis?"

"Only as long as it takes to have a good long look around. So, you may not see me again until this afternoon."

This new revised edition will soon be available on Amazon.

ABOUT THE AUTHOR

Pat Frayne, native of Philadelphia, is the author of the series: *Tales of Topaz the Conjure Cat*. These are fast-paced adventure fantasies about a large cat descendant from a special breed endowed with unique magical abilities. Topaz lives in a world inhabited by fairies, elves, and other mystical beings. Frayne's grandchildren have been her biggest creative inspiration. Her books are enjoyed by parents, grandparents, and children alike. She lives with her husband, Ron in a small town in Arizona.

About the Series

Tales of Topaz the Conjure Cat

These cleverly woven and original tales of a mystical Yellow Conjure Cat, his friends and the magical land they live in will truly captivate anyone who loves mystical stories of high adventure. The reader is drawn into the amazing Kingdom of Knownotten and introduced to unforgettable characters. The classic fight of good vs. evil is waged in a world inhabited by fairies, elves, gnomes, trolls, wizards and other mystical animals. All of these creatures coexist in a complex and beautiful land of peril and wonder. The author has crafted a truly well-rounded and enchanting story, rich with suspense, humor and tenderness.

These fantasy adventures are for parents as well as for children who wish to retreat into a world inhabited by mystical characters...... Child and parent alike will be able to relate to the difficulties these characters have to overcome in order to accomplish their objectives and yet remain true of heart.

www.patfrayne.com

Made in the USA
San Bernardino, CA
08 November 2015